D1825265

# *UNMASKED DESIRE*

Your fantasy just may get you killed

# *UNMASKED DESIRE*

Your fantasy just may get you killed

*KIM PRITEKEL*

SAPPHIRE BOOKS

SALINAS, CALIFORNIA

*Unmasked Desire*
Copyright © 2024 by Kim Pritekel. All rights reserved.

ISBN Book - 978-1-959929-05-5

This is a work of fiction - names, characters, places, and incidents are the product of the author's imagination or are used fictitiously. Any resemblance to actual persons living or dead, business, events or locales is entirely coincidental.

All rights reserved. No part of this publication may be reproduced, distributed, or transmitted in any form or by any means, including photocopying, recording, or other electronic or mechanical methods, without written permission of the publisher.

Editor - Heather Flournoy
Book Design - LJ Reynolds
Cover Design - Fineline Cover Design

**Sapphire Books Publishing, LLC**
P.O. Box 8142
Salinas, CA 93912
www.sapphirebooks.com

Printed in the United States of America
First Edition – April 2024

This book is licensed for your personal enjoyment only. This book may not be re-sold or given away to other people. If you would like to share this book with another person, please purchase an additional copy for each recipient. If you're reading this book and did not purchase it, or it was not purchased for your use only, then please return to your favorite book retailer and purchase your own copy. Thank you for respecting the hard work of this author.

All rights reserved under U.S. and International copyright conventions. Except for use in reviews, no part of this text may be reproduced, transmitted, downloaded, decompiled, reverse engineered, or stored in a storage and retrieval system, data base, including printing, recording either visual or audio, electronic and any future technology invented without written permission of Sapphire Books Publishing.

The author/publisher expressly prohibits any entity from using the production/publication for purposes of training A.I., artificial intelligence, to generate text that may replicate the author's style or genre similar to this work. The author retains all rights to use this work for purposes of generative AI training and development of any language learning system.

To the extent that the image on the cover of this book depicts a person or persons, such a person is merely a model and is not intended to portray any character feature in this book.

This and other Sapphire Books titles can be found at

www.sapphirebooks.com

# Kim's other books

**Standalones**
1049 Club
After Shadow
Blinded
Connection
Damaged
Shadow Box
She Who Would be King
Swann Song
The Gift
The Plan
Wild
Zero Ward
Control

**Dance with Me Series**
Curtain Call
Encore Performance

**The Traveler Series**
The Traveler - The Hunted
The Traveler - The Hunter

**The Wynter Series**
Finding Faith
Taking Liberty
Justice Won
Keeping Hope
Showing Mercy

# *Dedication*

To all the ladies out there making it happen.

# *Chapter One*

Ashton King stood in the kitchens of King-Kraft Chocolate. Her father, Jack King, had taken over the business from his father Townsend, who had founded the company with Milton Kraft, long dead. Now, as a third-generation chocolate maker, Ashton managed the London location, which was where most of their new flavors were created.

She focused on what she was tasting, the uneaten half of the truffle still clutched between her fingers. Shaking her head, she met the expectant gaze of their head chocolatier. "This is supposed to be…" Ashton reached down and picked up the little placard next to the plate. "Champagne?" she asked, making sure that was, indeed, the flavor that had been placed upon that plate. She shook her head again. "I don't taste it, Katherine."

Katherine turned away, tossing the white towel she'd been twisting between her hands to the counter. "It should, damn it!"

Rolling her eyes at the typical dramatics, Ashton popped the last half into her mouth to make absolutely sure her taste buds weren't off. She reached down and grabbed the glass of water she'd been sipping from to cleanse her palate between tastes. Setting it down, she looked at the angry brunette. "I'm sorry. You're amazing at this, but this one isn't there just yet."

Katherine reached up and tugged off her toque,

her frustration clearly displayed in every movement and expression on her attractive face. She stared at the empty plate and pursed her lips. "I'll have to regroup." She looked over at Ashton. "When do you need these by?"

Ashton took her phone from her pocket and, with a few taps and slides, pulled up the email from her father. "They want them for the New Year's celebrations," she murmured, reading over what she'd been sent. "So," she added, looking over at the other woman. "You still have a couple months." Sliding her phone back into her pocket, she headed toward the exit, high heels clicking on the tile floor. "Keep me posted, Katherine," she said, pushing through the swinging door.

Ashton had a small flat in London she used during the week, but on Fridays, like today, she opted to make the drive to Laddingford, a tiny hamlet just over an hour outside of the city. She yearned for the quiet of the English countryside, and for her small manor house. She'd dubbed it The Ashes—but not for the shortened name of Ash some used when addressing her. Nor was it only because of the veritable forest of ash trees that littered the four acres of the property. She'd named it mostly because the four-bedroom house hadn't been good for much more than firewood when she'd purchased it eight years before.

Now, she buzzed along the narrow roads and lanes as she left the city proper in her beloved 1961 MG MGA 1600 Mark II. The sleek little sports car was fun, and during the warmer months the convertible allowed the wind to blow through her hair, long and as black as the paint on the car's body.

The hedges on either side of the sometimes terrifyingly narrow lane were ten feet tall, turning the road into a little tunneled-off speedway where you had best know where your turnoff was, as it would suddenly appear out of nowhere, If you missed it, you had to keep going unless you were lucky enough to be alone on the road to attempt a U-turn without ending up in a hedge.

She slowed the little car as she got close to her house, waiting for a lorry to pass by, the big truck rumbling along, then turned into the long drive that led to the beautiful old house at the end.

The two-story Georgian-style house was built from stone and had two chimneys symmetrically set on either side of the structure, and two bay windows in the front on the main level. Each filled two identical rooms, one a formal dining room, the other a parlor, with natural light. The upstairs, with its four bedrooms and three bathrooms, was similarly symmetrical. But what had drawn Ashton mostly to the eighteenth-century manor were all the fireplaces, one in just about every room.

Though not all her time was spent in England, as she did have to hop back across the pond occasionally to King-Kraft headquarters in Colorado, she'd spent enough cold and rainy winters in England to know that a good fireplace was extremely handy.

She drove the car back to the only other building on the property, which had been the carriage house when the newer part of the manor had been built in 1763. The smaller building was also made of stone, and during its day was large enough to hold three carriages and their accessories. The horses were kept in the stables, which had vanished long ago.

Now, the musty building sheltered her car as well as all the tools and equipment the caretaker used on the property when she was back in the States. As she climbed out of the low-slung car, she pulled her peacoat tighter around her, even just for the walk to the main house. It was one of those chilly, rainy days in early November, kicking off what was usually a damp, dreary, and gray time of year.

She hurried to the house as quickly as she could, anxious to get out of her heels and into a warm tub of sudsy water, then into flannel pants, slippers, and a fleece pullover. Though getting dolled up was part of the job, it wasn't part of who she was. If it were up to her, she'd go to work with her hair in a ponytail, little to no makeup, and wearing tennis shoes.

Side door unlocked, Ashton let herself into the kitchen, which was large for a kitchen because it had once been the original building on the property. The eighteenth-century manor had been literally built around the stone cottage that had been erected in the mid-fifteen hundreds. Now, it was a kitchen worthy of any chef.

Ashton wasn't interested in food at the moment, so after getting the door closed, she stepped out of her heels and picked up the shoes, then padded through the room to the parlor, which was effectively her living room. She got a good fire started to heat things up downstairs before heading upstairs to change clothes and warm up.

When she'd taken over the house, she'd done her research to make sure that the renovations preserved its historical nature, keeping its character and charm.

She'd been able to purchase the property for so little that she'd been able to put a lot of money into its restoration.

When it had been time for her to go to college, she'd wanted to go into architecture and design, but her father had insisted she go into business instead, earning her MBA from Stanford and hating every second of it, even as she'd graduated top of her class. She hated the business aspect of the company, had no patience for it, but had come to enjoy the creativity of what she'd done in London.

The original business plan, and what was still the focus in Colorado, was the pure chocolate, both milk and dark variations, all produced on-site. Those were used in chocolate bars, syrups, and powders. They were sold in stores outright as candy, but also to coffee shops, bakeries, and such. What Ashton had created in England was the truffle and what she'd dubbed the "flavor pairing" arm of King-Kraft. Though Katherine's impatience and temper could sometimes get to Ashton, there was nobody better in the business, which was why she'd nabbed her from a Michelin-starred restaurant in Kansas to give her her own kitchen in London.

In her bedroom, Ashton stripped out of her women's-cut suit, tossing the blouse into the laundry basket and the jacket and trousers onto the bed to add to her dry-cleaning bag. First, she wanted a bath. She removed her bra and panties as she padded to the bathroom.

The large space had all that would be expected in a bathroom, though the centerpiece was the gorgeous claw-footed tub that was literally at the center of the large room. She reached out and turned the handles to get the water flowing and fill the tub before walking to one of the double sinks to wash the makeup off.

Being a woman who loved all things women, she certainly could appreciate the beautification of a woman through makeup and a nice dress. She equally loved a woman with a clean face, sleep-tousled hair, and an oversized T-shirt sagging off one shoulder.

Looking at her freshly washed face in one of the twin oval mirrors mounted above each pedestal sink, she studied her reflection. For a woman of forty-one, she supposed she looked good. She did her best to keep in shape, considering she dealt with unbelievably amazing chocolate creations all day every day.

She was the same age her mother had been when she'd died, and as she studied her long, brushed-midnight hair, gray eyes, and olive complexion, she saw her mother staring back at her. Though it hadn't technically been ruled a suicide, it may as well have been.

Turning away from the mirror, Ashton walked over to the tub, testing the water temperature before stepping one leg over the high wall and steadying herself before the other leg followed. She eased her nakedness down into the depths. She was beginning to recline back against the slanted back of the tub when she heard footfalls. She managed to stifle her irritated groan.

"Got room for one more in there?" Katherine asked, already undressing as she entered the room.

Ashton glanced over at her. "Of course." She scooted up a bit to make room. "After all, this tub is the size of a small efficiency in Manhattan."

The Brooklyn-born chef smirked as she tossed the last garment aside before she, too, gingerly climbed into the tub. "I didn't know you'd left," Katherine said, getting settled at the opposite end of the tub. Her dark brown eyes bored into Ashton. "Figured we'd come out here together."

Ashton studied the other woman for a moment before replying. "Frankly, I thought you'd stay in the city to continue your toils, considering how upset you got."

"Is that what you preferred I did?" Katherine asked.

This time, Ashton did sigh. "Katherine, please. It's not even quite dinner time yet. Can we hold off on arguing until at least dessert?"

Katherine said nothing, simply looked away. After a moment of pouting she let out a breath, then turned back to Ashton. "So, I was thinking about maybe us taking a drive this weekend," she said, her entire countenance changing as she moved through the water toward Ashton, straddling her hips.

Ashton's hands automatically went to rest on Katherine's thighs. "I can't," she said gently, so as not to anger the other woman. "We're heading toward the holidays, baby, and I have to get ready to head home for meetings to tie everything up with a great big Christmas gift-sized bow."

Katherine's eyebrows drew. "It's November. We 'tied up' the Christmas load here months ago."

"Yes," Ashton conceded. "But, and you know this because you've worked for us for six years, we have the whole gamut of holidays to tie up, plus New Year's coming, Valentine's Day, Easter—"

"Okay, okay," Katherine said, waving off her words. "I get it." She placed her hands on Ashton's shoulders, head slightly cocked to the side as she studied the face of the woman beneath her. "I think we need some time away from all this," she said, indicating the room around them. "We need to reconnect, Ash."

Ashton studied her for a long moment, noting that she truly was a lovely woman when she wasn't ruining it with her mouth or attitude. Finally, she nodded. "Okay. After I get back, we'll see what we can do. Okay?"

Katherine nodded. "Okay." She pointed a finger at Ashton. "I'm holding you to that."

As the plane touched down at Denver International Airport, Ashton felt her stomach begin to twist itself into knots. This was a side effect of the fact she didn't like to fly, as well as she wasn't looking forward to her trip home. At the moment, she intended to stay for a week, two at most, but it would depend on how well things were going stateside, and how much she would be blamed for it.

With a sigh, she leaned forward and grabbed her carry-on. Unzipping the smaller of the three areas, she grabbed her cell phone and powered it on, hers joining the symphony of other phones chiming to life all around her.

Noting she had a text from Leonard, she responded to it, letting him know they'd landed and she'd meet him at the car as soon as she collected her luggage.

An hour later found her sitting in the back of the town car her father had sent to pick her up. She sat in the back, her luggage stowed in the trunk as Leonard, her father's longtime driver, steered the polished black car through downtown Denver traffic. She'd purposefully planned her flight to try and miss the majority of the rush hour traffic.

"How are you, Miss Ashton?" the older Latino man asked, glancing at her through the rearview mirror.

She glanced up from her email messages on her phone to meet his reflected dark gaze. "Real good, Leonard. How are you? Did your daughter finally have her baby?"

He grinned, eyes returning to the road. "She did! Seven pounds, eight ounces. Little Lizbeth is a beauty."

Ashton smiled. "Congratulations, Leonard. The way she was headed, I thought she was having an elephant's pregnancy."

A bark of laughter escaped his lips. "Yes, Miss Ashton. Her husband said the same thing. Seemed like she was pregnant forever. Thank you for asking."

The town car made its way to what was known as Highlands Ranch, a suburb of Denver near Littleton. It had been wide-open ranch land when the house had been built in 1896, the same decade as most of the great big beauties in the Centennial state as monied families began to pour into the area. The Pittman House was built by one such family. Walter Pittman was a cattle tycoon from Canada and had the massive house built on his fourteen hundred acres of ranch land to show off his wealth.

By 1911, the Pittman family patriarch had died, the kids decided to move their cattle back up north to Montana and Canada, and the house was sold to the King family for a song, along with eight hundred of the acres. Ashton's great-grandfather had purchased the home but had kept the original name of The Pittman

House, hoping its prosperity and reputation would attach to the King family even as it was building its wealth.

As the car drove beneath the elaborate wrought iron archway of ivy with an ornate "P" hidden within, Ashton felt her stomach begin to roil. The palatial house was exactly as it had been last time she'd been there over the summer. And, as per usual, no Christmas decorations were hung outside the house as they had been when her mother was alive. The place used to be decked out for every holiday. When her life ended, so did that of the house.

The house was big, beautiful, and cold. As Leonard pulled up into the circular drive in front of the massive portico, a man dressed in the black slacks and white shirt and tie of Jack's hired help was already jogging down the stairs toward the car. She always thought they looked more like they were recent Brigham Young grads than employees to handle house and home.

"Who's that?" Ashton asked, unbuckling her seat belt.

"That's Dekayas," Leonard responded.

"Where's Andy?" Ashton asked, reaching for the door pull only to have the door whisked open by the smiling young Black man.

"Quit," was all Leonard was able to get out of his mouth.

She turned to the new staff member and returned his smile. "Hello, Dekayas," she greeted.

He looked surprised for a moment but quickly regained his composure. "Good afternoon and welcome home, Miss King."

"Thank you," she said, allowing him to take her

hand and, though unnecessary, help her out of the car.

"Your luggage will be in your rooms, ma'am," he said, scurrying to the back of the car as she headed up the stairs to the massive double front doors, the right side of which was already opening.

Ashton smiled. "Hello, Martin. Nice to see you."

"Madam," the older man said gravely as he clicked his heels and stepped aside to allow her entry.

Martin LeCroix had worked for the King family since before Ashton was born. He looked straight out of central casting. A man of about sixty-five now, his snow-white hair was combed straight back from his heavily wrinkled face. He was dressed, as always, in a traditional butler's outfit replete with black morning jacket with tails, gray pinstriped pants, and gray vest. His pristine white dress shirt had a winged collar with a perfectly knotted black tie.

"Mr. King will see you at six o'clock sharp for dinner in the north dining room," he advised, closing the door behind her entry.

She stopped and glanced at him. "North dining room? That's saved for guest visits."

"Indeed, madam," he said, hands behind his back as he stood waiting to be of additional service or to be dismissed.

"Damn it," she muttered. "Okay, Martin. Thank you." She gave him an affectionate smile and headed up the main staircase. She knew that her bags had been brought in through her private entrance, so they'd be there before she was.

The house was nearly twenty-eight thousand square feet, each floor had a different purpose. The main floor was where the kitchen was, the formal dining room, which was large enough to seat sixty, her father's office, and the sitting room and library. The grand staircase split off under the massive crystal chandelier, which hung down almost magically between the two staircases like the sun shining down through the clouds. The main floor also housed the ballroom and great room, which held a fireplace large enough for three grown men to stand in.

On the second floor was the unofficial living room where those in the house would go to curl up in front of the fire and watch TV and relax. There was also a recreation room, which held the pool table, a few arcade games, dartboards, and a wet bar. Many a business deal had been made in that space over the decades. All of that was off one side of the stairs while the opposite led to the guest bedrooms, four in all on that second floor.

A second set of stairs led to the family bedroom suites on the third floor. Her father's was considered the north wing while hers was the south, along with two other suites that were currently unused. The fourth floor held the servant's quarters, though most of the house staff lived off property.

When she reached the double doors that would open into the sitting room of her bedroom suite, she found one side left open for her, Dekayas long gone. A fire was glowing in the small fireplace in the sitting room, making it cozy and inviting. The bedroom beyond was large, the room she'd grown up in. A massive canopy bed was at the center, complimenting the large antique furniture that all belonged to the same set.

She was never allowed to personalize her bedroom but rather had to keep it in pristine, period-appropriate condition. After all, the house was essentially a twenty-eight-thousand-square-foot museum. She saw her luggage left on the side of the room by her dresser and armoire.

With a resigned sigh, she set about to unpack and get ready for dinner.

# Chapter Two

Showered and dressed in a dark blue suit, Ashton made her way downstairs to the north dining room. Her father was already there, standing at the credenza under the row of stained glass pouring himself a scotch. He was dressed impeccably, as she knew he would be. His salt-and-pepper hair was still thick and lush for a man of his age, nearly eighty. He was a well-cut figure for his age, tall, and could be intimidating in his bearing and deep voice.

"Hello, Father," Ashton greeted as she entered the room. The long wooden table, which could seat up to sixteen, was set for three.

"Wondered when you'd finally show," he said in lieu of a greeting, placing the crystal stopper back in the decanter.

"I'm here when you requested me to be." She glanced at the grandfather clock in the corner. "Seven minutes early, in fact."

"Drink?" he asked, sparing a glance at her over his shoulder.

"Scotch is good," she said. "On the rocks, please." She took her seat, noting the plating that was there, the fine white china.

Jack King walked over to the table, a crystal tumbler in each hand. He set the glass with ice in it in front of Ashton and the second at his own place at the head of the table, to her left. He was quiet for a moment before he glanced over at her.

"How're things going overseas?"

She reached for her glass and raised it to her lips, "Good," she said before taking a small sip. She let the burning liquid settle before continuing. "Katherine has worked on some amazing products, some still in the creation process, but I sent some samples of things before I left, so they should arrive in the next day or so."

He nodded, sipping his own drink. "Yes, that's exactly why our guest is coming tonight." A smile came to his lips as he raised his glass in salute. "Speak of the Devil, and he shall appear."

Ashton glanced over and was surprised to see Buck Reynolds, a man who had worked with her father for years. He was a well-known restaurateur in Denver and Colorado Springs. He was one of their biggest local buyers of King-Kraft chocolate as well as the desserts made in their kitchens to sell to his dining customers.

"So he does," Buck said, already extending a hand of greeting to Jack, who stood and took it, the two men sharing a warm one-armed hug and slap to the back. He walked around the table and gave Ashton a quick hug and kiss to the cheek. "Lovely to see you again, Ashton. Been a while."

"It has," she agreed, returning the hug and accepting the kiss. She liked the older man. She had no doubt he could be a little slimy as a husband, a man who loved women as much as he neglected the one he had.

As if a cue had been sent, the moment Buck went to his seat and sat down, the swinging door that was connected to the kitchen swung open and the first course was delivered by kitchen staff and Dekayas, whose position was essentially to be Martin's right-hand man, assisting the butler with many duties.

"So," Ashton began after they were left alone with their salads. "You've been working with my father and King-Kraft for years, Buck." She glanced across the table at him. "Why was I needed here? Not that I mind, mind you. Nice to see you and catch up. But, I'm a bit perplexed what business you'd have with me."

"Well," he said, chewing on the bite of food he'd just put into his mouth. He sipped from his cup of coffee before continuing. "I've gotten into a new venture these days that I want your expertise in." He smirked, glancing over at Jack before returning his gaze to Ashton. "Your father thought you'd be the best to advise. This isn't just my steak houses, seafood shacks, or microbreweries I've gotten into over the last decade."

She studied him with her full attention, intrigued as he talked. She also remained keenly aware of her father's reactions and attitudes during Buck's pitch, wondering where he was in all this. He didn't give away power or control of anything easily. He seemed amused yet a bit disturbed, the wrinkle of uncertainty she'd come to know appearing between his eyes.

"So," Buck said. "I'd like you to come see our location and get your take on what would be wise to do, what our customers would like."

She met his gaze and held it for a moment, then nodded. "All right," she acquiesced. "I'll come."

The building she stood before was completely

unassuming in the LoDo neighborhood, otherwise known as Lower Downtown. It was the oldest area of the city, which had been revamped over the past twenty years, turning the old buildings into hopping restaurants, clubs, and coffee shops.

The three-story brick building she stood in front of had an elegant wood door for entry at ground level, a simple carved wooden sign hanging from a brass pole above it. On the sign was a stylized image of a beautiful woman's face largely silhouetted in shadow, cat ears sprouting from her head.

"Alrighty then," she murmured, looking down at her phone for the key code she was emailed. She noted the keypad on the door in lieu of a doorknob or handle.

Punching in the five-digit code she was given, she heard a loud click and then the door swung slowly open. Looking around to make sure nobody was behind her, Ashton quickly scurried inside, closing the door behind her as prescribed in the email.

She had no idea why the cloak-and-dagger stuff but played along. Once inside, she found herself in an antechamber of sorts, the walls the same naked brick as the building outside. To the right stood a wall, straight ahead was another wood door, and to the left, a curtain of beads. Nowhere else to go, she pushed through those.

She found herself in a small room that looked very much like a coat check with a counter and a hotel bell. Nobody present, she walked up to the counter and lightly slapped the bell with her palm. A moment later, a man popped out of what seemed to be a back room to this sort of back room. He looked young with stylish dark brown hair, though he wore a mask over the upper part of his face, giving the impression of a modern Long Ranger. He looked at her quizzically but stepped up to the counter.

"Hi," she said. "Ashton King. I was asked to be here at four thirty to meet with Mr. Reynolds."

"Ah, yes," he said, nodding. "Did you bring a mask?"

She stared at him. "Mask?"

"Anonymity is key for our members," he explained. "You should have been directed in the key code email you received, but no biggie." He gave her a winning smile before turning to do a wonderful Vanna White impression as he waved at the wall behind him, masks of every stripe hanging on hooks. "Please pick one to borrow."

Pretty sure she'd fallen down the rabbit hole, Ashton pointed at a simple white mask that, like most of them, simply covered her upper face and sprouted into some feather floof at her hairline.

"Here you are," he said, handing her the mask from where he'd taken it from its hook. He went to the computer and typed a few things before the printer began to sputter to life. A few moments later, he tore off the waxy page and peeled off the sticker that read: *Hi, My Name Is Lavender.* "And," he said, holding out his hand, the name tag stuck to his index finger. "Here you are," he said again with a model-perfect smile.

She took the name tag and raised an eyebrow. "Lavender?"

"Our paid members choose a name to go by and that is their only identity here. For guests such as yourself, the computer randomly generates a name," he explained.

She nodded. "Okay," she muttered, about to

press the sticky side of the name tag to her peacoat.

"Oh, you must leave your jacket and any electronics here," he said hastily.

Glancing at him, she shook her head. "Why?" She was getting extremely irritated. She was there to talk chocolate, not meet the president of the United States.

He sighed, seeming to take pity on her. "Many of our members come here to discuss business, often multimillion dollar deals, and they expect privacy and discretion. They don't need a competitor or someone unscrupulous in their live streaming their business on some social media site. The expectation," he continued, accepting the jacket she shrugged out of. "Is that with their not-unsubstantial monthly member fees, they get privacy, anonymity, and, honestly," he added with a smirk. "A place to let their hair down without worries. Thank you," he said, indicating the heavy wool coat in his hands, which he placed on a hanger and hung on a rack at the back of the room, a handful of other jackets already there.

She handed him her phone, wanting to throw a good ol' fashioned fit about that one. Her father *better* appreciate this. "What is this place, anyway?" she asked.

He secured her phone in a lockbox, then grinned at her. "You're at The Black Pussy Cat."

She blinked at him before shaking her head. He indicated with a wave that she should head to the inner wooden door, which he buzzed open for her. She made her way up the narrow, steep staircase to a doorway curtained off by heavy, red velvet drapes. They reminded her of the type that were used for a theatrical production's stage curtains.

Through the curtains, she arrived in a rectangular room, a bit narrow but reaching far back. There were no windows, and the largeish room was done in rich, dark wood paneling with wainscoting up two-thirds of the walls, while a dark green satin-finish wallpaper covered the remaining top portion.

Brass and glass wall sconces were spaced out providing light pockets while Tiffany-style lamps were placed on the smattering of tables that peppered the area. There were also clusters of studded dark brown leather chairs with a small center table for drinks or whatnot. All the furniture was heavy and chunky, masculine. She could smell the sweet scent of cigar or pipe smoke without the cloud.

It very much reminded her of her father's office back at the family house. She noticed a mahogany bar that stretched the length of one of the shorter ends of the room, a man standing sentinel behind it. He, like other men she saw delivering drinks or cleaning tables, wore a starched white wing-collar shirt with bow tie and a red vest with black trousers. She wondered with amusement if they all shopped at the same store as Martin.

All the men were younger, well-kempt, and clean cut. It was so nice not to have to look at the wild, lumberjack beards so popular with men of their age group that she had to look at every day out in the world. All these young men were handsome and, as she herself, masked.

For a moment she wondered if she'd been summoned to a high-priced club for gay men, but then she saw the women. There were only a few, but they were magnificent. Two of them were standing with some suited men, and both held a drink in their hands, so she figured they must be members.

The women were dressed in evening gowns, hair in fancy up-dos. They both wore masks, though theirs were made of black leather and seemed to be fitted especially for the contours of their faces. They reached to just above the brow ridge and just below the cheekbones, revealing foreheads and lower face. Unlike the men's, however, the women's masks curved up at either corner to what appeared to be a small pair of cat ears.

"Ma'am, can I help you?"

Ashton turned to see one of the waiters standing next to her. "I'm here for a meeting with Mr. Reynolds."

"Ah, yes. If you'd like to step up to the bar and get a drink, I'll let him know you're here…" He glanced down at her name tag. "Lavender."

"Thank you," she said politely, though she felt she'd stepped into the creepiest game of *Clue* ever. *Lavender in the lounge with a highball glass.* She smirked at her thoughts as she headed to the bar.

"What can I get you?" The barkeep asked, a bright smile in place.

"Do you have white zin?" She rested her hand on the smooth, polished bar top.

He grinned. "Absolutely." He reached behind him to grab a wineglass from the collection hanging upside down by their base. "But here," he added, popping the cork from a chilled bottle. "We call it white sin."

She returned his grin. "White sin it is." She rested her elbow on the bar and glanced around the room. "What is this place?"

"On the record," he said absently as he poured her wine. "It's a place for wealthy businessmen to come and talk deals and relax among their peers."

He recorked the bottle and set the glass on the bar in front of her. With a twinkle in his dark eyes, he added, "Off the record? It's a place for ridiculously rich old dudes to come and gossip, brag, and pretend they're young and virile with gorgeous young ladies giving them the time of day in conversation."

She took the glass and chuckled. "Good to know." She brought the glass to her lips and, as she took a sip of the cold drink, she noted the most amazing behind she'd ever seen on a woman. It rivaled Pippa Middleton in her famous white dress.

This woman was in an emerald-green evening gown, backless with the halter strap visible around the back of her neck as she bent slightly over a table speaking to the man who sat there. Her back was to Ashton, who couldn't look away. The woman had dark auburn hair, pulled into a sophisticated chignon.

Typically, she wasn't a woman who was drawn to a great ass. Appreciative, sure, but not drawn to it. In that moment as she sipped her drink, all she could think about was grinding against that perfect ass, or even holding onto it as she took her from behind with a cock strapped to her hips. Warmed by such a thought and the white zinfandel beginning to move through her system, she was left stunned when the woman stood fully erect and turned in her direction.

Though she wore a black mask similar to the other two women's, it was easy to see that she was breathtaking. Her face had a beautiful bone structure, her skin the pale creaminess of a redhead. It looked so very soft and touchable. That dress looked as though it had been created for her body, clinging to her form in all the right ways, lovingly caressing womanly curves that Aphrodite herself would envy.

Ashton's gaze drifted back up to her face, slowing when she reached her cleavage and the beauty of her decolletage, which for Ashton was her favorite part of a woman. A black lace choker was clasped at the woman's throat, a single pearl the only decoration.

She noted the woman's mouth, which, like her facial structure, was perfect. The lips were full but not too full, perfect for kissing. Ashton loved to watch a mouth like that as the person spoke, the way the lips and teeth worked together.

Of all the amazing things she'd noticed about the incredibly beautiful woman, what she found most riveting were her eyes. Though seen only through holes in the mask, they were striking. She couldn't see much detail at this distance, but she could make out that they were green, further enhanced by the color of her gown.

It wasn't so much the color that caught Ashton by surprise, but their depth. As the woman looked back at her, she felt as though this stranger was looking into her very soul, and in turn, Ashton could see inside that of the woman. It was disconcerting, and the silent game of chicken ended when Ashton looked away.

"Delicious, isn't she?" was asked softly from beside her, startling Ashton.

She glanced over to see Buck standing there, a knowing smile on his lips. Feeling ashamed at gawking so openly, something she tried not to do as she respected women far too much to treat them as men treated them, she quickly schooled her features. "Hello, Buck. Nice to see you again."

"Indeed. Come," he said, placing a guiding hand on her lower back. "Let's go talk in my office."

# *Chapter Three*

Standing at the kitchen counter downstairs, Ashton poured herself a cup of coffee, watching as the dark brew filled her mug. The aroma was wonderful as it wafted up in the steam to warm her face. Task complete, she replaced the carafe onto the coffeemaker's hotplate and carried her mug to the huge cooking island so she could look in the fridge for flavored coffee creamer.

"What are you doing?"

She glanced up at the unexpected voice of her father, who stood at the entryway of the large room. "Making coffee," she said unnecessarily.

"Why didn't you have Dekayas or Maxine make you a cup?" he asked, stepping up to the opposite side of the island. It was large enough that three grown men could easily lay side by side atop the marble.

"Because I'm capable of doing for myself," she explained easily, finding a bottle of French vanilla on a shelf. She let the fridge door close as she headed back to her cup. "Want some?"

He looked down at her mug, then nodded. "I would."

"Spoke with Buck yesterday," she said, walking over to the cabinet where she found a mug and grabbed one for her father, filling it and setting it next to hers on the island. She raised the bottle of creamer and, at his nod, began to pour. "Say when."

"And?" he asked, placing a well-manicured hand on the cool island top. "How did that go? When."

She eased the bottle upright and used the spoon she'd grabbed for her own coffee and stirred the creamer in before sliding the mug across to him. "And, I think this is a strange bedfellow for us," she responded, turning to prepare her own coffee. She gave it an experimental sip before meeting his gaze. "His restaurants and coffeehouses, they absolutely make sense. But this one..."

He sipped his coffee, a thoughtful expression on his face. "What are your concerns?"

What, indeed? She considered his question before responding. "Well, he gave me a tour of the place. Beautiful location."

"But?"

"I don't see how it's beneficial for our brand," she said, bringing up her cup to blow on then sip the hot brew. "I don't know that we want to find ourselves connected to a gentlemen's club." She lowered her mug, sparing her father a glance. "However..."

Jack raised a bushy eyebrow as he sipped his own.

"What Buck wants is very different. What if we created an offshoot brand?" she suggested. "Like, how we have King-Kraft Chocolate here in Denver, which Brian heads, and King-Kraft Creations in London, which of course I head, all the under the larger umbrella of King-Kraft, which you head."

He studied her for a long moment before asking, "Why are you wanting this to come under its own LLC?"

"Because The Black Pussy Cat isn't exactly our regular client. Meaning," she added, "I'm not sure they'd be interested in our regular products."

He nodded. "Very different type of clientele, understood. You're right, it's not our normal wheelhouse, but the clientele has very deep pockets, and we could see a spillover effect into our mainstream products. Seems like it's worth exploring. So, what's your plan?"

"I think that we should see if this is a viable new market." She shrugged. "What do you think?"

"Was it open when you were there? Did you get to speak to the customers? Staff?"

"No, there were only a couple members there before Buck took me to his office, then he ushered me out as things picked up," Ashton explained.

Jack nodded. "All right. I want you to go back and observe a full service. Speak to the people, especially the staff. What would work, what would not be appropriate for the clientele, etc."

"I'm on it. I'll call Buck this morning and make arrangements."

"I like it," Jack said, grabbing his mug and turning away from the island. "I want you to get with Brian as well. Get his input."

"Will do," she promised.

"Thank you," Ashton said, smiling at the young man who had brought her up to the third floor.

"Someone will be with you in just a minute," he said at the door to the small room he'd unlocked for her. "Do you want anything brought up? Wine? Appletini, perhaps?"

She was going to decline, but said instead, "Surprise me."

"Yes, madam." With a smile, he softly closed the door behind him.

Left alone, Ashton looked around the small square room that was not much bigger than a walk-in closet. It was lit in hues of blue and green, calming even as she felt like she was on an underwater set piece. On one wall was an oversized couch of deep blue, and perpendicular was a matching armchair. A round, light-colored wooden table was in front of the two, the letters *TBPC* projected down upon it from above.

The third floor was a simple affair of a hallway with closed, open, or curtained-off doorways on either side. Based on the distance between the doors on her side of the hall, Ashton figured the line of rooms were similar in size to the one she sat in. After passing one that was open on the opposite side, she figured those rooms were larger, as there had been a group of men gathered around a table playing cards.

She sat on the couch, which was remarkably comfortable, and crossed one leg over the other. She yearned for a day off to be lazy in flannel pajama pants and a T-shirt as she read a book or watched some TV. Instead, she was in yet another pantsuit, as she despised skirts or dresses. She thought women looked amazing in both, just not her.

A moment later, the door opened and a woman stepped inside, a tumbler in one hand, wineglass in the other. Ashton sat up a bit straighter and her arm fell from where it had been stretched out along the back of the couch. The woman walked over to the table and set down her load. As she did, she glanced up into Ashton's eyes. Those eyes had been mesmerizing halfway across the room, but from two feet away, Ashton could see those emerald-green eyes were encircled by a dark blue ring. She felt her breath catch as they held eye contact for the briefest of moments.

The woman walked back to the door, pushing it closed with a soft click before returning, stepping around the table to take a seat on the couch mere inches from Ashton. The dress she wore was similar in style to the one the first night she'd seen her, though this one was a deep burgundy and had a slit up along the left leg that nearly reached her hip. The black mask was in place and her hair was pulled up, revealing the incredibly enticing column of her neck.

Ashton so wanted to lean over and bury her face in that perfume-scented skin. Her gaze again fell to the beautiful cleavage the woman possessed, equally enticing as her neck. As the woman brought her left leg up to cross over her right, the slit revealed much of a muscular thigh and calf. She wore black stilettos, one dangling off her left foot as it lazily swung to and fro.

"See something you like?" she asked, a bit of sarcasm in her tone.

Clearing her throat, Ashton looked away, feeling like a complete asshole. "I apologize," she said, meeting the other woman's gaze. "You're absolutely beautiful."

A small smile quirked that perfect mouth. "Thank you," she responded softly. She looked away for a moment then leaned forward, grabbing the tumbler off the table as well as the glass of white wine. "A surprise, as requested."

Ashton took the cocktail, decorated with a blackberry and mint leaf garland. It was a purplish-pink color, a small straw sticking out of the liquid. "What is it?" she asked as she sniffed, trying to identify its scent.

"A Purple Haze," the woman responded. "Since you were Lavender last time..." She glanced down at the name tag pressed just above Ashton's left breast. "Carlos?"

Ashton grinned. "Yes, that's me. For tonight." She studied the woman sitting next to her who sipped at her own drink. "What's your name? Are you the one Buck sent in to give me the lowdown on this place?"

The woman cocked her head slightly to the side as she studied Ashton. "Pearl," she said simply. "And, yes."

"Pearl," Ashton murmured, tasting the name on her tongue. "Is that why you wear the pearl choker?" She nodded to the black lace adornment once again clasped just above the hollow of her throat.

"Indeed," she said, reaching up and lightly fingering the gem. "We all wear them. Not exactly anywhere to place a name tag, is there?" she asked, indicating the cleavage-baring neckline of her dress.

Ashton grinned. "So, I assume then that Pearl isn't your real name?"

"You can assume that. You see," she added softly. "We're all Buck's gems. We have a Sapphire, a Ruby, and even an Onyx." She smirked. "And a few others that are a little less precious."

Ashton smiled. "And they wear a gem that is appropriate?"

Pearl nodded. "Yes. So, what is it you need to know?" she asked, studying Ashton over the rim of her glass as she took a sip.

"Well, I run—"

Pearl reached out a hand and gently placed two fingers over Ashton's lips. "Don't tell me the name," she murmured, allowing her fingers to lightly slide off

Ashton's lips, almost caressing her chin as her hand fell away. "Just tell me what your product is."

A little discombobulated from the touch, Ashton blinked for a moment. Finally, she said, "Chocolate." She needed a moment, so brought up the drink and took a sip from the skinny straw. The drink was cool and sweet, but she could tell she'd have to take it slow. It would not do her well at all to get buzzed around this woman, who was intoxicating all by herself.

Pearl studied her for a long moment, those eyes boring into Ashton like lasers. She reached out and ran her fingers through Ashton's hair, brushing it back from her face. "You have the softest looking hair," she said absently. "So dark."

Ashton felt as though she'd been touched by a live wire, electricity rushing through her. "Thank you,' she managed.

"So," Pearl said, her hand falling away from Ashton's hair, though it remained resting on the back of the couch just behind Ashton's right shoulder. "What do me and chocolate have in common?"

Ashton groaned inwardly. She could easily make that connection as she imagined licking some dark chocolate syrup from Pearl's cleavage. Instead, she cleared her throat and tried to focus on why she was there. "Buck wants us to create something that would make sense for this club," she explained. "We provide desserts and such for many of his restaurants, but this place is different, and a giant piece of Black Forest cake isn't exactly what this place cries out for."

"I'd agree with that," Pearl said with a nod.

"So, what I need from you is to know what this place is like. What do the men who are members here order? Why are they here? What role do you ladies play?" She looked around. "I have to admit, I was surprised by these rooms." She met Pearl's gaze. "Is this place..." She knew what she was thinking but somehow couldn't voice it.

Pearl cocked her head to the side a bit. "Is this place, what?" she asked, though the tone of her voice told Ashton she was playing with her, and that she knew exactly what was being asked.

"Are these rooms used for...um...Do the members here have some very hands-on privileges?" she finally managed, feeling stupid.

Pearl seemed amused. "Some try," she admitted. "Particularly the newer members. But, we have house rules here, and all of us have our own personal ones, too."

Intrigued, Ashton asked, "What are they? Both house and personal."

"House rules," she began, readjusting her position a bit on the couch, her leg grazing Ashton's. "Masks remain on at all times, no real names. No penetration of *any* orifice."

A bark of laughter escaped Ashton's lips. She brought up a hand to cover her mouth. "Sorry." She chuckled, trying to stop. "The way you worded that just amused the hell out of me."

"That's how it's worded in the employee handbook." Pearl smirked. "What you were wearing at 'hello,' you must be wearing through 'goodbye.'"

"Okay," Ashton drawled. "And, what are your own personal rules?"

Pearl brought her elbow to rest on the back of the couch then rested her temple against a closed fist as she looked over at Ashton. "Yes means yes and no means no," she said simply. "And," she added. "No kissing."

"Why?" Ashton asked, suddenly very interested in the other woman's response. "Why no kissing?"

"Because that's just for me and whomever I want to share that with. It's not a door prize, and neither am I."

"I can understand that," Ashton said quietly.

"I also don't drink when I'm at work," Pearl added.

Confused, Ashton nodded toward the wineglass that sat on the table next to her own drink. "You have wine right there."

That little smirk on her lips, Pearl leaned forward and grabbed the glass, holding it out to Ashton. "Take a sip."

Ashton glanced at her then the glass, taking it from her. For just a moment it occurred to her she was about to drink after a complete stranger, but it was also a bit of a thrill, knowing her lips and tongue had been there.

She brought the glass to her lips and took a tiny sip. Eyebrows drawing, she looked at Pearl. "Apple juice?"

Pearl smiled, white even teeth beautiful with those lips. She took the glass from Ashton and sipped from it, eyeing Ashton as she did. "So, what sorts of treats are you interested in providing for the club?" she asked, her tone changing, seeming to want to get back on track of the purpose for Ashton's visit. She forced herself out of the fog of arousal she was falling into, angry that she was allowing this woman to get to her so completely.

Ashton sat up a bit straighter, as she'd realized that, like a plant to the sun, she'd begun to lean a bit toward the woman sitting so closely to her. She could certainly see why the men returned to the club, not only for the industry talk and good booze, but for women like Pearl who were very good at what they did. She needed to be careful. Everything about Pearl dripped sex and the best fuck of your life, but there was something to the gorgeous redhead that went deeper, an intelligence and understanding within her that Ashton sensed could be dangerous to the heart, if nothing else.

"When I was downstairs earlier, I noticed a lot of top-shelf liquors. In fact, I think I only saw top-shelf liquors," she said.

Pearl nodded. "You won't find cheap vodka here. Has Buck told you about his bourbon?" she asked.

"No. You mean, his own label?" Ashton asked, very interested.

"I do. You should talk to him about it. May be something you can incorporate. The members here enjoy it quite a bit. Good seller."

Wheels beginning to turn, Ashton nodded. "Thanks for the information." She met the gaze of the woman who was staring back at her. She wished she could see the entire face. "And, what about for you ladies?" she asked. "What would be a nice bridge for you with the men you entertain, in your various ways?"

"Some of us are more interactive with the members than others." Pearl grinned. "Bigger tips," she explained.

"You ladies can take tips?" That got Ashton's curiosity. "How does the pay structure work for you? I'd assume a typical hourly wage, right?"

"Aren't you Miss Curious," Pearl said softly, her voice nearly a purr.

"You're right. I'm sorry, that's none of my business," Ashton said, waving off the question.

"No." Pearl leaned forward and set her wineglass down on the table before resettling next to Ashton. Her free hand moved across her own lap to rest on Ashton's thigh. It was absolutely extraordinary the effect this woman had on her. "I don't mind," Pearl murmured, her nails running random trails across the material of Ashton's pant leg down by her knee. "Yes, we make a wage, and yes, we accept tips. Like most in the service industry, tips are our bread and butter."

"So something interactive would be a plus, then?"

Pearl grinned. "What do you have in mind?" A single fingernail trailed dangerously close to the inside of Ashton's thigh before quickly moving away.

Ashton's breath caught, her heart rate increasing. "Well, I don't know," she sputtered. "I have no idea how far things are allowed to go."

"Each woman determines that for herself. But," Pearl said, uncrossing her legs and pushing to her feet. "I think something like that, to give the member an even better experience, would be a good thing for the ladies."

Ashton also got to her feet, following Pearl to the door. "Wait," she said, reaching into a pocket to bring out the slim wallet she carried that held cash and her bank cards. She took out a hundred-dollar bill and held it out toward the other woman. "For your time and the information. Thank you."

Pearl looked down at the money, then up to Ashton's eyes. That sexy little smirk crossed her lips. "This one's on the house," she murmured, bringing up a hand and brushing her fingers under Ashton's chin before turning away.

"How did you end up stuck talking to me?" Ashton blurted out. She had no idea why, as it didn't really matter. Perhaps she just wasn't quite ready for Pearl to leave.

Pearl paused at the door she'd just pulled open and glanced over her shoulder at Ashton. "I volunteered," she said, then was gone.

# *Chapter Four*

Okay, let's see what we've got here," Brian said, using an X-Acto knife to slice through the tape on the boxes sent over from Buck Reynolds. Brian, as average-looking a white guy as they came with blond hair and dull blue eyes, had worked with King-Kraft for fourteen years and had done a great job managing the Denver locale.

Ashton watched as he fished through the packing material and brought up the first of four bottles of BR Bourbon, the high-end label Buck had created for his club, restaurants, and liquor stores.

"What do you think?" she asked her father, passing him the bottle she'd just been handed.

Jack held the bottle up to the light, studying the liquid inside. "Good color," he murmured, almost as if to himself. Though a scotch man, Jack King was no stranger to the finest things in life, and whiskey was no exception. "Give me a glass," he ordered, tearing away the gold foil wrapping at the top before unscrewing the cap.

"Here you go, Mr. King," Brian said, scurrying over to a cabinet in the testing kitchen in the Denver location to grab the requested glass, setting it on the stainless steel table in front of the older man.

Ashton watched as her father did his usual ritual of opening a new bottle. He'd sniff it, look at it against a light source, sniff it again, pour some, sniff it, swirl it in the glass, then take a drink. She was always amused and bemused by it but said nothing, simply waited for the verdict.

Finally, he nodded, looking down into the glass with the little bit of the bourbon remaining. "Smooth," he said. "Good flavor." He looked to Brian. "I think it would be a good companion with our chocolate."

Ashton stared at the two men, from one to the other as they began to discuss options. "Excuse me, Father," she said, taking a step toward the table where they stood. "Brian and I already have a plan. We just wanted to make sure the bourbon was palatable."

They both turned to look at her, Brian quickly looking away, busying himself with opening the other boxes. At length, Jack cleared his throat and held out his hand with the glass in it. After Ashton took it, he grabbed the fedora he always wore with his ever-present suit and walked out of the room.

She looked down into the light brown liquid before she walked over to the sink and dumped it out, rinsing the glass and sink. She felt a mixture of anger and hurt, the common theme when her father was involved.

"You know," Brian said, voice a bit hushed as he began to break down the emptied boxes. "I've never understood sexism when it comes to intelligence."

Ashton glanced over at him from where she stood at the sink.

He met her gaze. "My daughter is every bit as important and brilliant as my sons are," he continued. "Equal opportunity to equal ambition."

She smiled at him. "Thanks, Brian. I appreciate that."

"This shit is smooth as hell," Brian said from

where he stood at the table. "I do agree with your dad," he continued, glancing over at her, the bottle cap in his hand that he'd used as a shot glass. "This will work well."

Ashton nodded in acknowledgment. "Excellent. Did you get the email I sent you?"

"I did. And," he said, reaching over and grabbing a box that had been sitting on the table when Ashton and Jack had entered the kitchen. He quickly sliced open the tape and pulled open the flaps. "This wasn't a great seller for us last Valentine's Day, but it might be able to give you or Buck an idea if it'll work for this place."

Ashton reached into the box and withdrew a product wrapped in clear plastic. It was an object made of a gummy-type material that was four inches long and red on one half and white on the other. It was just a little bit bigger around than the index finger of an average woman.

She looked at Brian for guidance, very serious doubt on her mind—and no doubt on her face as well. He laughed and took it from her.

"Okay," he said, tearing open the package and removing the treat. "This is that gummy dough made from chocolate your girl in London came up with a couple years back."

Ashton nodded. "Right, okay."

"So, this side is strawberry," he said, tapping the red side. "This one vanilla. Inside is strawberry jam here and a vanilla cream on the white side. So, the point is, you get two people on either end," he explained, turning the thing so one end was pointed at her, the other at him. "You both kind of gnaw your way to the middle, all the while pushing the strawberry and vanilla stuff to the middle, where it's weaker."

Ashton stared at the thing, imagining what he was explaining. "Keeps you pretty close together," she said.

"Yup. See, once you reach that weak point in the middle, which gets weaker all the while as the jelly stuff is smooshed against it, you're damn near kissing when it finally pops and explodes a mixture of the two flavors inside both people's mouths."

"Oh, wow," she murmured, taking it from him to get a better look at it. "What were the complaints?" she asked.

"Too messy. Not appealing looking," he said.

"Can see why. Pretty boring." She nibbled each side, curious of the flavor. "Tastes good," she said, though quickly brought a finger up as the jelly began to run down her chin. "Yes, messy."

Brian hurried to the sink and tore off a paper towel for her, which she used to wipe her face.

"Thanks. Okay," she said, putting the remainder back into the package. "For our clientele at the club, what do you think about making these the same basic size, but make them look like actual cigars? Then," she added, getting excited. "Let's create a filling that is based on popular cocktails, like amaretto on one end, sour mix on the other." She met his gaze. "That sort of thing. Thoughts?"

"I love it," he said, nodding his approval. "And, you know you could upsell him. We could create a version for his coffeeshops, too. You know, like coffee-flavored cream on one side and French vanilla on the other, something like that."

"Brilliant," she said, pulling out her phone and quickly tapping away a message to Katherine with their new ideas. "Brilliant, brilliant, brilliant."

The room was beautiful to be sure. Ashton was impressed as she toured the bedroom, massive bathroom, and living room area. King-Kraft clearly had spared no expense. Turning to the woman who also was perusing the area, she smiled.

"Looks mighty comfortable," she said. "And of course, anything you want or need, food, a ride, all that, just charge it to the room. We'll take care of it."

Katherine nodded, bringing up a hand to run through her hair. "It's beautiful, but I don't understand why I'm staying here and not with you." She met Ashton's gaze. "Would certainly save a few bucks."

Ashton tried her best not to get exasperated. "It's like I explained to you when I picked you up at the airport," she said as gently as she could. "This isn't pleasure, it's business. I've barely even been home since I got here. This new endeavor, which is why we brought your brilliance here, is sucking up the vast majority of my time."

"I understand that," the baker said, her gaze boring into Ashton. "But wouldn't it make more sense for us to have that pillow time together to talk about all this? After all," she added, a bit of bite to her tone. "Aren't we working on different parts of the same project?"

Ashton let out a sigh. "Katherine, by the time I get back to the house, I shower and crash. Today alone I've had six meetings, picked you up, and now I'm headed to the location to speak to our client and his staff about the upcoming product line."

She walked over to the woman she'd experienced a great deal of passion and creative genius with, but also nearly just as much strife and tumult. So often their relationship had been a battleground more than partnership.

"Baby," she said, using a conciliatory tone as she took one of Katherine's hands. "I need you this week." She looked into suspicious dark eyes. "I need you to do what I sought you out to do. You're at the top of your game in your field, and right now, with this brand-new and extremely exciting line we're starting, you have so much creative control it's not even funny."

Katherine looked down for a moment before she nodded. "All right."

Though relieved, Ashton knew it would be short-lived. So, she added, "Besides, I honestly don't want you to have to deal with my father. If I had my own place here, that would be different, but I don't."

Katherine's head snapped up, eyebrows drawn. "Your dad and I get along. What's the issue there?"

"My dad and I do not, however," she said quietly. "It's enough for me to have to deal with him and his consistent disappointment that I don't have a penis." She left a quick kiss on slightly pouting lips. "I have to go. I have to get over to the club."

"Do you want me to come with you?" Katherine asked, a bit of desperation in her voice as Ashton had turned to leave.

Her back to the other woman, Ashton closed her eyes for a moment, silently counting to three before she turned around, a smile planted on her laps. "You just got in from a long flight that I know is exhausting. I made sure you got a room with a massive sunken tub, Katherine." She reached around and smacked the attractive woman on the behind. "Use it." She turned back to the door and hurried toward it. "I have to get before I'm late."

Climbing into the car she'd left behind at Pittman House when she'd moved overseas, she closed the door and absently reached for the seat belt as she considered the last few moments in Katherine's suite. She felt like such a bitch. She'd said what she'd needed to say to get Katherine to do her job and not hop on the next flight back to London.

Getting involved with Katherine Whispell had been a mistake, she understood. Their time together had been nothing but a roller coaster of highs and lows, a cluster of breakups and make-ups, each more bitter than the last. It wasn't what she wanted. The good makeup sex used to be exciting and at times worth the drama, but that had long ago grown old and cold. She wanted off the roller coaster.

Letting out a heavy sigh, she started the car and pulled out of her space in the parking garage and headed to her next and final location for the day before heading home and taking a long, hot bath.

---

Ashton watched, waiting. She noted several expressions crossing the faces before her, the entire staff that would be working at the club that night, from bartenders to waiters to the ladies. That is, all except one, one very specific woman she would have liked to see. She'd forced herself to not look around expectantly or ask about her. Instead, she stayed focused. She was there for a particular reason, and Pearl wasn't it.

"I think this one is a little too strong," one of the women said, whom Ashton had come to know as Emerald, or Em for short. She held up the remainder of the bourbon truffle. "But I don't like bourbon, so..." She shrugged, handing the last of the candy to the bartender standing next to her, who popped it into his mouth.

"I think it's awesome," he muttered around the bourbon-flavored chocolate.

"So, this will seriously be made out of chocolate?" one of the waiters asked, holding up the mock-up of the little box that would contain either one of the assorted truffles Katherine was creating—chocolate cufflinks or a chocolate money clip.

"Yeah. It'll be an entirely edible gift," Ashton responded.

"Cool as shit," he muttered.

"Now, we have one more thing," she said, holding up the Cocktail Cigar. "This is something that is meant to be used between lovers, or even just something that..." She grinned and wiggled the cigar suggestively. "Can help you get a bigger tip."

"Um, where exactly are we supposed to put that?" the woman called Garnet asked, earning a round of laughter and a chuckle from Ashton.

"This end," she explained, tapping one side, "tastes like one thing, while this side," she continued to an utterly captive audience, "tastes like another. Together," she said, holding the cigar at the center, "It tastes like a popular cocktail. Each cigar is different."

"Fucking awesome." One of the waiters laughed, shaking his head. "In that little thing?"

"Yup."

"You have to show us how that works," Em said,

eyeing the cigar with uncertainty.

"Why don't the two of you do it," Ashton suggested, holding the sweet out. "It takes two." She smirked. "Unless one of you wants to volunteer?"

"Isn't that my job?"

Ashton looked over to her right and saw a vision in scarlet step into the room through the red velvet curtains. Her confidence, her bearing, the soft sway of her hips as she made her way over to them, all left Ashton speechless.

Pearl spared a searing glance to Ashton before turning to Garnet, who met her just before she joined them at the bar.

"How'd it go?" the tall blonde asked quietly, concern in her voice.

"Talk to you about it later," Pearl murmured, accepting the one-armed hug before turning back to Ashton, her sultry firmly back in place. "What are we doing?" she asked as she walked up to Ashton.

Instantly Ashton was enveloped in the redhead's perfume, just as sensual as the woman who wore it. She cleared her throat to get her bearings back and held up the Cocktail Cigar. "This is a little treat we whipped up for you guys. You start here," she said, pointing to the end closest to Pearl. "I'll start here," she continued, lightly pinching the end closest to her. "And, we'll meet here," she concluded, pointing to the center.

"My, my, Rosebud," Pearl murmured, a twinkle in her eyes. "That's mighty phallic of you."

Ashton smirked and took a step closer to the beautiful woman, looking her in the eye as she held the treat just an inch or so from those ruby-red lips. Eyes on Ashton the entire time, Pearl opened her mouth just enough to allow the sweet treat in. Forcing herself to hold that gaze, Ashton did the same.

The subtle flavor hit Ashton's palate, smoked whiskey with a hint of orange. She took small little nibbles, as did Pearl, the two moving ever so slowly toward the other. She could hear the little comments from the peanut gallery, snickers, and cat calls. The situation was so ridiculous, such an intimate thing to do with an audience, Ashton had to force herself not to start giggling.

She felt a hand rest on her hip and had to set her own on the bar top to avoid doing the same, as she knew she'd pull Pearl closer to her. As the cigar got shorter and shorter a nibble at a time, they were forced to tilt their heads a bit in the opposite direction or bump noses. She could feel Pearl's breath on her face and the heat of her hand through her clothing.

Distantly, Ashton heard someone say. "Shit..."

A soft gasp left Ashton's mouth when she felt the softest touch of Pearl's bottom lip brush across her own. That gasp from her turned into a small cry of surprise from Pearl when, with a small *pop*, the center of the cigar burst, the two flavors forced into both their mouths. They both laughed as the gooey insides began to seep out. It now became a mission of containment, but the containment vessel was both their mouths, working together.

Ashton started slightly when she felt Pearl's tongue glide against hers. She didn't think it was done on purpose, but then the soft sigh she felt more than heard made it clear that when it happened a second time, it wasn't an accident. Of its own accord, Ashton's hand slid along the bar until she felt the softness of Pearl's dress against the side of her thumb.

She turned her wrist, fingertips coming into contact with the material and heat beneath as she rested her hand gingerly on Pearl's waist.

"Fuck, that's hot," somebody said, which seemed to zap Pearl back into reality with a sharp gasp as she backed away.

Ashton met the wide, greenish-blue eyes and flushed face. She had no doubt her own was flushed as well, as her heart was racing and her body was on fire. After a moment, Pearl seemed to gather herself as she reached up a hand and trailed a finger along Ashton's bottom lip, gathering a bit of the filling from the Cocktail Cigar that had dribbled there. She brought the fingertip to her own mouth, parting her lips and poking out her pink tongue, licking off the bit of jelly from her fingertip.

"Very nice," she murmured, holding Ashton's gaze. "An Old-Fashioned." She turned to look at her coworkers. "What do you think, guys? Yay or nay?"

Hearing nothing, Ashton glanced over, too. The entire group was staring at them with mouths hanging open, one of the women fanning herself with a drink menu from the bar top.

"Guys?" Pearl said.

"Um," one of the bartenders said, reaching up and rubbing the back of his neck. "Total keeper."

Grinning, Ashton looked back to Pearl, who was already looking at her. "Are you planning to stay?" Pearl asked.

"Should I?" Ashton responded with a raised eyebrow in question, though it was hidden behind her mask.

"I don't know," Pearl murmured. "Should you?"

# *Chapter Five*

"You really think that helping her around the house, collecting trash, not just taking out the trash, will make a difference?"

Ashton nodded, bringing the hand that held her glass of ice water to her lips. "I know it will."

The man Ashton had been chatting with for more than an hour sat there in his comfortable studded leather chair, identical to the one she currently sat in. She'd essentially made the main bar her unofficial office in the club, chatting with various members and staff over the last few weeks to identify what additional products she could develop. Occasionally Brian would join her for a meeting with Buck, but she was doing most of the info-gathering footwork on her own. It didn't hurt that this arrangement also allowed her to catch a glimpse of Pearl on an almost daily basis. As hard as she tried, and as professional as she could muster, the beguiling woman drove her to distraction. Even when Pearl was not in sight, Ashton found it difficult to keep her mind on her work. She quickly refocused her attention on the man in front of her, hoping to rejoin the conversation without losing her place.

"So," he said finally. "Is that what you do with your…significant other?"

"I would," Ashton said with a nod. "If I had one."

He looked at her, eyes widening through the holes of his mask. "A beautiful woman like you?" he said, a genuine compliment as opposed to the sloppy come-ons she was used to. "Even as a lesbian, I figured you'd be taken."

She chuckled. "Thanks, Ken. I appreciate that."

He let out a heavy sigh, then slapped his own thighs just before pushing his bulk to his feet. "Okay. Guess I should head home and see if she's calmed down a little."

Ashton grinned. "Well, another bit of advice, and Mr. R," as Buck was known at the club, "May not like me saying this, but hanging out here probably isn't helping things. You may want to look into activities that serve you both."

He glanced down at her, chewing on his bottom lip before running a pudgy hand through thinning strawberry blond hair. He nodded. "Point taken. Have yourself a good evening."

"You do the same, and oh!" She smiled at the man who turned back to look at her as he'd begun to walk away. "Chocolate. Balm for the woman's soul."

He laughed as he turned back to head out. "Good evening, Pearl," he said as the lovely woman walked toward them. "It's so nice to see you." He stopped for a moment and left a rather chaste, almost fatherly kiss to her cheek.

"Hello, Ken," she greeted, allowing the kiss. "You're looking well, and it sounds like you got some solid advice." She glanced at Ashton. "Definitely go with the chocolate."

Ashton watched the interaction and how Pearl was with him. Ken was definitely not like many of the other men there, Ashton had found. He was kind and seemed quite lonely in an unhappy marriage, though it was one he wanted to work but wasn't sure how to do so. Gone was the sensual vixen that could level a grown man—or woman—with a look. Instead, the woman standing there in her place was kind, caring, an easy smile. She took his hand in hers, comforting, not seducing.

As the two parted, the older man heading toward the curtained-off doorway to the stairs, Ashton looked away, not wanting to seem like she'd been eavesdropping. A moment later, she smelled Pearl's perfume waft over her just before a hand nudged the leg crossed over the other to move. Ashton uncrossed her legs and looked up in time to see Pearl lowering herself down crosswise in her lap.

Automatically her right arm encircled the redhead's waist while her left hand rested on a thigh. She felt one of Pearl's hands lightly play with the length of her hair in the back, sending little thrills through her body. She looked up into the other woman's face, a difficult task considering her gorgeous breasts were so close to her face.

"I'm sorry I've neglected you tonight," Pearl said, the softness of her voice a lover's caress over Ashton's ears.

"You don't have to apologize," Ashton assured. Her hand on the gown-covered thigh ached to feel the warm flesh beneath. She had to use sheer willpower to keep her hand still. "You do have a job to do, after all."

"I know," Pearl murmured, her other hand coming up to lightly trail along Ashton's jawline with light, furtive touches. "But I all but asked you to stay after your demonstration earlier."

"It's okay, truly." Ashton gave her a smile. "I've

actually really enjoyed chatting with some of the members here. I can certainly see why they'd come here for business contacts."

"Uh-oh," Pearl said with a grin. "Are you considering joining? Hmm?" she added, a fingernail taking the place of that caressing finger a moment before.

Another little shiver passed through Ashton. "No," she said, shaking her head. "I do not. Besides, I'll be heading back home soon."

"Oh? Where's home?"

Ashton chuckled. "Is Rosebud allowed to say?"

Pearl gave her that saucy little grin she'd come to expect and love. She took that fingernail from Ashton's jaw to the name tag stuck on her upper chest. "Not entirely sure if the names are getting better or worse. Flowers to Orson Welles."

"Don't forget Carlos," Ashton said sagely.

"Of course. Never forget Carlos." Pearl was quiet for a moment, her gaze studying Ashton's face for a long moment. "So, where is home? And," she added. "I won't tell if you don't, being bad and breaking the rules of nondisclosure."

"London," Ashton responded. "I run things out there for our company."

"Goodness," Pearl said, surprise in her voice. "You're far from home, sailor."

"I am."

"Well," Pearl said, leaning down and murmuring into Ashton's ear. "I was thinking that maybe we could go upstairs and spend some time together."

Ashton felt warmth engulf her, then consolidating squarely between her legs. It was deeply disconcerting how Pearl was able to affect her with such little effort. It made her feel out of control and, she had to admit to herself, guilty.

She looked up into Pearl's face and, as though her brain had stopped having an opinion, her mouth said, "Okay."

Pearl climbed off her lap and reached out a hand, which Ashton took. As if in a dream, she was guided through the club to the staircase that led to the third floor. They went to the same room as the first time, Pearl unlocking the door and letting Ashton enter before she followed, closing the door behind them.

Feeling like an awkward teenager, Ashton shoved her hands into the pockets of her trousers as Pearl passed by her, lowering herself to sit on the couch. She patted the cushion close to her. Letting out a long, slow breath like a balloon with a slow leak, Ashton walked over there and sat down, their legs not quite touching. Apparently not good enough for Pearl, she scooted over the last little bit so they were.

"I've been wanting to ask you a question," Pearl said, resting her hand on Ashton's thigh with her right hand as again, her left found Ashton's hair. "I love your hair," she said absently. "So soft. Thick."

"Thank you. I'd love to see yours down sometime," Ashton responded, looking up at Pearl's hair. The style varied, but it was always in an updo. "What's your question?"

Pearl smiled. "Perhaps you will someday. My question is," she began. "That first night I saw you, I was talking to someone, and when I turned around, you were looking at me like I was dinner."

Ashton looked away. "Yeah," she drawled, feeling like an ass being called out on her piggish behavior that day. "I apologize for that."

"Why?" Pearl asked, her nails beginning to run lazily up Ashton's thigh. "I loved it."

Ashton met her gaze and saw the truth there, as well as a well of desire. She decided to be honest. "I saw you and thought you were absolutely stunning," she began softly. "And, I wondered what it would be like to fuck you with my cock."

Pearl didn't say a word, didn't much react, which made Ashton's blood go cold. She was worried she'd gone too far, no better than the men who sniffed around after women like Pearl like dogs in heat. But Pearl's hand began to slide across to the inside of her thigh by her knee, slowly but with a firm touch, pulling that thigh up and over to drape across Pearl's own, effectively leaving Ashton's legs spread and her feeling quite vulnerable.

"Let's see here," Pearl murmured, meeting Ashton's hooded gaze as her fingers began to run up the inside of Ashton's thigh to her crotch, where they stroked up and down the seam of her trousers. Ashton gasped as her clit jerked at the huge influx of arousal. "I don't feel a cock," Pearl said teasingly.

Ashton couldn't speak as her heart rate began to pick up. She noted that Pearl, for her part, also seemed to be affected as her lips parted ever so slightly and her own breathing increased. Everything in her was telling her to make Pearl stop, that it wasn't right. What about Katherine?

"Maybe it's in here," Pearl said, her voice now low and husky. Her hand moved up from Ashton's crotch to the button and zipper, deft fingers releasing both before her hand wormed its way down inside the pants and her panties. She leaned in a bit, her lips close to Ashton's ear. "Nope," she said, breathy and hot. "But there is an extremely wet pussy in there."

Ashton gasped softly as two of Pearl's fingers ran through the immensity of volcanic wetness between her legs.

"Is this for me?" Pearl murmured, her fingertips finding the hard, slick clit that pulsed.

Ashton nodded, unable to speak. Pearl rested her forehead against the side of Ashton's head, her breathing heavy against the side of her face and neck adding to Ashton's arousal as the fingers worked against her need. She turned her head a bit toward Pearl, eyes closed as she concentrated on what was happening to her body. Her hips were moving with the fingers that were ruthless in their drive to make her release.

Mouth falling open and eyes squeezing tightly shut, Ashton gasped loudly, even as she tried to hold in her cry as she orgasmed, her body unloading weeks of pent-up lust toward the woman next to her. Her hand reached down and gripped Pearl's forearm as her body was rocked by a second orgasm. She was left sitting limp against the couch, her chest heaving as she tried to catch her breath.

Pearl eased her hand out of Ashton's panties as Ashton's hand fell to the couch. "You're beautiful when you come," she whispered, leaving a kiss on Ashton's cheek before moving away from her.

After several moments, the world began to come back into focus for Ashton, who took several deep breaths from where she slumped on the couch. She looked over and saw Pearl standing next to a small cabinet against the wall opposite the couch. The door of the cabinet was open, revealing bottles of cleaner, hand sanitizer, and a container of premoistened disposable towelettes—what amounted to baby wipes for adults.

Pearl had pulled a few of the wipes from the container and was wiping away the remnants of Ashton's passion from her fingers and hand. Watching that and the almost cold, removed expression on Pearl's face from what she could see of her profile, Ashton was brought right back down to earth with a loud thud.

Sitting up fully, she got to her feet and adjusted her clothing. She felt so dirty at that moment, and very lonely, even as she stood in a small room with another human being. She saw Pearl drop the soiled towelettes into the small trash can placed at the bottom of the floor cabinet, return the container, and shut the door.

"Um," she said quietly, reaching into her pocket for the slim wallet she'd made sure to keep on her when visiting the club. She opened it and withdrew three hundred-dollar bills. "Here." She took a small step toward Pearl, who shrunk back from her a bit. "I hope this is enough."

Pearl glanced down at the extended hand that held the bills, then spared a glance up at Ashton. "Thank you," she murmured, taking the money and looking down for a moment before folding and tucking the bills into her cleavage. She met Ashton's gaze again, her own unusually shy. "I hope you get home okay," she said. "Once your business is finished here in the States." With that, she turned and left.

It was a beautiful Colorado night. The snowflakes were big and fat, the kind that you could easily catch on your tongue. The well-lit property was a veritable winter wonderland, and every single light along the pathway that Ashton strolled was a halo of light-tinted snow.

She loved the snow and certainly missed the Colorado Christmases. England had rain—lots of it—and even snow at times, but not like Colorado. The air was crisp and cold as she wandered along the lit path, gloved hands shoved into the deep pockets of her long peacoat. Her hair blew back away from her face as the soft breeze stirred the snow from the ground and the rooftops and trees, making it snow gently from every direction.

She thought over the last six weeks or so, which had flown by, taking Christmas and New Year's with it. What was supposed to be a two-week trip had tripled in size. Even so, she was proud of what she and Brian had managed to do. Their new line, Top Shelf Creations, had been a screaming success not only at The Black Pussy Cat, but also at Buck's other endeavors, making a big splash as a high-end line exclusive to Buck's properties.

The last time she'd been to the club had been two days before Christmas, when Buck had held a small get-together for his staff and some of the staff of King-Kraft who'd made it all happen. She and Katherine had gone together, and Ashton had held her breath. She hadn't come clean to her on-again, off-again girlfriend, but for a very logical, if not cowardly reason.

Katherine could be extremely vindictive, and Ashton knew that if she'd told her what had happened that night with Pearl, as unexpected as it had been, Katherine would have not only smeared Ashton, but the company as well. King-Kraft deserved better, and her orgasm wasn't worth destroying generations of work.

They'd arrived for the celebration of the new products and Ashton had already been working out what she'd say if confronted by her time spent with Pearl. She'd worried about it, sweated about it, lost sleep over it. All for naught. As relieved as Ashton had been to not be found out or revealed, she left the party equally disappointed; Pearl hadn't been there at all. She knew better than to ask any of the staff, as they seemed to protect their own and questions about what others did in their time off the clock weren't welcome.

For Ashton, the silence of Pearl's absence had been deafening. Now, it was the beginning of a new year and she would be flying home soon. In two days, she'd catch a flight with Katherine back to England.

As she strolled around the property, her breath coming out in little white puffs of steam, she thought about Pearl. She hadn't let herself think about her much, not nearly as much as she wanted to, but some things couldn't be helped. Initially, she'd been hurt by Pearl's seeming indifference to her after their intimate encounter in that little room. She hadn't seen her since.

But, with some time and distance, Ashton had a different perspective and went from hurt to anger—at herself. Pearl was one of, if not *the* most beautiful woman she'd ever seen. Her face, her body, and an aura that drew people in…all those things the woman possessed, yes, but she'd learned how to harness them into a skill set.

Ashton hadn't been lied to, she hadn't been bamboozled, she'd simply gotten exactly what she'd wanted. Pearl was a master at reading people, understanding what they needed, and creating the fantasy for them. Even for Ken, in that moment he'd needed a friendly smile, calming voice, and comforting hand, Pearl had provided it.

Ashton had needed passion, to feel wanted, a quiet presence with a big appetite for an exciting experience. Pearl had provided it. After their encounter, Pearl had simply removed the name tag and mask, a job well done.

She smiled and shook her head. She'd fallen for it hook, line, and sinker. The problem was, once she'd figured it out, she wanted more. So much more. Pearl could make her drain her entire savings over a year's time, her need for her was so intense. It was best she was headed back home. Besides, since Pearl hadn't been at the Top Shelf celebration, it was entirely possible she'd left the club altogether.

# Chapter Six

It's something, isn't it?" Ashton asked, amused as the three people standing next to her looked on with mouths open in stunned silence. Smiling, she looked back to what lay about thirty feet or so from where they stood at the rail that had been erected to protect the historic site.

"I always wondered what Stonehenge would feel like," Brian said absently, never taking his eyes off the massive stones.

"What do you think now that you're standing in front of it, freezing your ass off?" she prodded.

A burst of laughter escaped his lips, breaking the silence of the cold, February afternoon. "That I am," he admitted, glancing over at her, only half his face visible from the winter scarf he had wrapped around his neck and mouth. "But it's incredible. Absolutely incredible."

Ashton leaned forward to look past Brian and at his wife who stood behind their nine-year-old daughter. "What do you think, Pam? Bella?"

"The energy is electric," Pam said, glancing past her husband to meet Ashton's gaze. "You can feel the history here."

"Me, too," Bella said, her gloved hands holding her mother's, who had them crisscrossed at the girl's upper chest.

"Well," Ashton said. "If you guys want to see

some really cool history, let's catch the bus back to the guest center." She nodded toward the bus that picked visitors up at the guest center, which included a dining area, gift shop, and restrooms, and drove them the mile out to the site, then back again. "And I'll take you guys to Salisbury, just about fifteen minutes or so away. We can get some lunch at a sixteenth-century pub."

"Cool!" Bella exclaimed.

For Ashton, the cathedral city, so-called for Salisbury Cathedral, a gorgeous thirteenth-century structure, was the quintessential time machine. For her, to drive into the town of roughly forty thousand souls was to go back in time. So much of England was, but Salisbury spoke to her in a special way.

She took her guests to the Ox Row Inn, a quaint little pub that oozed history and charm. They were seated and settled with drinks ordered.

"Mom, can we go look around?" Belle asked, indicating the plethora of framed pictures and historic artifacts on the walls.

"Of course." Pam pushed her chair back from the table, as did her and Brian's daughter. "We'll be right back."

"How are things going back in Colorado?" Ashton asked.

"Real good," Brian said, meeting her gaze. "Jack and I have been talking about some changes at the factory, maybe getting rid of some older, less popular product, adding some more." He smiled at the waiter/barkeep who brought them their drinks, including his Guinness. He grabbed the dark brew and brought it toward his lips as he said, "Went to talk to Buck the other night."

That caught Ashton's attention. She glanced over at him as she sipped her water. "Oh?"

"Your friend asked about you," he said before taking a long swallow of his ale.

"What friend?" she asked, setting her water down.

"The redhead, one of Buck's ladies. Opal?" he asked, eyebrows drawn.

"Pearl?" Ashton offered.

"Pearl! Yeah, that was her." He grinned. "Too many damn gems and shit to keep track. But yeah, the really gorgeous one. She asked about you." His smirk was lecherous. "Didn't know you had something going with anyone there."

Panic fluttered at her rib cage as she tried to think of how to respond. She snorted. "I haven't been there in over a month, Brian."

"Yeah, but you were there for nearly two," he reminded with a raised eyebrow.

"Most of which was spent with your ass," she said, playfully shoving at his arm. "In the weeks I was there I got to know a lot of Buck's staff. Good people."

Ashton watched as Katherine explained to a wide-eyed Bella how everything was done, from the beginning of the process of creating a flavor to cooking it, making the chocolate, filling it, setting it, and, Belle's favorite part, eating it. To her credit, Katherine had one ready for Belle at every stage, considering that to actually make one truffle, it was a multi-day process before it ended the journey on the production line.

"This is amazing," Bella said, happily munching on the chocolate she'd been given.

She noticed Katherine hadn't once looked her way, totally keeping her attention on Bella and her parents. After the tour today, the Lewises would head back to The Ashes and pack up for a final night in the UK. The following morning Ashton would drive them to the airport to return stateside.

She'd been surprised they were coming, but she respected Brian wanting to understand the entirety of the business. She'd held his position for years, so she knew it well, and in truth, knowing that aspect of things had helped greatly in creating the division she had. So, no doubt after helping create Top Shelf, quite the undertaking in such a short amount of time, Brian had been thirsty to learn more. She respected that.

Ashton could feel eyes on her so glanced up as she stretched the fitted sheet over the corner of the mattress on the side of the bed she was working on. Katherine, also working on smoothing out the fitted sheet, was looking at her.

"What do you want me to say, Katherine?" Ashton asked.

"Well, an answer to my question would be appropriate, for one," Katherine said, yanking her side a bit harder than need be, popping the corner off on Ashton's side. "Sorry," she muttered.

"We've been on shaky ground for the lion's share of our relationship," Ashton said, irritated as she fixed the sheet. "Why would you think it's a good idea for us to move in together?"

"Because, quite honestly, I think the main reason we argue so much is because we have such little time together," Katherine said, accepting the top sheet that Ashton had whipped out over the bed and was slowly floating down.

Ashton considered her words as she straightened and tucked the top sheet over and under the heavy pillow top. "Katherine," she said softly, looking across the expanse of the queen-sized bed that had been used by Brian and Pam during their stay. "Do you realize in the month we've been back in England, this is the first time we've seen each other outside of work?"

The baker didn't respond for a long moment as they began putting the blankets on the bed. "That is true."

"And you know the worst part?" Ashton asked, not cruelly, just as a matter of fact. When Katherine met her gaze, she answered her own question. "It didn't bother me that much. What does that tell us?"

Katherine turned away as if she'd been slapped. She cleared her throat, almost as though she were trying to gather her composure as she walked over to the window, arms crossed pensively over her chest. Finally, she turned to face Ashton, who had moved to Katherine's side of the bed to finish with the blanket.

"Is there somebody else?" she asked.

Ashton brought her hand up to brush her hair behind her ear, a nervous gesture, as she walked over to the rocking chair in the corner of the room and grabbed the quilt that would top the sheets and blankets and finish the bed. She considered how to answer that question.

"There isn't," she said, not a lie.

Katherine walked over to the rocking chair and

sat down. She crossed one leg over the other, and Ashton was silently amused as she considered the position. When Pearl did it, she could make a man ten years dead sit up and take notice. When Katherine did it, she looked like a petulant child.

"So, it's just over then?" Katherine said, glaring over at Ashton, who grunted as she maneuvered the heavy quilt. "You're throwing us away?"

"Damn it, Katherine!" Ashton shoved the quilt away from her as she turned on the other woman. "Are you happy?" she asked. When there was no response, she demanded, "Are you happy?" Ashton's cell phone began to ring from where it sat on the dresser. She spared another glance at Katherine, and when it seemed she'd get no response, she walked over to the dresser. Seeing it was the house phone back in Colorado, she answered the call.

"Really?" Katherine gasped, getting to her feet. "In the middle of breaking up with me, you're going to take a call?"

Ashton ignored her. If her father was going to call her, he used his cell phone or his home office phone. This was the main number, used only by the house staff. "Hello?…Hello, Martin. How are—… What?" She leaned back against the dresser, a hand going to her forehead. "I see." She glanced at the clock on the bedside table to see it was nearly ten in the morning, which meant it was the very early morning hours in Colorado. "All right. Yes, I'll leave as soon as I can…All right. Thanks for calling, Martin. Please keep me updated…" She nodded, even though he couldn't see her. "Thank you. Bye."

"What's wrong?" Katherine asked.

Ashton clicked off her phone and ran her hand

through her hair. Looking down at the floor, she let out a heavy sigh. Finally, she looked over at the other woman. "Can I have a ride to the airport?" she asked softly. "My father has had a stroke."

The big man who had intimidated her her entire life, whom she'd watched her mother cower from, lay motionless. Somehow, his six-foot two-inch, two-hundred-sixty-pound body looked small and frail lying in that narrow bed. Lines were attached to various parts of him and machines strategically placed up near the head of the bed beeped softly, an indicator every few seconds that Jack King was still alive.

Ashton stared down at him, unsure what to feel. She'd spoken to the doctor before coming into her father's room in the ICU, and he'd given her the uncertain news. More tests would need to be run to quantify the amount of damage to the brain and exactly where it had hit the most. She was told he could recover fully, partially, or not at all.

She hugged herself as she blew out a breath. She felt such a strange mixture of things in that exact moment: uncertainty, sadness, concern, and, most notably, numbness. It was a strange dichotomy of emotions, as they should cancel each other out, but they didn't. Each seemed to battle for dominance, making her feel a little manic.

Nothing more she could do as more tests were scheduled for the morning, she decided to go to the house.

Ashton waited until everyone assembled in the massive foyer. Some of the staff sat on the stairs of the grand staircase, others leaned against the wall, while others took advantage of the fine chairs and benches placed around for one to sit down and remove or put on shoes.

"Is this everyone?" she asked as Dekayas scurried in from the kitchen, rubber dish gloves still on his hands. Ashton smiled, then sobered. "Okay," she said, looking over the crowd of about a dozen house staff, half-dozen garden staff, and the two drivers. "As I assume many, if not all of you, know by now," she began, standing at the center of the foyer, making sure to make eye contact with everyone at one point or other. "My father has had a substantial stroke." She heard a couple quiet gasps from those present. "Doctors don't have a lot of answers yet, but he's under the best care he possible can be."

"Is there anything we can do?" a woman asked, who Ashton recognized as one of the housekeeping staff who'd worked for the family for nearly a decade.

"Honestly, Nora, I want you all to take a few days off." She again looked at the individuals spaced around the room. "My father will be in the hospital for a week or more, his doctor said, depending on what they find. When he comes home, and you know he'll insist on it," she added with a smile that many of the staff returned, as well as nods. "He's going to need you more than ever. So, with pay, I want you to finish your day today, then I don't want to see you again until Wednesday. Okay?"

"So, we're not fired, right?" a gardener asked skeptically.

"Absolutely not," she responded, shaking her head. "Just enjoy a little downtime." She raised her hands in supplication. "That's it." She watched with a heavy heart as the staff, so many of whom she knew very well, cleared out of the foyer and back toward their area in the house. Many gave her a sad smile or a squeeze to the shoulder as they passed.

Ashton headed to her father's office, intending to see if she could find paperwork on his power of attorney or if he had any sort of special instructions if he were to become incapacitated. She planned to call his attorney the following day.

Jack King's office had initially been the smoking lounge when the house was built. It's dark wood paneling gave the room a heavy, almost somber feel to it, even as it was beautiful. The colors from the octagon stained glass window up high on the wall behind the massive desk painted a rainbow across the wood. At the right time of day, the refracted light glinted magically off the crystal figurines in the curio cabinet against the opposite wall. Sometimes the ghostly scent of cigars could be smelled from decades gone by.

She walked around to the business side of the desk and sat down in the leather captain's chair. There was no computer on the desk, no laptop or keyboard or tablet. Her father detested computers, and to her knowledge had never used one. He was a man who believed pen and paper and leather ledgers should still be the way.

She noticed some unopened mail on the corner of the desk, which wasn't entirely unusual. Focusing on her task, she opened the second to bottom drawer on the left-hand side, which she knew held all his most personal paperwork. She wasn't disappointed.

The handwritten page was notarized and titled: *Should I Need A Voice*. Ashton read through it, noting the name and phone number of his attorney—who should be called immediately, according to Jack King—and his wishes for absolutely no resuscitation under any circumstances. "If I'm dead, let me stay that way. If I'm dying, bring me home to do so."

"Okay," she muttered.

Pushing back from the desk, she took the page with her as she closed and locked the door to the office, then headed upstairs to her suite. She could smell the freshness as soon as she opened the double doors. The vacuum marks were evident, and she smiled at the fresh-cut flowers that were placed in a vase on the table in her sitting room. She knew that meant Stella had been the one who'd cleaned her rooms.

Walking into the bedroom, she saw her luggage by the armoire and felt the warmth from the fire that had been built in the bedroom fireplace. She set her father's paper on the dresser top and began to strip. It was such a long flight from London, let alone all the rigmarole in the airports to get from Country A into Country B. After, it had been a long day at the hospital speaking to doctors, and then the travel to her family manor.

Due to the seven-hour time difference, it was only seven thirty at night Colorado time, but it was two thirty in the morning back home in London, and she was exhausted. She wanted a long, hot bath and then bed.

Naked, she padded into the bathroom and pulled open one of the drawers in the cabinet, looking to see if she had any bath bombs left. She left a certain amount of clothing and toiletries at the Pittman

House in case she forgot anything during trips back. If she was coming home, she'd be dealing with her father and that was a guaranteed stressor, therefore she always tried to keep either bubble bath or bath bombs at the ready.

When she opened the drawer, she was thrilled to see a brand-new, unopened package of bath bombs, but something else caught her attention. She reached in and grabbed the white mask, looking down at it. She wondered if perhaps whoever had cleaned her rooms last had mistaken it for something used with a facial and tucked it away with her tubes and jars of mud and such.

As she looked down at it—a mask she'd picked up from an adult toy site so she'd have her own—a facial was the last thing she was thinking of.

# *Chapter Seven*

"The good news is, there is normal brain activity around where the stroke occurred," Dr. Brightman explained, holding a model of the human brain in his hand as he sat behind his desk, Ashton in one of the two chairs opposite. He whirled his hand around the area affected. "So, while that's good news, this area here, where the stroke occurred, will profoundly disturb the right side of the body, and we could be looking at hemiplegia."

"Which is what, exactly?" Ashton asked, a bit nervous by the answer.

"Total paralysis of that side of the body and face," he said. "We'll know more, of course, as time goes on and how he begins to heal."

She nodded and blew out a long, shaky breath. "I came across some paperwork last night," she began. "He wishes to be brought home in the event of something like this happening."

The older man sat back in his chair, clearly not pleased. "I would highly recommend against that."

"I share your concern, but you know my father, Dr. Brightman. He won't stop until he gets his way, so what needs to happen?"

"This was an ischemic stroke, so there's quite a bit of swelling in the brain. That needs to go down so we have a much better idea of what we're looking at. Let's agree to let that happen and then reexamine options. He's simply not stable enough to go home just yet. Okay?"

Ashton nodded. "All right. I agree. Thank you, Doctor." She pushed to her feet but paused when he said her name.

"If he comes home, you'll have to essentially create a hospital room environment in the home with round-the-clock medical staff. So, keep that in mind."

She nodded. "Lovely. Noted."

Carrying the hand basket with the store's logo printed on the side, Ashton tossed a few things she knew she'd eat over the next few days into it, including some fruit and yogurt. She hadn't shopped for herself while living in the US since her college days, and it felt strange. It also felt strange with the staff gone. The huge house was so quiet and empty. A few of the hardcore staff, like Martin, insisted on staying around, but overall, everyone had gone off on a mini-vacation just as she'd asked them to do.

Indecisive on exactly what she wanted, Ashton found herself wandering around the grocery store. Finally, she decided the aimless approach wasn't working, so she looked up at the signs that headed each aisle listing the core offerings. Chewing on her bottom lip, she walked down a couple aisles when a category caught her eye.

She strolled down the juice aisle, taking in the shelves of plastic bottles lined up like colorful little soldiers. One type in particular made her stop in front of it. A small smile spread across her lips as she reached out to grab one.

Her stomach was in knots as she looked up at the nondescript brick building she'd become fairly familiar with for a short time. After feeling ever the fool the last time she left The Black Pussy Cat, she'd never intended to return unless Top Shelf had required it purely for business purposes. The good thing about being in business with Buck was that she had a permanent keycode to get into the building.

Wearing her newly found white mask and sporting a permanent pseudonym for her visits to the club, Ashton smoothed out the name tag on the upper chest of her suit jacket. She was there with a singular mission, which included a new understanding and respect of the parameters.

"Good evening, madam," the bartender greeted with a wide, welcoming smile. "So nice to see you again."

She grinned at him as she walked over to the bar. "Nothing, thank you," she said as he waved a hand at the collection of liquor bottles behind him. "Is Pearl working tonight?"

"She is," he said with a nod and knowing smile. "She just took drinks up to the poker game in room seven."

"Thank you, sir," she said with a smile, then headed for the stairs.

She stepped out of the purple hue of the staircase to the dim lighting of the third-floor hallway. It looked as it had the last she'd been there, including the boisterous laughter of the men playing their card game. She heard Pearl's voice as she joked with them, brilliantly sidestepping their flirtatious comments and suggestions.

"Come on, Pearl! Let me change that pearl to a diamond. Marry me," one of them said.

"Bill, Bill, Bill," Pearl said, that sexy tone in her voice. "And then you woke up." This, of course, earned a round of laughter by the other men and a smile from Ashton as she headed down the hall.

"All right, boys. Behave, now. Good luck." Pearl stepped out of the room and gasped in surprise when she nearly ran headlong into Ashton. In that moment, she seemed to steel her spine and took a half step backward, raising her chin defiantly. She was as stunning as ever in lime green. "What are you doing here?"

It was the first time Ashton had ever seen Pearl seem to not fully be in control. She seemed a bit shaken, certainly surprised. "Good evening to you, too."

Pearl looked away, a hand coming up to cup the back of her neck for a moment before returning her gaze to Ashton, that look of cool indifference solidly back in place. "My apologies. Good evening."

"I came here to talk to you. Business," Ashton was careful to add.

Pearl hugged herself and looked down for a moment before nodding. "All right." She turned to her right and unlocked the all-too-familiar door, allowing Ashton to enter first. Ashton stepped into the room just far enough so Pearl could close the door but did not sit on the couch. She didn't even look at the couch.

Pearl leaned back against the door, head slightly cocked to the side as she studied Ashton, as though waiting to hear what she had to say.

Realizing the floor was hers, Ashton cleared her throat softly. "I want to spend some time with you," she began. "Outside of here." She indicated the room around them with a hand. "I'd like—"

"No." Pearl pushed away from the door and turned to open it. "I can't do that," she said quietly over her shoulder before walking out of the room, leaving the door open behind her.

Surprised by her own reaction, Ashton felt the sting of emotion behind her eyes. She took a deep breath to stop it from forming into anything more than a sting. She wasn't sure if it was the cold, detached way she'd been treated, or the absolute, foot-down rejection. She decided it didn't matter. She had her answer, and it was time to move on.

Pulling herself together, she stood straight and held her shoulders back just like her father had taught her, and walked out of the room. She trotted down the stairs and into the main room on the second floor, then headed to the final staircase to take her out of The Black Pussy Cat and Pearl's life.

She waved a goodbye to the barkeep with a small smile and pushed the curtain aside, her fingers running along the wooden rail as she made her way down.

"Wait!"

Ashton stopped, hand grabbing the rail as she turned to look over her shoulder. Pearl was hurrying down the wooden stairs, heels tapping her progress. Ashton stayed put until the redhead reached her.

"I'm sorry," Pearl said softly. "I'm sorry I was so rude."

Ashton nodded but said nothing.

"I wasn't expecting to see you, and it just..." She shrugged. "It shook me a bit."

"Why?" Ashton asked, turning to look up at her as Pearl stood on the step up from Ashton's.

Pearl looked away for a moment before responding. "It shook me at how glad I was to see you."

Ashton slowly shook her head. "You're just full of surprises, aren't you?"

Pearl smirked. "Something like that." She looked away again before meeting Ashton's steady gaze. "I'm still not sure it's a good idea, but what do you have in mind?"

Ashton shrugged, this unexpected turn in events leaving her a bit flatfooted. "I'll send a car to pick you up at your house, bring you to mine. Spend a few hours together, then get you back home safely."

Pearl tucked her full bottom lip beneath white teeth before letting it go. She seemed torn, if the expression on her face said anything.

"I'll give you three thousand dollars for your time," Ashton added. She sensed Pearl wanted to know but felt it impolite to ask.

"That's a lot of money," Pearl said softly. She held Ashton's gaze for a long moment. "What do you expect me to do? What do you want from me?"

"I want to touch you," Ashton said simply. "I understand and respect that they have house rules here, and that you have rules of your own. But I want some time with you. In private."

Pearl nodded. "Why me? You're an absolutely gorgeous woman, and somehow I don't think you need to pay for company."

"Fine, then," Ashton said with a smirk. "Let me take you to dinner and then back to my house."

A bark of laughter escaped Pearl's lips as she shook her head. "That would be a no."

"Well, then you answered your own question," Ashton grinned.

Pearl nodded, laughter gone. "Okay. Do you have a pen?"

Ashton reached inside her suit jacket and pulled one out, clicking it into life.

Pearl took it then grabbed one of Ashton's hands. The tip of the pen tickled Ashton's palm as the ten digits were carefully written on her flesh. "Text me," Pearl said, clicking the pen back into hibernation and handing it to its owner. "We'll work out details."

Ashton glanced down at her hand to make sure she could read the numbers, then nodded. "All right. I'll text you tomorrow."

"Have a good night," Pearl murmured, the sexy vixen returning. She turned and headed back up the stairs, Ashton watching her until she disappeared through the curtains.

Blowing out a nervous breath, Ashton continued down the stairs. She pushed through the front door of the building and was about to remove her mask when she saw a man standing on the sidewalk on the opposite side of the street.

He looked to be in his forties, perhaps early fifties. His short brown hair was a bit scruffy, and she couldn't tell if he cut it himself or if he was growing it out from a shorter style. He had a bit of beard stubble, which was growing gray on his chin. He stood there in baggy jeans and an army-green T-shirt with a single breast pocket, jeans that sagged in the crotch, and worn cowboy boots.

Ashton felt uncomfortable as he stared,

completely not dressed for the weather. Though it wasn't snowing, it was February in Colorado, which meant cold temperatures. She met his gaze for a moment before looking away and walking briskly toward her car.

Wearing simple cotton yoga pants and a tank top with her hair pulled back into a ponytail, Ashton worked to remove the framed pictures and artwork from the wall. She'd wheeled a cart into the room to make it easier, as some of the works were family heirlooms.

"Might I help you?"

She glanced over to see Martin standing in the doorway, dressed in his typical uniform. "Of course you can," she said with a welcoming smile.

The older man entered the large bedroom and began to gather the trinkets and knickknacks displayed around the room. "How do you think your father will feel to be put in your mother's old bedroom?" he asked at length.

Ashton grinned as she carefully removed another picture, this one above the fireplace mantel. "He'll hate it," she said. "But I think he'd appreciate it a whole lot more if we turn this one into a hospital room rather than his own bedroom."

"I definitely agree with that assessment," the butler said. "Honestly, I think the one who would be most angry at this point is your mother."

Ashton chuckled. "'Get the hell out, you old fool,'" she said, mimicking her mother's voice. To her surprise, she heard the man she'd known her whole life chuckle.

"She would have insisted he be set up in the carriage house, I'm afraid," Martin said.

"Why did they hate each other so much?" Ashton asked, carefully wrapping the framed picture she'd just removed in a blanket made for just such a purpose before loading it onto the cart.

Martin let out a heavy sigh. "There's a very fine line between love and hate, madam. Your mother tried to love your father, but he just wouldn't have it. Once Jackson was killed," he added, "Your mother served no real purpose anymore."

Ashton absorbed what she'd been told as she was joined at a particularly large painting, the two of them working together to lift it off the wall. Once it was down, she stared at the woman in the picture, no clue who it was. Her mother had always loved the painting.

"Do you think when my brother died, he took my mother with him?"

Martin looked at her for a long time, his expression pensive. "May I be plain with you?"

"Of course," she said. "Hell, I'd love it if you went up to your rooms and changed into some sweatpants and an old T-shirt."

He waggled a finger at her. "*That* will not happen, madam."

Ashton chuckled. "I know, I know. Yes, please just be honest with me. Since the age of seven, my father has been busy sending me off to private school in Connecticut, college in California, and now to work in London. I feel like my whole life has been spent with him pushing me out of his way."

He gave her a sad smile. "You're not entirely wrong, madam. I've always seen Jack King as a bit of Henry VIII. His whole life he was searching for an heir, and the first three wives weren't able to produce it for him, for this reason or that, and finally your mother comes along. Much younger than he, then you arrive."

"Not the boy to take over the business, huh?" Ashton asked. It had never been spoken outright, but had been made known.

"Exactly," Martin confirmed. "When Jackson came along seven years after you, well..."

"I'm shipped off to private school and he's groomed," Ashton murmured.

Martin nodded. "I believe that was when things began to truly break down. Your mother was furious when he shipped you off. She was furious he got rid of her daughter, and he was furious she only gave him one son."

"Hysterectomy after Jackson was born, just to save her life," Ashton said softly. At the nod of the butler, she let out a heavy sigh, hands on hips as she looked around the room. "Looks so different in here, doesn't it? So empty, even though it's still loaded with furniture."

Martin nodded. "Indeed. I'll make arrangements to get movers in here tomorrow, madam, and get these stored properly," he added, patting the handle of the cart.

"Thank you, Martin. I truly appreciate it. I'll speak with Father's doctors more about what I need to have ordered and moved in here for him."

He nodded. "Good night, madam."

"Good night, Martin."

# *Chapter Eight*

Standing at the window of her bedroom, Ashton watched as the sleek black town car pulled into the circular drive in front of the grand house, Leonard behind the wheel. He parked the car, headlights still shining as he climbed out from behind the wheel and hurried to the back passenger door, opening it for the woman tucked inside.

Satisfied that Pearl had arrived safely, Ashton moved away from the window, blowing out a nervous breath. Looking around the large space, she felt everything was as she wanted it to be. She was freshly showered and spritzed with her favorite perfume. She wore no mask, no longer wishing to hide her identity from Pearl. She only hoped they'd reach the place where Pearl eventually felt the same. She had no intention of making the evening a onetime event.

Moments later, she heard the outer doors of the sitting room open. "In there, miss," Martin said, his voice muffled behind the thick closed doors of the bedroom proper. "Have a nice evening, miss."

"Thank you," she heard Pearl say before the sound of Martin closing the doors softly behind her.

Ashton's heart was racing; she could feel it in her throat. There was a moment of silence before there was a soft knock on the bedroom doors. Wanting to vomit, Ashton swallowed her nerves down as best she could before padding over to the door, the silk robe belted at her waist flowing out around her legs with every step.

Taking one last moment to breathe, Ashton reached down and took the door handles in hand and pulled open both doors at once. Before her stood a fantasy in the proverbial little black dress with thick straps over beautiful shoulders. It reached just above her knees, finally revealing gorgeous legs. The curve-caressing black material showed off her body to perfection.

Mask in place, her hair was pulled up but auburn tendrils framed her face, giving her the look of sophistication she wore so well while not as severe as it was at the club. Her makeup wasn't as heavy, either, lipstick a touch and not a demand for respect. She was even more beautiful, and Ashton honestly hadn't thought that was possible.

"Please come in," she said, stepping back out of the way. She noticed a London Fog jacket lying across the couch in the sitting room along with a small clutch. She closed the door after Pearl had passed. "Welcome."

"Thank you," Pearl said, stopping at the center of the room, near where Ashton had created a nest on the floor for them. The many pillows and a thick, fluffy rug were all situated close enough to the burning fireplace to be cozy, but far enough away to not get overheated. "This is incredible," she continued, glancing toward the bed. "That is the biggest bed I've ever seen in my life."

Ashton grinned. "You should see my father's."

Pearl turned toward her as Ashton walked over to a small table near the floor nest where an ice bucket had been placed, two wine goblets next to it, as well as a sealed envelope with Pearl's name printed on the outside. "Oh?" Pearl asked. "Bed envy?"

Ashton's grin grew as she shook her head. "Hardly." She reached into the ice bucket and brought out a chilled bottle of apple juice. "I hear Welch's is a fine vintage."

Pearl's smile was genuine. "I would agree." The smile turned into that sexy little smirk that always hit Ashton low. "Perhaps after we work up a bit of thirst, hmm?"

"I like the way you think," Ashton said, placing the bottle back into the ice before walking over to the other woman.

Pearl reached a hand up, lightly caressing the side of Ashton's face. "You are so beautiful," she murmured. "I hope you'll forgive me for keeping mine on."

"I told you," Ashton said. "I know you have rules you work by." She moved around behind Pearl, placing her hands on her hips. She leaned down, murmuring in Pearl's ear. "Here are *my* rules." She nuzzled Pearl's neck, Pearl's head moving to give her access to more creamy skin. "All I want is for us to enjoy each other," Ashton continued, leaving a soft kiss just below Pearl's ear, earning a soft sigh in response.

Encouraged, her fingers took hold of the zipper at the back of the dress, slowly pulling it down, the sound electrifying and full of expectation. She nearly groaned when she saw the smooth expanse of Pearl's back and, it seemed, no panties.

"I don't need my ego stroked," she continued, her hands moving to the warm nakedness of Pearl's sides, creeping beneath the loosened material of the dress. One of Pearl's arms had lifted, her hand burying itself in Ashton's hair. "If you don't like something," she murmured, "tell me." Her hands moved up over her rib cage, the rounded undersides of her breasts touching her fingers, garnering a soft sigh of pleasure from Ashton. "If it feels good," she continued, her hands moving up to cover naked breasts, hard nipples pressing into her palms. "Let it."

Pearl's neck arched more as Ashton lightly bit the muscle there. She pressed her breasts into Ashton's touch.

"Is this a yes, then?" Ashton asked into her ear, fingers lightly pinching hard nipples.

"Yes," Pearl whispered. "God, yes."

Flicking Pearl's earlobe with her tongue, Ashton removed her hands from inside of the dress, bringing them up to brush the straps from her shoulders, allowing the garment to fall to the floor. She groaned deep in her throat when she saw that, indeed, Pearl was completely naked beneath that little dress.

Her left hand found its way back to her breast while her right hand trailed down to the closely trimmed patch that rested between muscular thighs. She pressed her own hips into Pearl's perfect ass as her fingers slipped between slick, swollen folds.

Pearl's hand tightened in Ashton's hair and she leaned farther back into Ashton's body as Ashton's fingers began to stroke her, her clit already rock hard, which told Ashton that the gorgeous woman in her arms was just as affected by her. That turned her on all the more. She knew it wasn't going to take long, and it didn't.

Pearl's hips bucked as a loud gasp escaped her throat. Volcanic wetness covered Ashton's fingers and palm. She nearly purred as she held Pearl back into her, nearly holding her up until the other woman seemed to calm a bit, gathering her wits and her strength.

"My god." Pearl chuckled breathily.

Ashton grinned, whispering in her ear. "Now we're even."

Pearl chuckled, turning in her arms to face her. "Do I have to go home now?" she asked, teasing in her eyes.

Ashton shook her head. "Nuh-uh." Her hands slid down to cup Pearl's ass, pulling them closer.

Pearl's hands wormed their way between them, tugging at the belt to Ashton's robe. The garment fell open, Pearl's gaze dropping to feast on Ashton's naked form. The hunger Ashton saw in those eyes made her nearly quiver. Pearl looked up into Ashton's eyes before her gaze dropped to her lips, just a flicker of longing in them before she looked away, her mouth moving to Ashton's neck as her hands brushed the robe off Ashton's body.

Pearl's mouth was hot and hungry, her hands deceivingly gentle, almost loving, as they caressed Ashton's back, arms, stomach, and breasts. When her mouth found her left breast, Ashton's head fell back, eyes closed.

"Baby." She gasped, pushing against Pearl's shoulders as the redhead began to suck hard on her nipple, sending white-hot lightning bolts of pleasure between her legs. "I need to lie down."

Pearl released the nipple with a wet *pop* as she helped Ashton recline on the thick rug. "Comfortable?" Pearl asked softly, kneeling next to her, adjusting the pillow gently beneath Ashton's head. She stretched out next to Ashton, looking down along the length of her body. She ran her hand over her skin, again finding her breasts. "You have the most beautiful breasts I've ever seen."

"Clearly you haven't been looking at your own body, then," Ashton murmured.

The smile that genuine compliment brought to Pearl's lips was absolutely worth the price of admission sealed in that envelope. Pearl moved on top of Ashton, insinuating a thigh between her legs, making Ashton hiss as she pressed that thigh where she needed it most.

"I love how wet your pussy gets for me," Pearl said into Ashton's neck. "I want to taste you." She reached her hand down, lifting her hips a bit as she ran her fingers through Ashton's wetness, bringing up the glistening fingers and using them to paint one of Ashton's nipples.

Ashton moaned softly, her hand cupping the back of Pearl's neck as her mouth returned to her breast, tongue as deft as her fingers as it licked Ashton's nipple clean, lightly tugging at it with her teeth for good measure.

Before Ashton could even wonder what was next, Pearl was on the move again. She licked and kissed her way down the length of Ashton's body, making it very clear what her intention and destination was. Ashton's legs fell open at Pearl's urging.

"Oh, fuck." Ashton groaned as Pearl settled between her legs, her tongue moving slowing from Ashton's opening up to her clit, then back down and up again before settling on her clit. Ashton's hips rocked with the ruthless tongue.

Pearl hummed into her task and wrapped her arms around Ashton's spread thighs, pinning them open and down. She sucked her clit deep into her mouth, wrapping her lips around it as her tongue batted at it, eliciting breathy whimpers from Ashton as her hips began to rock harder.

Finally, Ashton's body gave in. Her neck and back arched, a cry ripping from her throat as she came hard, Pearl humming in approval as she continued to lick Ashton's clit, sucking intermittently, milking every ounce of pleasure. Finally, Ashton begged for mercy with a hand pushing against Pearl's head, and Pearl stopped.

Resting back against the rug, Ashton's chest heaved as she tried to get her body under control. Warm sensation rippled through her as she lay there, helpless. A smile came to her lips when she felt the soft, gentle touches of Pearl's body and hands as she made way back up, leaving a trail of comforting kisses up Ashton's neck and on her face. She knew mouth kisses weren't an option, but she wished they were.

Instead, she wrapped her arms around the beautiful woman and urged her to lie atop her. Pearl moved so her legs rested on the rug between Ashton's legs, her head resting on her chest.

"Am I too heavy?" Pearl murmured.

"Nope. I just need a minute," Ashton said, running her hands over the smooth skin of Pearl's back. "You're so soft."

Pearl let out a contented sigh as she settled in against the woman beneath her, her breath washing over Ashton's right nipple, making her gasp softly. "What do I call you tonight?" Pearl asked.

Ashton smiled, her fingertips trailing down to Pearl's lower back and the swell of her behind. "By my name. Ashton."

There was silence for a moment, then, "That's your real name? Ashton?"

"It is." Ashton looked into the eyes of the woman she was sharing such intimate space with as Pearl raised her head. She placed an elbow on the rug next to Ashton's right shoulder, her head braced against an upturned palm. "I hope you don't mind, but I just want to be real with you. I'm not good at games or pretending." She gave her a small smile, bringing her hand up to run the backs of her fingers along a proud jawline. "That's why I wanted to bring you here, outside the walls of the club." She smirked. "That, and I wanted you naked."

"I think you managed that one pretty easily," Pearl responded with a grin. "I'm also beginning to think the house rules, as it were, dissolve pretty quickly around you."

"Oh?" Ashton asked, raising her eyebrows.

"Definitely," Pearl murmured, her hand running down along Ashton's side and down to her hip, nails trailing as far along Ashton's raised thigh as she could reach. "I seem to remember you mentioning something about a cock."

Ashton felt instant arousal bloom in her crotch. "I did." Her hands ran down to cup Pearl's perfect ass, remembering that first sight of her leaning over that table. "Is that what you want?"

Pearl pushed herself up until she was straddling Ashton's hips. She looked down at her with eyes that looked as though they could eat Ashton alive at any moment. She ran her hands over Ashton's stomach and cupped her breasts while her hips moved just enough to mimic riding such a cock. "I'm ready and very willing."

Ashton sat up, her mouth going to Pearl's neck. She moaned when she could feel just how wet Pearl already was for her. "Looks like I'm not the only one who gets incredibly wet."

"Mmm," Pearl hummed, head tilting to the side as Ashton explored her neck, her hands buried in long, dark hair. "So true."

"You smell so good," Ashton murmured against Pearl's neck.

She could get addicted to the taste and smell of Pearl's skin, the sound of her whimpers, and the feel of her touch. She had to be careful. In the meantime, she gently urged the woman in question to move off her lap so she could get up. She walked over to her armoire, surprisingly comfortable in her nakedness even as she felt Pearl's eyes on her.

Pulling the doors open, she opened one of the drawers inside and pulled out the satin drawstring bag that held her dildo and leather straps to attach it. Stepping into it and getting everything buckled and tightened, she glanced over to their little love nest and saw Pearl reclined at the center, one leg bent at the knee with foot flat on the rug, the other straight out in front of her. She was watching Ashton, hands tucked behind her head.

"It is so hard to look sexy or even remotely competent in one of these things," Ashton said, heading back to the sexy woman who awaited her, the cock bouncing obscenely with every step.

"Oh, I don't know," Pearl said, arms moving down to her sides as she raised her other leg, thighs spread to reveal just how ready she was for Ashton.

Nearly purring at the sight, Ashton lowered herself to the rug between Pearl's thighs. She could smell her need and it made her clit jump in sympathy. Unable to help herself, cognizant of the addition at her crotch, she lowered herself to her belly, mouth watering to lick and suck at the heart of Pearl's need. She felt fingers in her hair as her tongue ran up the length of Pearl's seam, gathering the tangy wetness that was unique to the woman she so wanted to please. She made the same, slow journey a second time, Pearl's low, guttural groan encouraging her to make a third pass, this time dedicating time to the hard clit at the top of the road.

She was getting lost in her task, loving every soft cry and whimper until she felt a hand on her shoulder. Worried she'd hurt her, Ashton lifted her head and looked up to see a flushed but amused Pearl looking back at her.

"You're going to make me come, baby," Pearl gasped. "If that's your goal, nice work."

Ashton grinned, taking one last swipe before she pushed up to her knees, hands moving to rest on Pearl's thighs. "No. Not my goal. Well, not like that, anyway." She grabbed the cock in her hand, guiding the tip through the swollen, saturated folds, easing the length of the phallus inside. Hips flush with Pearl's as she was all the way in, she remained on her knees but lowered her upper body to rest against the woman beneath her, who immediately wrapped her arms around her. "So much for the no penetration rule."

Pearl grinned as she raised her knees, inviting Ashton to go deeper. "Baby, the fact that I'm here at all shows just how much of my personal rules have gone out the window since I met you."

Ashton began to slowly move her hips, pulling the long shaft out before lazily pushing it back in.

"Oh yeah?" she murmured, resting on a forearm as her other hand reached back, fingernails trailing up the underside of Pearl's thigh, eliciting a long sigh from the gorgeous woman she was slowly fucking. "You haven't met with a member outside of the club before?"

"Never," Pearl responded, voice breathy as she ran her hands over Ashton's shoulders. "I've never touched anyone there, either."

Ashton was surprised to hear this, remembering their night in that little room, Pearl's hand inside her panties. She lowered her mouth to Pearl's neck as she continued her slow, measured thrusts inside of her. She wanted nothing more than to initiate a slow, passionate kiss but instead settled for the warmth of her neck.

"Baby..." Pearl whispered, fingers once again buried in Ashton's hair, her soft moans and whimpers close to Ashton's ear.

Ashton raised herself to her hands, looking down into Pearl's face. Despite the mask covering half of it, she could see the beauty there, the desire in her eyes, and knew it reflected her own. As Pearl looked up at her, eyes hooded, something passed between them. Suddenly, it was as if the world receded and it was just the two of them, Ashton's cock gently thrusting inside of Pearl's pussy, and nothing else mattered.

It almost felt like making love.

Forcing that thought out of her mind, Ashton raised herself higher and began to increase her thrusts, forcing reality back to what it was: she was paying this woman beneath her, paying her to let her fuck her, and that was okay.

The haze seemed to have lifted off Pearl as well,

as gone were the loving caresses and soft, breathy moans. In their place was a viselike grip on her sides as Pearl's hips moved to meet each thrust.

"How does my cock feel?" Ashton panted, her hips slapping against Pearl's as she pounded into her.

"Fuck yeah," Pearl managed through her constant, high-pitched cries. Suddenly, her neck arched and mouth opened, though no sound came out for a long moment.

Ashton's own orgasm washed over her violently, causing her to yell out as she continued to slam into Pearl. "Fuck," she ground out through clenched teeth, her hips jerking with the intensity of the experience.

Both of them were panting heavily as Ashton's arms gave out and she lay against Pearl, who slung a limp arm across her back. "Jesus," Pearl gasped.

Ashton nodded, forehead resting against the pillow Pearl's head lay upon. "I concur."

Pearl chuckled, her other hand coming to cup the back of Ashton's neck. "I think I want that apple juice now."

# Chapter Nine

Here you are, madam," Ashton said, holding out a wine goblet with cold apple juice in it.

"Thank you," Pearl said, accepting the goblet. She patted the space next to her.

"Un momento, por favor," Ashton said, pouring her own. She replaced the bottle in the ice bucket and made her way over to where Pearl reclined against the pillows they'd stacked to lean back against. "That fire feels amazing," she said, getting settled. She lifted an arm to allow Pearl to cuddle in next to her. Now that their bodies had calmed down, the cold February night put a chill on naked skin.

"It does. So beautiful." Pearl took a long drink of her juice. "Oh, that's good," she whispered. "I have to tell you, I never in a million years thought I'd get to see the inside of Pittman House."

Ashton stared at her. "Well," she said, surprised. "I must say, I love a girl who knows her history."

Pearl hid her thoughts behind her Mona Lisa smile as she sipped more of her juice and settled in against Ashton. "How long had you been back in town before you came into the club?"

"Not long, a few days," Ashton admitted.

"Why are you here?" Pearl asked softly, absently running her fingers over Ashton's forearm, which was wrapped around her shoulders.

"My father had a stroke."

"Oh no," Pearl said, pulling away just enough to be able to look over at Ashton. "I'm so sorry. Is he okay?"

Ashton took a drink, staring into the flames. Finally, she said, "I don't know. We're moving him into the house soon. We'll basically create our very own private ICU here at the house."

"You can do that?" Pearl asked, turning in Ashton's arms to place her goblet up on the table before returning and snuggling in closer now that she didn't have a drink to keep from spilling.

Ashton smiled, holding her closer. She closed her eyes as she turned her face to bury in her hair, her updo now messy and partially coming out of its style. She inhaled the scent of Pearl's shampoo before she left a kiss on the side of her head. "To be blunt, when you have money, you can do anything." She snorted. "My father certainly has the money."

"Do you like coming back here?"

Ashton considered the question. "Not really," she finally said. "My father and I don't get along and I don't really have any friends here anymore. No other family. So…"

Pearl was quiet for a long time, so long Ashton wondered if perhaps she'd dozed off. But finally she said, "I'm sorry."

The clock on the mantel began to chime the hour. Ashton groaned, displeased. "Hate to say it," she murmured into Pearl's hair. "But it's eleven o'clock. You're officially paroled."

"I can't believe the three hours are already up," Pearl said. After a long moment of silence between the two, she pulled away and got to her feet. "Do you mind if I use your restroom?"

Ashton looked up at her, knowing it was possibly the last time she'd see that glorious body. "Of course."

Pearl smiled down at her, bringing her hand out to caress her cheek before she walked over to her dress and high heels, carrying them to the bathroom with her before quietly closing the door behind her.

Blowing out a breath, Ashton also got to her feet. She looked down at the space where they'd spent three amazing hours together, her body still humming with sexual contentment. She did, however, hate the fact that she'd be going to bed alone. That sparked a thought in her mind.

She lightly tapped on the door. "Do you need to take a shower or anything?" she asked through the thick wood. "If so, feel free."

She picked up her robe, swinging it around so she could push her arms into the sleeves and wrap it around her chilled body, belting it. She walked over to the small table and grabbed the envelope, sliding it into her pocket. The toilet flushed and the water in the sink ran before the bathroom door opened and a fully dressed Pearl stepped out. Her hair had also been fixed.

"No," she responded belatedly. "I don't have anyone at home to question."

For reasons that shouldn't matter, that made Ashton happy. She opened her arms to indicate the room around her. "Clearly I don't, either."

Pearl walked over to her, her high heels putting them at an even height. She brought her arms up around Ashton's neck and initiated a hug, with Ashton immediately responded to. She held the smaller woman, her heart racing. For the first time, though, it wasn't lust on her mind, but sadness.

"Thank you for coming," she murmured into the hug.

"Literally," Pearl replied with a small laugh, which made Ashton smile. "I'm glad I did."

"Me, too. Leonard will be waiting for you down where he dropped you off," she offered.

Pearl pulled out of the hug and nodded. "Okay."

The two walked together to the sitting room where Pearl grabbed her long coat, Ashton holding it for her so the redhead could slide into it. "Thank you," Pearl said, pulling it closed and belting it much as Ashton had done with her robe not long before.

Ashton reached into her pocket and pulled out the envelope of money, gingerly tucking it into a pocket in the coat. Pearl smiled at her, though Ashton sensed that she, too, was reluctant to leave.

Finally, Pearl reached up, cupping Ashton's face, holding her steady as she leaned in and placed a lingering kiss at the corner of her mouth. "Good night," she murmured into the kiss, then turned and let herself out of the sitting room.

It was quiet. So very quiet. That is, save for the soft beeps of the machines that had been leased from a medical equipment company, along with the hospital bed that now rested where the large canopy bed had been. It had been the bed where her mother had slept for the entirety of the twenty-eight years she'd been married to Jack King. Now, the space embraced the very man who had forced it upon his wife rather than sharing his own bed—or heart—with her.

Her father slept peacefully—that is, she assumed. He'd yet to regain consciousness since the stroke, and his doctors were beginning to prepare her for the worst. As she sat in the chair next to his bed, she didn't know what to feel. At least with her mother, she'd killed herself over the span of two years, a slow-motion train wreck. This time, though, her father was in his eighties, it had been quick and unexpected.

"Miss King," Maddy, her father's live-in nurse, said as she came out of the smaller, adjoining room. It had once been used as a nursery for both Ashton and her brother, let alone previous generations, but now housed the ICU nurse. "I just spoke to the doctor and he said he'll be by tomorrow morning to go over the latest MRI and EEG with you."

Ashton met the older woman's gaze and nodded. "All right. Do you have a time? I have some appointments to keep."

"He said no later than ten, ma'am. I can see if I can tighten that timeframe for you."

"I appreciate that. Thank you, Maddy. Is there anything I can get you?" she asked, pushing up from the chair. "Anything you need?"

"No," Maddy said, hands on her scrubs-covered hips. "I think I have everything Mr. King and I will need, though thank you."

"Okay. Just know that's not a onetime offer," Ashton said with a smile. "If you need anything, give me a call or tell Martin."

"Yes, ma'am. Have a good night," the nurse said with a friendly smile.

"You do the same."

Ashton walked to the other wing to her own suite, tired yet restless. She stripped once she got to her bedroom, tossing her clothing into the laundry basket before heading to the bathroom for a long, hot shower.

Forehead resting against the cool tile in the large walk-in shower, she let the water, just this side of too hot, beat down on the back of her neck to try and release some of the tightness so she didn't end up with a migraine later, a problem she and her mother shared. After a long moment, she turned and raised her face to the spray, reaching up to smooth her hair back from her face.

Tomorrow she and Brian were headed to the club to talk to Buck. She needed to fill them both in on the latest of her father's condition. Buck also wanted to rework the contract for Top Shelf, said he had some products he'd like to add and that he wanted to rework the partnership. Ashton wasn't thrilled about it, but she figured they owed it to him to hear him out.

It had been five days since her encounter with Pearl, and she ached for another one. They'd be at the club during the day, so she figured the chances of seeing her there were slim to none, but she hoped. She wished Pearl were on her way over to spend some time with her that evening, truth be told. Her body warmed at the thought, nipples tightening. She hissed as the hot water rained down on the sensitive flesh.

Her eyes closed as she ran her hands down over the soft skin of her own breasts, cupping them. She was amused as she was pretty sure her nipples could cut glass. She saw Pearl's breasts before her mind's eye. They were perfectly shaped, soft, yet firm. Pearl was a small woman, well-proportioned. She wondered how she looked in regular, everyday clothes. She wondered what she looked like without the mask, without the fancy chignon.

What was it like to spend a normal day with her? What would she want to talk about? What was her sense of humor? Favorite movie? Song? At The Black Pussy Cat it was easy to see Pearl as nothing more than an object of desire, with her mask on, the ultimate Catwoman fantasy. Even when Pearl had been at the house, it was all about sex and desire.

But so many times Ashton had seen the woman beneath the fantasy. She'd felt her gentleness, felt her own need to be close when they'd shared the hug before she'd left. Ashton craved that, now.

Sex was wonderful, and sex with Pearl was amazing. And, yes, her body was humming with the need, but in truth, all she wanted was to cuddle in bed and talk. She wanted to just be human, something she felt like she hadn't had a lot of opportunity to do in her life. There was always expectation in her head.

She considered texting her after her shower, see if perhaps she was free. But then, she decided not to. She needed to get some sleep for the next day's meeting. It was better to have business on the brain and not Pearl's perfume.

"I'm thinking we should bring in Doug Bainbridge and run the numbers by him," Brian said as the two headed down the long, narrow staircase to the ground floor and front door.

"I agree with that," Ashton said. "I think Buck actually had some decent ideas."

"Agreed." They were silent for a moment when he added, "Look, I need to drop you off anyway, okay if I go in and see Jack?"

"Yes, I think he'd like that," Ashton said.

"Really glad to hear he finally opened his eyes. Still nothing, though?" he asked, concern in his voice, their footfalls hollow thuds on the wooden stairs.

"Nothing. Hasn't spoken. He's alert, but not sure how much."

Brian shook his head. "Such a shame."

Ashton was about to respond when the wooden door opened at the bottom of the stairs and the person about to step through froze. Ashton's smile was slow but wide. Pearl seemed to relax from her startled state, pressing her back to the wall for the two to pass.

"Brian," Ashton said, glancing at her companion. "I'll meet you at the car in just a minute."

He looked from Ashton to Pearl then back to Ashton, a knowing smirk on his lips. "'Kay." He nodded at Pearl as he passed her by, the heavy wooden door slowly closing behind him, leaving Pearl and Ashton alone in the stairwell.

"Well, hello there," Pearl said, walking up to the stair Ashton stood on, having halted when she registered who had opened the door. "What a nice surprise."

"I'd agree with that statement," Ashton said. "And here I was all upset I wouldn't see you today."

"I'm mad at you," Pearl murmured, moving toward Ashton until she was against the wall of the staircase, the railing digging into her back.

"Oh?" Ashton was taken yet again by the immensity of the woman's presence who was nearly pressed up against her. "What did I do?"

"You gave me four thousand dollars," she said quietly.

"Yes, yes I did." Ashton's gaze followed Pearl's hand as it reached out, a finger toying with the waistline of her trousers.

"Our agreement was three," Pearl insisted, sparing a glance up at Ashton, the look in her eyes mischievous.

"Are you complaining?" Ashton raised her eyebrow, even though she knew it was hidden behind her mask.

"No," Pearl purred, her fingers deftly tugging down the zipper.

Ashton gasped, surprised. Her gasp turned to a whimper when that hand pushed its way inside, cupping her pussy and squeezing. The fingers relaxed and her index finger began to stroke her through the satin of her panties, which were becoming saturated, easily finding her swelling clit.

Pearl buried her face in Ashton's neck, her breath hot. "You're so fucking sexy," she murmured.

Ashton couldn't respond as her body was thrust from surprise to pleasure, her brain still stuck back on surprise. A groan managed to escape her lips as Pearl's fingernail rubbed vigorously over her clit through her panties, her hips slamming back against the rail as she came from the pleasure/pain of that fingernail, though mostly pleasure.

Pearl's fire seemed to cool as she lightly stroked the lips of Ashton's sex before removing her hand and gently pulling the zipper back up. She left a series of kisses on the side of her neck and her jaw.

"I have to go," she whispered.

Ashton nodded, her brain finally beginning to catch up to the situation. "When can I see you again? At my house."

Pearl met her gaze, her hand cupping Ashton's cheek, thumb rubbing her lips, which her eyes watched before her hand fell away. "I'll text you." She met Ashton's gaze again. "Okay?"

Ashton nodded. "Okay." She watched as Pearl was about to move away from her and just wasn't ready for her to go. "Wait." She grabbed the other woman's arm and swung her back toward her, taking her into a tight hug. She needed to feel her. Pearl returned the hug, their bodies pressed together. "I'm glad I got to see you," she whispered into the hug.

Pearl said nothing, simply gave her a firm squeeze before letting her go, hurrying up the stairs.

The drive south from downtown Denver to Highlands Ranch was largely done in silence. Ashton felt Brian's gaze on her from time to time. Finally, he cleared his throat.

"Everything okay?" he asked, flicking the turn signal to go down the road that would lead to the house.

She met his gaze and nodded. "Yeah. Fine, thanks."

Brian pulled his car into the circular drive of the big house and cut the engine. He blew out a breath as he pulled the key from the ignition and released his seat belt. "I can't believe it's come to this," he said quietly.

Releasing her own seat belt, Ashton glanced over at him. "With my father?" At Brian's nod, she said, "Yes, I know. We can only hope he pulls through this."

Twenty minutes later, they stood in the bedroom that had been turned into a hospital suite. They'd been told that Jack had been resting peacefully for a couple hours, as he still was. Brian looked down at his boss, arms crossed over his chest as the fingers of one hand stroked at the goatee he was growing.

Ashton stood next to him and looked from her father's still form to her colleague. "Come on," she said quietly. "Let's let him rest. Let's go work out some numbers before we get Doug involved."

Brian nodded. "Good idea."

Ashton led the way back downstairs to her father's office. She hadn't set foot in it since the day she'd looked for the letter of instructions. "Okay," she said, flicking on the light as she entered, leaving the door open for Brian to enter. Walking to the desk, she gathered the stack of mail from the corner of the desk and moved it to one of the drawers, replacing it with a yellow legal pad, which she slapped to the desktop, setting a pen in front of him and one in front of her.

Brian sat down and grinned, taking the pen. "What's this for?"

Ashton grinned, removing the cap from hers. "Right?" she laughed. "I need to bring my laptop down here, bring this office into the twenty-first century." She indicated the notepad with a hand. "You want to be the notetaker, or shall I?"

He grinned and shook his head. "I will," he said, sliding the pad to him. "Your handwriting looks like a serial killer."

# Chapter Ten

*Pearl: Good morning. ⊠ How's your dad?*

*Ashton: Good morning to you, too. Literally waiting for the doctor right now.*

*Pearl: OK. Please let me know what he says. If you need to cancel or postpone tonight, I understand.*

*Ashton: I'll definitely let you know, and I definitely want to see you.*

*Pearl: OK. All the best with the doctor. Talk soon.*

*Ashton: Talk soon.*

Ashton smiled at the unexpected text message. They'd been exchanging them on occasion, and her heart swelled each time she received one out of the blue. She lowered the phone, her knee jiggling incessantly with nerves as she waited to hear the results of the newest batch of tests. Finally, the door to the office opened and Dr. Brightman entered, followed by a small Indian woman in a white doctor's coat whom Ashton hadn't met.

"Good morning, Miss King," Dr. Brightman greeted, extending his hand, which she shook. "This is Dr. Sunku, whom I've brought on for her extensive expertise in vascular neurology and can be of great benefit in your father's case."

"Dr. Sunku, please," Ashton said, shaking the woman's small, soft hand.

Dr. Brightman took his place behind his desk

while the second doctor took the seat next to Ashton. "Together, Dr. Sunku and I have gone over and discussed the results and," Dr. Brightman said, lacing his fingers atop his desk as he studied Ashton with a serious gaze. "I have to be honest with you, Miss King. We don't have good news."

Ashton nodded even as her stomach somersaulted. "All right," she said quietly, steeling herself for what she was about to hear.

"Your father," Dr. Sunku began, her words clipped by the accent of her native land. "Had a significant cerebrovascular accident, otherwise known as a stroke. A stroke can either be a blockage and therefore lack of blood supply to the brain, or the rupture of a blood vessel, thus causing a lack of blood supply. Your father falls in camp two."

"Preliminary tests weren't able to truly show us the amount of damage due to the blood from the rupture," Dr. Brightman explained.

"But now," Dr. Sunku continued. "This new set of tests reveal that your father's brain has less activity than it did during the last round of tests."

Ashton felt emotion squeezing her throat, which she tried to swallow down. She nodded, taking a moment to absorb what she was being told. "What does this mean, then?" she finally asked. "Can he regain any ground?"

"Unfortunately, no," Dr. Sunku said, shaking her head. "At best, even if the damage stopped right now, your father would face extensive brain damage and paralysis. You need to prepare yourself for the inevitable," she added, reaching out and taking one of Ashton's hands.

Looking down at her father now, Ashton felt differently than she had before. When she'd been there as the paramedics had unloaded him from the ambulance after returning from the hospital for his tests, she'd felt as she'd felt all along—unsure of her feelings. Sad, but unsure, and numb in many aspects.

But now, knowing that the prognosis was essentially set, she felt that wall of numbness beginning to buckle. She sat in the chair next to her father's bed, looking down at her hands, which dangled from limp wrists that rested on her knees.

"Tomorrow is fine, George," Ashton said into her phone, pacing over to the window and looking out before turning to start pacing in the other direction. "I should be here, but if I'm not, Martin can let you in. I'll make sure my father's office is left unlocked for you." She smiled at the kind words being spoken on the other end of the line. "Thank you, George. You've been King-Kraft's attorney since God was a boy, so if anyone can make heads or tails of his, shall we say, unique way of recordkeeping, it'll be you." She laughed at his response. "All right, George. Thanks for everything. See you tomorrow. Good night."

Ending the call, she set her phone down on the table where the ice bucket was, a fresh bottle of apple juice inside and Pearl's labeled envelope lying next to it and the wine goblets. Blowing out a breath, she walked over to the fireplace, staring down into the flames. She was stressed and a bundle of emotions. She felt like the weight of the world was on her shoulders. Not too far off the mark, considering the entire weight of her family's world and her business's world *was* on her shoulders.

She was startled by the knock at the door. A glance at the clock told her it was just a few minutes before eight, their agreed-upon time. Running a hand through her hair, she turned from the fireplace, walked over to the double doors of her bedroom, and pulled them open. Pearl stood on the other side, as expected, beautiful and looking deceptively innocent in white.

But it wasn't luscious curves or enticing cleavage that had her attention. It was looking into her eyes. She didn't know what her own expression was, but the compassion and understanding she saw in Pearl's eyes, the depth of which even a mask couldn't hide, was her undoing.

Pearl took her in her arms, holding her close. "It's okay," she murmured. "I understand."

Ashton buried her face in Pearl's neck and let the tears come, her entire body shaking with the power of her grief. What made it worse was, it wasn't grief of losing her father, it was grief that the tiny flame of hope that someday her father would love her and treat her like a daughter would now be forever gone. It was grieving the dream.

After several minutes, her tears dried up, Pearl caressing her back the entire time. "Come on," Pearl murmured into her ear. "Let me hold you."

Ashton started to object, as she hadn't called Pearl there to have to comfort her like she was a child, but stopped when Pearl placed two fingers over her lips. She shut up and looked into Pearl's eyes.

"Just be with me," Pearl said softly, her hand moving away from Ashton's mouth to caress her cheek before that hand fell to grab Ashton's hand and lead her over to the bed.

Ashton said nothing, simply acquiesced. She hadn't set up the little floor nest as they both had gotten chilled last time. Instead, she'd already turned down the bed. Stopping next to it, Pearl quickly stripped out of her dress, again nude beneath it, and pushed Ashton's robe off her shoulders.

"Go ahead," Pearl said, indicating the massive four-poster.

Ashton climbed in, sliding beneath the covers, Pearl following. She scooted over to Ashton, worming her arm under Ashton's shoulders and gently urging her to lie against her. Ashton rolled onto her side and rested her head onto Pearl's shoulder, their naked bodies as close as possible beneath the covers. Pearl felt amazing, her skin so soft and warm. She smelled incredible, and as she ran her fingers lightly through Ashton's hair, Ashton felt the comfort that she hadn't been aware she needed.

"Tell me," Pearl said softly,

Ashton heaved a heavy sigh, her fingers lightly running down along Pearl's side, simply for the tactile bliss. "My father will never recover," she said. "Too much damage has been done."

"I'm so sorry, Ashton," Pearl whispered, her hand reaching under the covers and grabbing Ashton's top thigh, bringing it up and over her own and resting her hand there. "How long do they think he has?"

"They don't know." Ashton reveled in the closeness. She hadn't cuddled with someone like that in a very long time. Katherine wasn't the cuddle type, and besides, she never felt as comfortable with Katherine as she did with this woman that she'd known such a short time. "His doctors said that eventually the brain would shut down, a mass termination event, she called it."

"Are you close to him?"

Ashton didn't respond for a moment, then said, "That's the hard part, and I was actually thinking this a bit earlier. We're not close, he's always held me at arm's length. Always. He tolerated me for a long time I think because he had my brother, Jackson. His plan was to groom him, the boy, to join the company and someday take it over."

"Was Jackson not interested?"

"No, he was. Bright kid, but he was killed in a motorcycle accident when he was nineteen. That would've been bad enough, but it was his fault. He was a reckless kid, always taking unnecessary chances. I always wondered, if he had lived, would he have destroyed the company or taken it to new levels?"

"How old were you?" Pearl asked. "When he died."

"I was twenty-three. Getting my MBA. So, he had no choice but to turn to me."

"Do you like it, working in the chocolate business?" Pearl asked softly. "How is your mother handling all this?"

"There are aspects of the business I like, I suppose," Ashton said truthfully. "I get to be creative, especially in the division I run in London. And," she added with a sigh. "My mom died when I was twenty-five. She never recovered after Jackson's accident."

"So much tragedy," Pearl said. "In such a huge house, it must get lonely."

"Yes, it can," Ashton admitted. "You met Martin, he's been here since my father was a young man. He's always been almost like an uncle to me. Watched out for me and my mom."

"What happens, once your father..." Pearl left a kiss on Ashton's head. "Do you go back to London?"

"I'm not sure. After he passes, we'll have to see what he called for in his will." She snorted. "It's entirely possible he left the whole thing to Brian."

"Brian from the club the other day?" Pearl asked, her fingers drawing lazy patterns on Ashton's thigh.

Ashton nodded. "He's basically my equal stateside," she explained. As her emotions had calmed, she was becoming very aware of the woman she was pressed against, a naked breast very close to her mouth. "Pearl?" she whispered.

"Hmm?"

"Tell me something about you, something about the woman beneath the mask."

Pearl was quiet for a long time, so long that Ashton thought she wasn't going to respond. Finally, she cleared her throat and said, "Tristan."

"What?" Ashton asked, lifting her head and looking down at the other woman. "What's Tristan?"

Pearl studied her for a long moment then said, "My name. it's Tristan."

A slow smile spread across Ashton's lips. "Tristan," she murmured, tasting the name on her tongue. "I like it. It's beautiful, like you." She brought her hand up and ran her fingers along the jaw of the woman looking up at her. "Can I call you that? When we're not at the club?"

The smile that Ashton received was blinding. "I'd like that," Tristan whispered. She reached up and tucked Ashton's hair behind her ear before she gently urged her to lie back, which she did. Tristan followed until she had moved atop her.

Ashton looked up into the beautiful woman's face, wanting so badly to kiss her, but she wasn't going to push it. Finding out Pearl's true name, Tristan, was a wonderful discovery. Her hands ran down the strong, smooth back as Tristan used a knee to nudge her thighs open. Tristan settled her hips between Ashton's spread thighs, adjusting her position until her clit rubbed against Ashton's, which sent a bolt of white-hot pleasure slicing through Ashton.

Gasping, Ashton's eyes slid closed as her hands moved up to cup the back of Tristan's shoulders as the redhead began to move her hips in slow, measured thrusts against her. The bed beneath them creaked softly with each graceful move of her hips.

Ashton looked up into Tristan's flushed face, her hands moving from her shoulders to run along the smooth skin of her side and around to cup her breasts as Tristan held herself up on her hands. Her eyes fell closed and lips slightly open as Ashton rolled her nipples between her fingers. Her hips never picked up their rhythm as soft moans left her lips as Ashton gently tugged on her nipples before running her palms over them.

It wasn't long before the large room was filled with the sound of the popping flames from the fire and heavy breathing of the two in the bed as Tristan kept the slow thrusts, which was nearly torture as Ashton's body kept threatening to release, only if she had a little bit more, a little bit more...

"Fuck!" she exclaimed as her body exploded, the slow buildup winding her body taut until it finally snapped, pleasure shooting through her like a firehose that got away from the guiding hands of the firefighters.

Tristan wasn't far behind as her hips jerked into Ashton's, her upper body falling on top of her even as she continued to grind their clits together, Ashton holding them tightly together with her arms. Finally, Tristan grew still, her chest heaving as she panted into Ashton's neck.

Needing to hold the woman in her arms, Ashton whispered for Tristan to turn on her side, which she did, rolling off Ashton, who spooned up behind her. It was the only way she wouldn't take her in a desperately needed kiss. She held Tristan against her with a possessive arm over the smaller woman's stomach.

Intending to simply catch her breath, Ashton's eyes fell closed.

Some time later, Ashton woke up. She was alone in the expansive bed, and the room was dark. The lights had been turned out, the fire burned down to embers. Sitting up in bed, she brought her hands up to brush her hair out of the way. It was unsettling when the last thing you remember was holding someone in your arms yet you wake up alone.

She pushed back the covers and scooted to the edge of the bed before getting up. Walking to the fireplace, she used the poker to ensure the fire was out before continuing to the bathroom where she did her business and then washed her face and brushed her teeth.

She looked at her reflection in the mirror. Her eyes were red from crying earlier, the skin tight. She so rarely cried, always an unpleasant thing for her, especially in front of Pearl… A slow smile came to her lips when she remembered.

"Tristan," she said softly.

Turning from the mirror, she flicked off the bathroom light as she left the room, wandering back to the bedroom, which was still dark, though her eyes had begun to adjust. Something caught her attention and she stopped. Walking over to the small table where the ice bucket was, which was now largely cool water with pea-sized bits of ice floating around, she saw the bottle of apple juice had been opened and one of the goblets had been used. She also saw the sealed envelope of money with *Pearl* written across it.

# Chapter Eleven

Ashton heard the gasps and even a few sniffles in the large audience gathered before her. They'd put in a theater-style addition to the Denver factory and first King-Kraft store years ago. They found it was the easiest way to show new products to employees, from factory workers to those who ran the stores, before letting them taste the merchandise.

Standing on the stage with microphone in hand, she waited for reactions to wash through the audience, even as her own heart was heavy. "I know my father's death comes as a shock," she said, scanning over the sea of shocked faces. "But even as we work through this as a company, Brian and I, as your management team, want you to know you have nothing to worry about. Your jobs are safe. My father, without exception, loved each and every one of you." No matter how he may have treated his own daughter, Jack King's employees were everything to him. "Right, Brian?" she asked, indicating the man who stood just back from her on the stage.

"Absolutely," he agreed.

"Now," she continued. "Before I hand things over to Brian, I wanted to tell you all something. We're still going through paperwork and everything, lord knows my father loved paperwork." She smiled as that got her some chuckles, especially from the old timers in the crowd. "Our lawyers came across a provision that even I didn't know about," she said, placing a hand on her chest. "In the event of his death, my father asked that every single King-Kraft employee, from the stores to the factories to the test kitchen, from here to England, receive a twenty-five-hundred-dollar thank-you bonus from him personally, for working for him." Thunderous applause and surprised cheers rent the space. "Be looking for those," she concluded, turning and handing the microphone to Brian.

Ashton stepped back, allowing Brian to address his people. She stood there like a good little soldier, hands clasped in front of her as she tried to pay attention to what he was saying. Her mind, however, kept wanting to return to that morning three days ago. She'd been getting ready for her day, taking her time as she had appointments later in the morning, so had enjoyed a long, lazy shower and a bit of reading, and was finally getting dressed.

Responding to the frantic knocking on the door to her sitting room, she'd ended up with her arms full of sobbing housekeeper. He was gone. It was done. After the medical examiner had come and signed off on death by natural causes, the funeral home had come to gather Jack King so the self-styled King of Chocolate could begin his journey to the family crypt on the property.

The funeral would be a massive affair, held at the Basilica of the Immaculate Conception, a beautiful cathedral that Titanic's own Molly Brown was instrumental in raising money for to ensure its completion. Her seat was still reserved in the pews, more than eighty years after her death.

Luckily, his wishes were widely known, so it just took some phone calls and emails to get things moving for a very successful member of the business community to have his farewell.

❧

George and a few of his law clerks sat around the massive table in the north dining room with Ashton, the fireplace at one end ablaze as they went through what seemed to be unending boxes delivered via courier from Jack's office.

"This is nuts." One of the men chuckled, looking around at the boxes. "Like, all of this," he said, indicating it all with the wave of his hand. "Could fit on this," he added, holding up a thumb drive, drawing a laugh from the group.

"Well, this all came out of sixteen file cabinets," George added from where he sat.

"Plus," another said, entering the room carrying two more boxes, one stacked atop the other. "More filing cabinets here."

Ashton smiled, beginning to go through the box of files closest to her. "He hated computers and technology in general."

"Let me guess," one of the clerks said. "He had a flip phone, right?"

"You kidding me?" she said, glancing over at him. "Did you not *see* the rotary phone in his office?" That earned another round of laughter, which Ashton felt was what they all needed—a little levity to begin their long day to break the ice. She knew nobody present minded the boxes or hundreds upon hundreds of files; it was their job.

As they got more focused on their task, silence fell over them, only the sounds of shuffling papers and boxes as well as popping flames sounded. For her part, Ashton couldn't help but think that, if her father had already been in his grave, he'd be turning in it with the fact they were using the north dining room, *the formal place*, for such a task. She almost stuck her tongue out and chanted, "Nanny nanny boo boo!"

After an hour or so, the clerk who'd gathered all the contents from the home office spoke. "Um, George?" he said, fingers stroking his dark brown beard as he read over something he'd removed from an envelope.

Ashton glanced over at him and recognized it as one of the pieces of unread mail that had been atop her father's desk when she'd arrived at the house after the stroke.

He pushed back from his chair and scurried over to the other side and the older man. "Have you seen this?" he asked softly, glancing quickly at Ashton before focusing on his boss. "Did Mr. King know about this?"

A look of concern passed across George's face as he read over the page, which made Ashton concerned. He glanced at her over his glasses. "Ashton," he said quietly. "Would you mind joining me in your father's office, please?"

"Certainly." Ashton stepped away from the table and, waiting for the older man to get his cane under him, walked with him to the room in question.

She helped him get settled in one of the chairs before closing the office door. The man's body might have been getting frail, but his mind was still as sharp as a tack. She sat down in the matching chair to his. "What's up?"

"Have you seen this?" he asked, holding out the

page.

Ashton took it, eyebrows drawn as she began to read. She read the short missive twice and then a third time, unable to believe what was being asserted. She shook her head, looking at the man who waited in silence. "This is absolutely bullshit. Forgive my language, George, but no way. Who sent him this? It's not signed."

"I don't know. It must have come in anonymously. None of this is accurate?"

"Katherine Whispell and I have had an on-again, off-again relationship, but it was certainly not an affair. Neither of us are married, and it was a known fact."

"And the embezzlement?" he asked. "That's a huge accusation, Ashton. If I hadn't known you your entire life, I would never have asked you, I simply would have begun an investigation."

"A thousand percent no," she said, shaking her head. "Never."

He nodded. "As I thought." He met her gaze. "I do believe you. Anyone in the King-Kraft Creations division who has a grudge against you?"

She considered and shook her head. "No. Things didn't end up well for Katherine and me, but I can't see her doing this," she said, holding up the page.

"All right. Well," he said, slapping his own thighs before grunting as he began to stand. "We'll investigate this, get to the bottom of it."

"Yes," she said, holding his arm to steady him as he steadied his cane. "I welcome it, George. I have absolutely nothing to hide."

It was cold, terribly cold. She'd never forget that. She stood on the grounds of the Pittman House property huddled in her long black peacoat. The heavy wool helped, but still, the cold cut through her like a knife.

As expected, the church service had a massive turnout, as Jack King was a business leader in the city and had employed thousands of locals over the years. Many of those people came out to show their respects, people Ashton hadn't seen for years.

After the service there, Jack's casket was taken back to the house, as well as a small group of invite-only mourners to be present during the graveside ceremony, which was where she was now. They'd opted to have the graveside outside the crypt to allow more people to be there.

She stood there, looking at the shiny black casket. No flowers, per her father's orders. He hated them, felt they were a waste of money. The casket was as cold and black as his heart was. For those who had shown up for the mass and funeral service, and those standing around her now, he had treated all of them with respect, and often kindness.

His cruelty had driven her mother to an early grave, just inside the very crypt her father would be placed by end of day. He'd driven Ashton away, sent her to work on a totally different continent. She mused that once the will was read, chances were she'd lose everything. She'd planned for this. Despite her expansive home in the English countryside, she'd been sure to make very responsible investments and financial decisions over the years, never wanting to depend on her father's whim for her future.

Feeling like she was being watched, Ashton pushed her thoughts away and looked up and around. Standing by the giant cottonwood tree just outside the wrought iron fencing that surrounded the family cemetery was a lone figure.

She wore a long, dark green coat which revealed the lower portion of legs covered by black trousers. Her hands were covered by black leather gloves, one of which reached up to brush long auburn strands blown in the cold breeze out of the loveliest face. Little to no makeup revealed natural beauty and femininity that was breathtaking.

The eyes Ashton knew, but they were looking back at her from a face she'd dreamed of seeing but could never have imagined. There was a purity and vulnerability that belied the deep well of passion that she knew all too well was beneath the surface. The face of an angel with the touch of a seductress.

The smallest of smiles touched her lips, and Ashton smiled back.

The little room was as it always was: same lighting, same furnishings, same nervous feeling in the pit of Ashton's stomach. She'd come to see Pearl, yes, but she'd come to ask if she could spend a day with Tristan.

Sitting on the couch, she crossed one leg over the other, foot bouncing nervously as she reached up to adjust her mask to a more comfortable position. A few more minutes had gone by when finally the door opened and Pearl stepped through, looking as sexy as ever.

Ashton smiled and pushed to her feet. "Hey," she said, meeting the other woman by the round coffee table.

"How are you doing?" the redhead asked softly as they embraced, her hand going into Ashton's hair. "I'm so sorry."

"Thank you for being there, Tristan," Ashton whispered into her neck, where she left a small kiss on the warm skin.

"Of course," was whispered back. "I'm sorry I couldn't do more."

Ashton smiled, pulling back to look into her face. Though she was used to the mask, used to Pearl's countenance, she desperately wanted to see Tristan again. Bringing up a hand, she lightly caressed the other woman's jaw and the side of her neck before her hand fell away. "You've done plenty." She took her by the hand. "Sit?"

"So," Tristan said, her Pearl voice fully intact, though the softness in her smile didn't quite match the vixen in her tone. "What can I do for you tonight?"

Ashton smirked. "Gee, I'm sure I can think of something."

Tristan grinned. "Naughty, naughty."

Ashton looked down at their laced fingers for a long moment, trying to garner the courage to ask. Finally, she blew out a breath and said, "I want to spend a day with you. Just us, no Pearl, no masks. Just us."

Tristan looked away, her free hand reaching up and playing with the earring that dangled from her ear for a moment. "I don't know, Ashton," she said softly.

"What aren't you sure about?" Ashton asked.

She was trying not to let herself become immediately disappointed, instead opting to get to the root of uncertainty.

After a moment, Tristan looked over at her. "I love the time we spend together," she began. "I honestly do. It's not just about the money—"

"Why didn't you take the money last time you were with me?" Ashton asked. "I know you saw it by the glasses."

Tristan met her gaze then looked away again, nodding. "Yes. I did."

"It was why you were there," Ashton said gently, no accusations, no judgment. Just a simple statement of fact.

"It was," Tristan murmured. "In the beginning." She swallowed, her throat working with the motion. Abruptly she pushed to her feet, moving away from Ashton and the couch but remaining in the room.

Ashton could feel her confusion rolling off her in waves. The smaller woman hugged herself as she leaned back against the wall next to the little cabinet where she'd wiped Ashton's passion away that first time.

"Talk to me," Ashton urged. She stayed seated, as clearly Tristan needed distance between them for whatever she was dealing with.

Tristan looked up from the spot she'd seemingly been staring at on the floor. "I'm afraid if I see you, outside of this," she said, indicating her dress, the mask, their surroundings. "I'm afraid that, for a woman like you, it could never be enough."

Ashton took a moment to absorb her words, initially stung by them, but then she thought she understood what she meant, what her fears were.

Getting to her feet, she sidestepped the table and walked over to the other woman who, in that moment, looked so small, so vulnerable, a child playing dress-up in Mommy's makeup and dress.

"Tristan," she began, placing her hands on the redhead's hips. "This," she said, running her hands around and down over an incredibly shapely behind, squeezing before running her hands there. "Is incredible. You are the sexiest woman I have ever set eyes on. But," she added, removing her hands and placing one on Tristan's chest, just above her left breast. "I want to know what's in here." She moved her hand and lightly placed two fingers on a pale forehead, just above the line of the mask. "And in here."

Tristan looked deeply into Ashton's eyes as Ashton's hand once again fell away. She seemed to be looking directly into Ashton's soul, which made her feel unsettled. But, after a moment, Tristan nodded. "Okay."

# *Chapter Twelve*

Dressed casually as instructed, Ashton made her way down the main staircase in jeans and a heavy sweater, her coat draped over her arm with wallet and phone tucked into the pocket. Never one for purses, she loved wintertime as she always had a jacket with large pockets. It was supposed to be a mild day with chilly temperatures but sunny skies.

Reaching the bottom of the stairs, she heard a car pull to a stop in the circular driveway. Her stomach flipped as nervous butterflies battered her rib cage with their wings. Hand to her stomach, she blew out a slow breath as she walked to the front door, Martin already waiting to open it for her.

"Have a nice day, madam," he said.

She smiled at him. "Thank you, Martin. Not sure when I'll be back."

He nodded, stepping aside for her to exit.

Parked out front, engine still running, was a dark green Toyota Rav4. She made her way to it, raising her hand in a wave, the woman behind the wheel returning it. Pulling open the door, Ashton felt the warmth inside the small SUV waft out to caress her face.

"Hey there," she said, climbing into the passenger seat.

"Hey, yourself," Tristan greeted. "What?" she asked, suddenly looking a little uncertain.

Ashton, who had been gawking at her, smiled and slowly shook her head. "You're just so beautiful," she said, again taken aback by this woman.

Her hair was once again down, brushed to a shine in auburn waves around her shoulders, no bangs, as they'd grown out to the length of the rest of her hair. Ashton so badly wanted to run her fingers through it. She wore no makeup, absolutely no need for it. Her skin was like porcelain, and flawless. Her eyes were even more gorgeous without the benefit of a mask to isolate them.

Smiling shyly, Tristan looked away. "Stop," she muttered, getting the car moving.

Ashton let it go, excited to see what the day would bring. "So, where are we off to?"

"Well," Tristan said, sparing a glance over at her before returning her gaze to the road. "I figured we could get some breakfast. Are you hungry?"

"I am. Sounds great." Ashton looked forward to sitting across the table from her, talking, so utterly intrigued by this woman. "Where do you want to go?"

"There's actually a place I want to take you to," Tristan said, glancing shyly at her. "Is that okay?"

"Very okay. Today, I'm yours. Do your worst," Ashton quipped. The devilish grin she got in return made her squirm in her seat.

Eventually, Tristan maneuvered the Rav4 into the parking lot of a little hole-in-the-wall bakery that Ashton had never noticed before. There were a few cars in the parking lot. The banner sign claimed: *BEST BREAKFAST BURRITOS IN COLORADO!*

Tristan pulled the SUV to a stop in a parking space and cut the ignition, glancing over at her passenger. "This okay?"

"Absolutely. I love breakfast burritos," Ashton exclaimed.

"You're in for a treat, then," Tristan said with a winning smile. "Come on."

She placed her hand on Ashton's knee for just a moment before climbing out of the car. Feeling like a teenager, Ashton gasped, the quick, innocent touch feeling like a zap of electricity.

"Jesus," she muttered, gathering her coat—and herself—before opening the car door.

The little place was rather cute and smelled heavenly. A smattering of tables peppered the small dining area only broken by a cutout in the wall where a woman was standing in front of a register. On the wall behind her was a menu board. There was a single door marked with the unisex bathroom sign and a swinging door to the kitchen.

"Tristan!" the woman said through the open window, a Latina woman with long black hair pulled back into a ponytail. "What are you doing back here? Thought you were long gone."

Tristan leaned against the small bit of overhang from the serving counter atop the cutout. "I was gone. Left at my normal six. Came back to introduce my friend Ashton here to the best breakfast burritos and donuts she'll ever eat in her life."

"Ohhh," the woman said, glancing over at Ashton, who was amused. "She tryin' to sweeten you up. She's never brought nobody here."

Ashton glanced over at Tristan, an eyebrow raised, but said nothing.

"So?" the woman said expectantly, pen at the ready over her order pad.

Minutes later, the two women were seated at a

table near the window with a coffee for Ashton and hot chocolate for Tristan, a mountain of homemade whipped cream atop it.

"You work here?" Aston asked once they were settled. "Also?"

Tristan nodded. "Two to six, five days a week."

"Two to six in the morning?" Ashton gasped.

Tristan grinned, mouthing the top of the whipped cream mountain off as she nodded. "Yup." She licked a bit of the whipped cream off her lip, Ashton's gaze very focused on that quick flash of tongue. "I get off at the club and head here. I change in that bathroom right there." She smirked. "Not exactly easy to make dough and tortillas in an evening gown."

A bark of laughter escaped from Ashton's lips at the image of that one. "Sorry," she murmured when a woman at a nearby table glanced over at her. "No, no I suppose not." She looked back to Tristan. "Why the second job?"

"Because I need the second money," Tristan replied easily. "This place takes care of my car payment and phone bill."

Ashton nodded, sipping her coffee. "I can respect that." She considered the other woman sitting across from her, trying to figure out her age. Seeing her in the light of day, she suspected she was in her early thirties somewhere. "How long have you worked at the club?"

"Just over three and a half years," Tristan said, smiling up at the woman from the window who brought over two plates of food, one in each hand. "Thanks, Maria."

"You two enjoy," she said, then left them alone

Ashton stared down at the giant burrito that

nearly filled her plate. "This thing is the size of a newborn."

Tristan chuckled. "This will make about three meals for me."

"No, kidding. Jeesh."

"My advice is cut that puppy into two or three pieces, what you think you'll eat. It's a little less intimidating." She laughed.

Ashton nodded, eyeballing the burrito. "Good plan." Doing as instructed, she asked, "Do you like it?" She glanced up at her breakfast companion. "Working at the club."

Tristan had just taken a bite, so she chewed the food as she seemed to consider the question. "I've met some very interesting people," she began, giving Ashton a pointed look. "Some good people, some not-so-good people. I don't know," she said, cutting another bite off the third she clearly intended to eat. "I think 'like' is too strong, though I don't necessarily dislike it. It's a means to an end, I suppose."

Ashton nodded. "I very much understand that." She looked down at her plate as she chewed her first bite. "Very good," she muttered around the food. Feeling eyes on her, she looked up to see Tristan studying her. "What?"

"What is it that you exactly do?" the beautiful redhead asked. "Besides pimp chocolate at gentlemen's clubs."

Ashton grinned. "You think that's what I do, huh?" She loved the grin that earned her in return. "I'm in charge of King-Kraft Creations, based out of London, which is a division of King-Kraft Chocolate. I was in town last fall for our annual meeting here to discuss upcoming promotions when my father,

President and CEO of King-Kraft, nominated me to work on the deal with Buck."

"I see," Tristan said. "The big boss sends his gorgeous, lesbian..." She raised a questioning eyebrow. "Daughter to the club where the women work to make a deal."

"Yes, and yes."

"You don't like what you do, pimping chocolate aside?" Tristan said, cutting another bite after she'd finished the last one.

"There are aspects of it that I like and aspects that I don't. I hated working for my father."

"How are you doing with that now?" Tristan asked, her voice soft and filled with compassion.

Ashton let out a quiet sigh as she sipped her coffee. "My relationship with him was very complicated," she said after swallowing the warm brew and returning the cup to the table.

"Do you miss him?" Tristan asked gently.

"I really hope you don't think I'm a bitch for saying this," Ashton said, meeting an understanding gaze. "But I miss the idea of him."

"I don't think you're a bitch at all," Tristan said, shaking her head with a smile. "Not at all."

"Hold that, please?" Tristan asked, holding out a second bouquet of flowers.

Confused but acquiescing, Ashton took the flowers, a tissue-paper-wrapped bouquet, in both hands, watching as Tristan carefully picked out a third. "Um..."

Tristan smiled at her as she took the two from

Ashton. "Come on. I'll explain."

The flowers paid for, the two walked out of the small flower shop and to the green SUV where Tristan lovingly tucked the bouquets upon the back seat behind the driver's side before climbing behind the wheel, Ashton getting settled on her own side. She looked to her companion for an explanation.

After a long moment, Tristan glanced over at her, the keys still held in her hand, which rested on her denim-covered thigh. It was as though she'd made a decision. "Can I take you somewhere?"

"Of course," Ashton said, tilting her head a bit as she met the other woman's gaze. "Anywhere." On instinct, she reached over and covered the hand that still clutched the keys and squeezed lightly with a small smile.

"Okay." Tristan returned the smile and, once Ashton took her hand away, she inserted the key into the ignition and started the engine.

The grounds were expansive, a snow-covered landscape of hundreds upon hundreds, if not thousands, of stone and brick monuments to the dead. Ashton carried one of the bouquets she was asked to, Tristan holding the other two as they made their way through the rows, Tristan clearly knowing the way by heart.

Ashton had been to Littleton Cemetery a couple times before over the years for funerals of friends or colleagues. It had a few famous inhabitants, including alleged murderer and so-called Cannibal of Colorado, Alferd "Alfred" Packer, and some of those lost in the horrific 1999 Columbine High School shooting. She wasn't sure who they were there to see or what tale Tristan intended to tell, but Ashton was intrigued.

Finally, they stopped at three graves: Ronald P. O'Toole and Regina R. O'Toole shared the same large stone, as well as date of death: May 23, 2015. The third grave was for Sophie Louise Delgado, twenty years younger than the O'Tooles and her date of death was two days later.

"Hey, Mom and Dad," Tristan said quietly, placing the bouquets she held into the brass holders on either side of the wide stone. She turned to Ashton, giving her a small smile as she took the bouquet she'd carried for her. "Thank you." She placed it in the brass holder at the Delgado grave. "Hey, Sophie. Sorry I'm late this month. Been crazy.

Ashton's mind was whirling as she realized what she was looking at, and what Tristan had lost, and all in an extremely short amount of time. She had to take a deep, steadying inhale as it nearly took her breath away to contemplate.

The chilly morning's calm was broken by Tristan's soft voice. "I don't do what I do because I want to, or because I love it, or because the money I make is worth it. I do what I do because I have to."

Ashton said nothing, simply gave Tristan her full attention, nodding from time to time so Tristan knew she was taking in every word, which she was, even as Tristan stared down at the graves before them.

"Six years ago I was in my eighth year teaching high school history and government. My partner Sophie and I owned our own home here in Littleton where we both taught. She taught fourth grade."

Ashton felt nauseous as she began to understand

the enormity of Tristan's loss. Her eyes fell closed for a moment as she swallowed down her rising emotion.

"So, it was nearing the end of the school year, and as we always did," Tristan explained. "My parents, my little sister Christine, Sophie, and I were going to go on our annual Memorial Day weekend camping trip." She shoved her gloved hands into the pockets of her jacket, words coming out in white puffs of steam.

Ashton wanted to reach out and put her arms around her, but she felt it wasn't the time as Tristan was lost in yesterday.

"I had managed to get a really severe stomach bug," Tristan continued. "Barely made it through the last couple days of class. Sophie fought with me, wanted to stay home and take care of me, but honestly, I prefer to be alone when I'm sick. I'm so miserable and I just don't like taking it out on those around me."

Ashton smiled in understanding. "I'm the same way."

Tristan met her eyes and gave her a small smile before continuing. "So, Chrissy rode with Sophie, planning to share the little camper we had. You know, the kind that goes in the back of a truck?"

Ashton nodded.

"At sixteen, I think my sister was excited to get away from my parents and sleep in the big kid tent, as it were." she smiled, then blew out a long breath before continuing. "So, they headed out, Dad driving he and Mom, pulling their fifth wheel in front of Sophie and Christine in the truck and camper."

Ashton braced herself for what was to come.

"Something…something went terribly wrong," Tristan said, her voice still quiet but now flat, as though she were merely reciting facts from a report.

"Authorities theorized the welding on the truck bed hitch for the fifth wheel was insufficient and gave way. It caused catastrophic insecurity in the F-250 my father was driving, and it sent he and my mother over the edge and into a ravine."

Ashton's hands came up to cover her mouth. *Oh god.*

"The fifth wheel trailer, all thirty-two feet of it, was flung back into the truck Sophie and Christine were in." She grew silent for a long moment. "Sophie was declared brain dead on Memorial Day."

Ashton reached up to wipe away the tear that had managed to escape her left eye, followed closely by one out of the right. She sniffled again, wiping at her eyes. Finally, she managed to ask, "What happened to Christine?"

Tristan looked over at her, eyes filled with a profound sadness. "You want to meet my little sister?"

Ashton met her gaze, her own watery. She nodded. "Yeah."

"Okay." Tristan turned back to her family. "I love you guys," she said softly. Turning to Ashton, she said, "Let's go."

# Chapter Thirteen

The walls were painted a warm beige with a cream chair rail along the way. The floors were a combination of highly polished linoleum and berber carpeting in deep brown. The long hallways were dotted with doors to rooms filled with patients in varying states of wellness. Some doors they passed were open, the inhabitant inside the room sitting in a wheelchair knitting, other times lying in bed watching TV.

They turned left down another hallway, which looked like the others in the maze of a facility, this time the nurses at the nurse's station at the center of that wing smiling greetings to Tristan, a few calling her by name. Finally, they reached room 213, the door closed. Tristan glanced over at Ashton and gave her a soft smile before turning the handle and pushing the door open.

The room was dim with the curtains drawn. There were few machines, only those to keep track of the basic vitals, with no real sound inside the room. In the hospital-type bed was a single figure lying on her back. She looked to be asleep. Her long, blond hair had been brushed and looked clean. Her face was pale with the smoothness of youth. She wore a simple blue T-shirt, the sheet and blanket folded down just under her breasts, her arms resting down at her sides, hands in a relaxed position.

Ashton followed Tristan inside the room, the door slowly easing closed behind them. She noted a chair in the corner of the room near the window, a giant teddy bear sitting in it looking very friendly and huggable.

"Hey, Chrissy," Tristan greeted, walking over to the bed. She leaned over it and placed a kiss on the young woman's forehead. To Ashton's surprise, Christine didn't respond, didn't open her eyes, didn't react in any visible way. "How about some sunshine?" Tristan asked softly, reaching down to take the younger woman's malleable hand in her own. She turned to Ashton. "Would you mind opening the curtains?"

"Certainly." Ashton turned away from the bed and walked over to the window, reaching over the large head of the teddy bear to the cord pull, tugging the heavy blackout curtains open, spilling light across the room as they shrilly slid across the curtain rod.

"Thank you." Tristan turned back to her sister. "I'd like to introduce you to someone, Chrissy," she said, thumb running across the back of her sister's hand. "This is my good friend, Ashton. Ashton, this is my little sister, Christine, or to those of us who love her, we torment her with Chrissy."

Ashton smiled as she walked over to the side of the bed closest to the window, which put her on the opposite side as Tristan. The two met eyes for a moment before Ashton's gaze fell to the woman in the bed. "Hi, Christine," she said. "Not sure if I qualify to call you Chrissy just yet." She smiled over at Tristan. "But it is an absolute pleasure to meet you." She didn't touch the young woman as she felt like she would be rude on some level. "How long has she been like this?" she asked, not entirely sure what she was seeing.

"Since the crash," Tristan whispered. "Doctors tried to get me to..." She glanced over at Ashton, the look in her eyes pleading for understanding.

Getting it, Ashton nodded. "Why don't you?"

"I don't know." Tristan shook her head as she looked back down at her sister. "Every time I made up my mind to do it, thinking I'd be letting her go finally, something just..." She shrugged, again looking to Ashton. "Stopped me." She let out a tired sigh. "I had to move her here out of the hospital once she was able to breathe on her own."

Ashton shook her head, feeling so much sadness for three lives lost and one on pause. Well, she amended the thought, glancing over at Tristan. Two lives on pause. "Can she hear you?"

Tristan shrugged her shoulders. "Doctors have told me over the years that they think they can. So, I talk to her when I come. I try at least three times a week, just depends on how hard I crash after work, what kind of time I have before work at the club. Sometimes I'll just come in and doze in the chair and play music that she loved before the accident."

Ashton nodded in understanding. She cleared her throat, again trying to push emotion down that threatened to rise. "Thank you for bringing me here, Tristan. For helping me to understand."

There was a knock on the room door as it was being pushed open. A woman with a head full of tightly wound braids pulled back into a ponytail entered the room. "Knock knock," she called out.

Tristan looked over her shoulder. "Hey, Tanisha."

"Well, hey, big sis!" The woman entered, her plump body dressed in scrubs with circus clowns printed all over them. She looked past Tristan to

Ashton. "Who's your lovely friend?"

"Tanisha, this is Ashton. Ashton, Chrissy's main nurse, Tanisha."

"So nice to meet you," Ashton said, extending her hand toward the woman who looked to be somewhere in her forties.

"Likewise, likewise," Tanisha said. She looked at Christine from where she stood at the foot of the bed. "Okay, blondie. You ready for daily exercise?" Ashton could tell from the woman's tone that for her, *blondie* was a term of endearment, specific to the woman's personality. "Red is here to help out this time."

Ashton moved over to the chair and set the bear on the floor next to it as she sat down so she could get out of the way.

"Ashton," Tristan said softly. "Do you mind?"

"No, of course not."

As the two women began to work on Christine, slowly bending her arms, legs, turning her over, it was a strange thing to watch. It was like Christine was a life-size, lifelike doll they were playing dress-up with. It was heartbreaking to know that it was no doll, but a twenty-one-year-old woman who had lost what was left of her teenage years, missed getting a driver's license, prom, high school graduation, college, getting a job. The list went on and on, let alone what her parents and Sophie missed out on.

As she watched Tristan chat with the nurse as they worked together, clearly something she'd helped with many, many times before, she thought about what she'd learned that day. Had the accident not happened, Tristan and Sophie would likely still be together, still be teaching, and still have their home together. Had a horrific twist of fate not taken the lives of Tristan's family, this day, and whatever came of it, would never have happened.

She wasn't entirely sure how she felt about the fact that three people had to die and one young woman's life had to be completely derailed in order for that to happen.

Tristan gave Ashton a side glance once they got back into the car from picking up the pizza they'd ordered for pickup. "Um," she said. "You know, we can always take this back to your place."

Ashton grinned and shook her head. "Nope, you promised me a full day in your world. Besides," she added coyly. "You've already been to my house."

The shy smile that curled Tristan's lips was absolutely adorable and damn near made Ashton burst into laughter. "Okay, fine. But," Tristan added, holding up a finger for emphasis. "It's not Pittman House."

Ashton gave her a smile as she leaned her head back against the headrest. It had been a long day and she was feeling it catch up to her. "I'm glad. Pittman House is my father's world. I want to see yours."

Tristan held her gaze for a long moment before nodding and letting out a breath. "Okay. Let's go to my world, then."

The apartment where Tristan lived was in a small complex that had fewer than twenty-five units. It was one where the apartment was accessed from the outside as opposed to one central door to enter the building itself. A block of mailboxes was bolted into cement near the arched entryway into the outdoor courtyard where the tenants could hang out on a few wrought iron chairs around a table, and a few barbecue grills were available as well.

It was a cute building, landscaped nicely, but not a lot of amenities. Tristan parked her Rav4 and together they gathered the pizza and the grocery bag with the few things they'd picked up at the store.

Ashton followed Tristan to the third floor, which was the top, climbing two flights of metal stairs, and waited patiently as the redhead unlocked the doorknob and dead bolt before pushing the door open.

The two-bedroom apartment was small, but like her car, clean and neat. The living room was small with a full-sized couch as the centerpiece to sit on among a mass of bookcases that sat against every inch of free wall space there was, including into the little nook set aside for a kitchen table off the galley-style kitchen. All of them were filled to bursting with books of every size, topic, and stripe.

The first bedroom was used as just that, and contained a queen-sized bed, dresser, and bedside tables. The second bedroom had more bookcases in it but also seemed to be her dressing room with three racks of the dresses she wore for the club. Ashton recognized several of them.

"That's one thing I don't like about working at The Black Pussy Cat," Tristan said as they stood in the opened doorway together during the short tour of the apartment. "Having to spend money on the dresses." She met Ashton's gaze. "I really don't like having to have so many of them. Dresses are fine, beautiful even, but…" She'd rolled her eyes.

After the tour ended, they ended up in the

kitchen, which Tristan called a "one-butt kitchen," and Ashton stood off to the side, watching as Tristan got them plates and two wineglasses from the cabinet over the fridge. She looked at Ashton. "Do you prefer a sweet red or the white zinfandel we bought tonight?"

Ashton leaned her shoulder against the doorframe. "Sweet red might be good with pizza, but..." she added with raised eyebrows. "I thought you don't drink."

A Mona Lisa smile appeared on Tristan's lips as she applied the corkscrew to the bottle she'd grabbed out of the fridge. "I don't drink when I'm working," she said sweetly, popping the cork and pouring a glass. She set down the bottle and held the glass out to Ashton. "I'm not working tonight."

Ashton took the glass and met her gaze before nodding. "True enough."

Wine poured and pizza on plates, they headed into the living room where Tristan flipped on the gas fireplace and they made themselves comfortable on the couch. Shoes off and feet up, they mirrored positions, sitting with their back to the couch arm facing each other, plates set on the middle cushion.

"Okay, so if you weren't in the chocolate business, what would you be doing?" Tristan asked, popping a piece of Italian sausage into her mouth.

"An architectural engineer," Ashton said easily, bringing her glass up to her lips.

Tristan looked at her with a look of surprise on her face. "Really?"

"Absolutely." She lowered her glass as she swallowed the sweet, slightly tangy wine as she sat back into the corner of the couch, angling herself a bit so her back was supported better. "I love old houses and

I'd love to be able to rebuild them as their structure begins to fail. Bring them back to life."

"Do you think that comes from growing up in the house you did?" Tristan asked, moving her empty pizza plate aside to the coffee table as she, too, relaxed back against the couch.

"Probably. It's a really beautiful place. Way too much house for just me, though. I don't know what my father decided to do with it, if it'll even go to me." She shrugged, bringing up her glass again. "I just don't know."

"Do you want it?"

Ashton considered the question as she sipped her drink, enjoying the warmth that was spreading through her body on such a cold night with an amazing woman. "I don't know," she said at length. "It's been in the family forever. Be kinda lonely." She smiled.

"Well, you could fill it with a bunch of kids," Tristan suggested.

"I'm already forty-one. That ship has largely sailed," Ashton said with a chuckle.

"Well, then you'd better find you some young chickadee and get reproducing already," Tristan said, raising her glass in salute.

Ashton grinned. "Got anyone in mind?"

Tristan glared playfully at her. "How are you doing? After your father's death, I mean." Her voice was gentle and understanding.

Ashton shrugged a shoulder. "I'm doing okay. His lawyer will read the will this coming week, and I'll be glad when he does. Right now, I really don't know where I stand in any of this."

Tristan studied her. "Will you be okay?"

"I will," Ashton assured with a nod. "I just want

it all to be over. Find out what he did so I know where I'm going next."

Tristan smiled at her, leaning forward and lightly tugging on Ashton's foot. "I believe in you."

"What about you?" Ashton asked. "If you could, would you go back to teaching?"

The smile that graced Tristan's lips was heartbreakingly soft. "Yes," she said. "In a heartbeat. I loved teaching." She let out a heavy sigh, resting her head to the side against the back of the couch. She had a wistful look in her eyes. "I kept at it for two years after the accident, but Chrissy's care was insanely expensive. I sold my parents' house, their cars, Sophie's car, and finally my house," she said with a heavy sigh.

"I'm so sorry, Tristan."

The redhead smiled at Ashton's genuine sympathy. "Finally, I had to make the most difficult choice of any of it. Had to leave teaching. There was just no way I could take care of my sister on a teacher's salary. I had nothing left to sell." She indicated the bookshelves full of books all around them. "These are mostly what I took with me. Sold the furniture. I have some things in storage, but for the most part..." She shrugged. "I did what I had to do."

"And that's when you started working at the club?"

"It is. I knew Lisa, otherwise known as Garnet, and she began working there. She told me about it, the kind of money she was making. So, I took the plunge. Now," she added quickly, "I could make more, in a place that like you can pretty much decide what you want to bring in. A lot of the girls do, and some of the guys, too. We get members in with all sorts of interests."

"Oh, no doubt. But," Ashton hedged. "You don't." She stopped, not entirely sure how to proceed with what she wanted to know, despite the little bit Tristan had mentioned before.

"I don't," Tristan said, shaking her head. "I made a deal with myself that, if I was going to go into this business, essentially an escort for a couple hours, I would have my boundaries. Luckily, Buck stands behind us. His thing is, as long as we can entertain the members while observing house rules, and keep them coming back, how much money we want to make is up to us. Since I refuse to get physical," she added, eyeing Ashton. "Under normal conditions, I've had to learn how to be a really good talker, really good listener, and learn how to flatter the shit out of those men. Honestly, that's mostly what they want."

"To be flattered?" Ashton asked, surprised.

Tristan chuckled. "To feel important. Many of them have been in marriages for decades and the spark has long since gone. Having someone like me on their arm for a couple hours saves them money and scandal." Tristan's words were punctuated by a large yawn. "Oh my gosh, I'm sorry."

"It's okay." Ashton got to her feet and began to gather up her plate and wineglass. "I'll call for an Uber and let you get to bed."

Tristan followed her into the kitchen with her own dishes and began to rinse them off before loading them into the dishwasher. "Do you want to just stay?" she asked. "It's late. I hate to think of you out there."

Ashton met her gaze. "You sure?"

"Yeah. I can give you something to sleep in." She reached out and tugged on Ashton's sweater.

"As beautiful as it is, I doubt it would be all that comfortable to sleep in."

Ashton smiled. "Guessing not. If you're sure," she said, looking into Tristan's eyes, making sure there was no discomfort there. "Okay. I'll stay."

Tristan smiled. "Excellent. It's settled, then. I'll get you a T-shirt and sweats."

As Tristan headed toward her bedroom, Ashton headed to the living room and gathered her socks and shoes, carrying them in the direction of the bedroom. She nearly ran into Tristan in the hall, who held a folded comforter and sheet with pillow atop it, and folded clothing. She held it out to Ashton, who looked down at it, then up into her eyes.

"I'm not working tonight," Tristan said softly.

Saying nothing, Ashton took the bundle and gave her a small smile and a nod.

"Good night, Ashton."

"Good night, Tristan."

# *Chapter Fourteen*

Ashton looked up at the ceiling. She'd been lying on the couch for the better part of an hour, not sleeping. The apartment was quiet, a couple dogs barking outside in the distance now and then. She was desperately trying not to think about the woman sleeping in the other room, within those seven hundred square feet of space.

Instead, she pondered what she'd seen and learned that day. She thought about Christine and the facility she was in. She knew that sort of care had to be close to a hundred grand a year. What a horrible burden. Her thoughts ceased when she heard movement in the bedroom, something shuffling, then footfalls through the darkness, headed her way.

"Hey," she said to the silhouette in the darkness.

"Hi," Tristan whispered, stepping up to the couch and looking down at Ashton. "Did I wake you?"

"No," Ashton responded. "Just lying here. Thinking."

"I can't sleep, either," Tristan said, lowering herself to sit on the edge of the couch. "Are you comfortable?"

"This is one of the more comfortable couches I've been on, yes," Ashton said with a smile. "Are you okay?"

"Yes," she finally said. "No." She snorted ruefully. "I haven't had someone stay in my home like this in six years."

"I can go home, Tristan," Ashton said gently. "It's really okay if my being here is upsetting you—"

"No." Tristan shook her head. "That's part of the problem." She looked down at her hands resting in her lap before finally looking to Ashton again, her face barely visible through the dim lighting. "Ashton, would you be willing to…I mean, I know it's childish, but will you…"

"Do you want me to sleep in there with you?" Ashton asked softly. She didn't take that as anything more than it seemed to be: an invitation for comfort.

"Please?" Tristan took hold of the comforter and sheet that covered Ashton and pulled it back. She got to her feet, stepping back as Ashton brought her legs up and out from beneath the covers and turned so she was sitting on the couch. "Take the pillow."

Doing as directed, Ashton got to her feet and her hand was grabbed as she was led through the darkness to Tristan's bedroom. She was urged to the right as they approached the foot of the bed, while Tristan took the opposite side.

It felt wonderful to be in Tristan's bedroom and her bed as Ashton got settled on her back. The mattress was soft and comfortable, the bedding warm. She felt the mattress shift as Tristan turned to her side, looking at her. Ashton glanced over and met her gaze. She wanted to open her arms to her, but she wasn't sure what would spook her.

Tristan studied her for a long time, her face able to be seen by the moonlight coming in through the window over the bed. She brought up a hand and reached over, lightly caressing Ashton's face. "You're so lovely," she whispered.

Ashton smiled, turning her head to leave a small

kiss on the palm of her hand as it rested on her cheek. She turned back to look into Tristan's eyes, wondering what was in her head.

"I was doing just fine," Tristan whispered, almost as if to herself. "I was making it happen." She shook her head a bit against the pillow. "Then you come along. You made me remember what it's like to touch someone, to be touched," she continued. She scooted slightly closer, her cotton-clad breasts brushing against Ashton's arm. "You made me remember what it's like to be wanted, to want. To need."

She scooted a bit closer yet, her hand sliding down from Ashton's cheek to her neck. Ashton reached up and covered that hand. "I thought you weren't working tonight," she said softly, seeing the desire grow in Tristan's eyes.

Tristan moved until she was lying atop Ashton, holding her upper body up on her forearm as she looked down into her face. "I'm not."

Ashton's eyes fell closed at the first soft touch of Tristan's lips against her own. They were so soft. Tristan sighed into the kiss, settling her body more fully atop Ashton's as their lips brushed against each other, the very tip of a tongue asking for entry, which was immediately granted.

Kissing Tristan was unlike anything Ashton had ever experienced. Yes, Tristan was a very talented lover, passionate and giving, but there was more to it than that. The emotion and feeling she brought out in Ashton was confusing, comforting, and terrifying, all at once. As their kiss continued and deepened, her hands moved down to Tristan's shapely behind, covered by the fleece pajama pants she wore, and slid upward. She felt the warm skin of Tristan's lower back as her T-shirt was pushed up just a bit.

Ashton moaned into the kiss as her hands pushed up underneath that T-shirt and smoothed over the strong back, the skin so soft. Finally, Tristan pulled out of the kiss, leaving them both breathing heavily.

"I've been wanting to do that since the moment I saw you," Tristan murmured, readjusting her body and sitting up, straddling Ashton's hips.

"Just for the record," Ashton said, placing her hands on Tristan's thighs. "I wouldn't have objected."

"Oh, I'm sure," Tristan said with a grin, her hands running up along Ashton's sides to her shoulders, across her collarbones and down between her breasts, still hidden beneath the borrowed T-shirt she wore. Tristan took hold of the hem of her own T-shirt and pulled it upward, whipping the garment up and over her head. She shook her long hair to free it from the material before sending it off into the darkness of the floor. "Come'ere."

Ashton was urged to sit up by a tug on the front of her shirt, so she complied. Immediately her own T-shirt was pulled up and over her head. Once the shirt was gone, Tristan buried her hands in Ashton's hair and pulled her in for another devastating kiss.

Pushed back to the bed, Ashton hugged Tristan to her as their kiss continued. She thrust her hands in the thick mane of auburn hair that she'd longed to see free, longed to touch. It was soft and smelled amazing. It also felt amazing against her naked flesh. As their kiss deepened, Tristan's hair fell around them like a curtain, shutting out the rest of the world.

Finally, Tristan left Ashton's mouth, moving to explore her jaw and neck. She lifted her head long enough to whip her hair to one side, meeting Ashton's gaze in that moment before going back to her task.

Ashton's head fell to the side, giving those questing lips and tongue all the access they wanted. She hissed as that mouth made its way to her left breast. The feel of Tristan's hair trailing down across her chest as her nipple was licked and sucked heightened her arousal. She arched her back encouraging Tristan's touch. She was so wet, she could feel her panties sticking to her.

Tristan brought her hands up and pushed both of Ashton's breasts together, bringing her mouth to suck in both nipples at the same time, earning a long, languid groan from Ashton as a new round of arousal bloomed between her legs. It was a total assault on her breasts as Tristan's passion consumed her. It left Ashton's head spinning.

Finally, Tristan left her breasts and continued down, running a hot trail with her tongue down the center line of Ashton's torso, ending at her belly button. She glanced up Ashton's body and met her gaze, Pearl on full display in those eyes. The sexual intensity in that look made Ashton gasp then lift her hips as she was urged to, Tristan removing her pajama pants and panties. She quickly removed her own before making her intentions very clear.

Ashton watched as her thighs were spread and Tristan settled between them. She brushed the length of her hair down the sensitive skin of the insides of Ashton's thighs, drawing a long, sensuous sigh from her lips as her head fell back to the bed. The sigh turned to a groan when she felt something small and hard rub against her clit. Opening her eyes, she looked back down the length of her body and saw that Tristan had one of her own breasts held in her hand, using the hard nipple to tease Ashton's clit, which felt amazing.

"Fuck," Ashton whispered, her head falling back to the pillow yet again. Her hand reached down and tangled in Tristan's hair as her mouth replaced the nipple. Her tongue was focused and hot against her need.

Tristan hummed into her task, her tongue dancing and teasing across and around a hard clit before licking down, slicing through the plethora of wetness until she reached Ashton's opening, making her groan as she pushed inside, fluttering against her inner walls near the opening.

Lost in a world of pleasure, Ashton's hips rocked with the rhythm Tristan's tongue set, thrusting inside her before trailing back up to her clit again, which was rock hard and throbbing. Her whimpers and sighs were turning into all-out cries, becoming longer and louder as the assault became narrowed down to just her clit, Tristan's very capable tongue batting ruthlessly at it

It didn't take long before Ashton's body stiffened and an earth-shattering shudder rocked her world, literally making her lose track of time and place from the intensity of the orgasm. It took several moments for her body to relax, feeling as though it fell back down to the mattress from somewhere up in the clouds. Her legs fell open fully, her limbs feeling like Jell-O.

Tristan made her way back up Ashton's body, finding her mouth. Their kiss was slow and lazy, Tristan's tongue warm and slick with Ashton's passion. Tasting herself on Tristan's tongue made Ashton sigh in pleasure and very much wanting to return the favor.

"Climb up, baby," she murmured, indicating she wanted Tristan to kneel over her face, which she did.

Holding onto the headboard, Tristan looked down at Ashton, who met her gaze as she lifted her head just enough to be able to feast. As wet and hard as Tristan was she knew it wasn't going to take long. She wrapped her arms around the spread thighs on either side of her head.

Tristan's breathy whimpers floated down to her, egging Ashton on to suck harder before pressing Tristan's clit firmly with the flat of her tongue as she moved her head quickly from side to side, rolling her clit with each aggressive shake.

With a loud cry, Tristan's hips jerked as she came, Ashton milking every ounce of pleasure for the woman above her as she sucked her clit into her mouth, swirling her tongue until another cry was heard from above, Tristan's thighs trembling as she seemed to lose her strength for a moment.

Ashton moved out from beneath her and helped her to lie down, spooning her from behind. It took awhile, but eventually Tristan was able to relax back into Ashton, who held her tightly. She kissed the side of her neck.

"You're amazing," she whispered into her ear.

Tristan sighed with contentment as she wiggled her butt back as far into Ashton's crotch as she could, making Ashton smile. She luxuriated in the softness of Tristan's skin, her hand roaming randomly, just to feel, to touch, to bask in tactile connection.

"Can I ask you a question?" Tristan asked, her hand reaching back to rest on the side of Ashton's thigh, tucked up behind her own.

"Of course," Ashton murmured.

"What was your last relationship?" Tristan asked. "What happened?"

Ashton let out a sigh as she considered where to begin on that one. "Well, my last relationship of any length was Katherine. She works for me at the London location. She's brilliant as an expert in chocolate and her work as a pastry chef, but she's a very broken woman when it comes to any sort of interpersonal relationships."

"Lisa told me about her," Tristan said. "Was she the one who was at the Christmas get-together that Buck held at the club? I wasn't there, but Lisa said a woman was there with you."

"Yup. That was her. In all the years I've known Katherine, the years that we've been involved, we've literally not gone more than two days without fighting." She left a small kiss on a very tasty shoulder that just happened to be in front of her mouth. "Now, I'm not blaming her for that, just saying that we were always so terribly mismatched."

"Why do you think that was?" Tristan moved away from Ashton just enough to turn over so she was facing her, scooting in close as she could, their bodies becoming a tangle of legs and arms.

A little groan of approval escaped Ashton's throat. If she could, she'd invite Tristan to dive inside and literally become one with her. She'd never felt so close to a human being before. "We're just too different of people," she responded, loving the way Tristan's breasts felt pressed against her own. "I'm more quiet, prefer things to be calm and under control. Don't like loud noises, big bursts of a crowd to stimulate me. Katherine, on the other hand, needs that stimulation of a crowd of people, which usually means drama."

"I hate drama," Tristan murmured, hands running down along Ashton's side, over her hip, and to her thigh, which was pulled up over Tristan's hip, the redhead's thigh tucked snugly between Ashton's legs. Her hand absently moved back along the path it had just taken, reversing the course, then starting all over again.

Every touch from Tristan caused Ashton's heart to speed up, and the feel of her body, so intricately and intimately woven with her own, kept her in a constant state of arousal, like a low hum that vibrated in her lower belly.

"I do, too." She felt her body becoming restless, hands beginning to move. Everything about Tristan electrified her. She leaned forward the scant few inches to initiate a slow kiss, which Tristan responded to. "You know what I *do* like though?"

"What's that?" Tristan murmured, rolling to her back as Ashton gently nudged. She spread her legs as Ashton moved in between them like a well-choreographed dance they both knew the steps to.

"Kissing you..." Ashton whispered, adjusting her hips as she pressed them between Tristan's legs. They began to move together. "Touching you..."

Tristan sighed into their kiss as her hands roamed over Ashton's back and down to cup her behind. "What else?"

Ashton grinned at the playful and sexy tone in that question. "I like how wet your pussy gets," she began. "How your pussy feels against mine." She ground herself against Tristan to illustrate her point.

"I like it when you do that," Tristan said, pulling a grin from both of them.

"How about this?" Ashton raised herself to her

hands and used the power of her body to increase her movements. With short, quick thrusts she slapped their clits together, adding a new dimension to the sensation.

Tristan's eyes fell closed as she spread her thighs wider and raised her knees, which pushed her clit forward. Her groan was fire to Ashton's arousal. The sound of skin slapping against skin rent the air, sharp and loud. She could hear the headboard banging against the wall with each aggressive thrust.

Close to coming, Ashton slowed down, rolling her hips as she rubbed their mutual need together. Tristan reached up and buried her hands in long, dark hair, bringing Ashton's head down for a breathy kiss as their hips moved together, bringing them both closer to orgasm. It didn't take long before they were breathing too hard to kiss but remained in the bubble of combined personal space they'd created, breathing in the other's air as they clung to each other, Ashton's hips never stopping their movements.

Ashton's mouth opened and eyes closed as her release bloomed over her like a warm blanket, beginning at her clit and exploding outward. Tristan's claw-like grab on Ashton's shoulders foretold her own release, which erupted from her lips as she wrapped her legs around Ashton's hips, using their strength to hold them together, her hips moving as she grinded against Ashton.

"Oh," Ashton said, forehead resting against Tristan's as they held each other. "I like you."

Tristan burst into laughter, a hand coming up to caress the side of Ashton's face. "I like you, too."

# *Chapter Fifteen*

"Do you have any questions?" the attorney asked as Ashton gathered up the pages he'd just gone through and tucked them into the manila envelope from which they'd come.

Ashton sat there for a long moment, not quite sure what to say. She brought up a hand and ran it through her hair before finally letting out a long, shaky breath. "I honestly never thought he'd do this."

The attorney eyed her for a moment before continuing to pack up. "I was your father's personal attorney for thirty-three years," he said. "Do you know what he said to me when I asked him why he'd chosen you to get things going in England and not somebody else, or why he hadn't paired you up with one of the men in upper management?"

She shook her head, afraid to hear the answer.

"He said, 'Because I want it done right.'"

She stared at him. "He said that?"

The bald man nodded, glancing at her as he stood by the desk, briefcase open as he loaded it with the paperwork of the day. "I don't understand why Jack acted as he did toward you, Ashton, but I know he was proud of you." He slapped the case closed, studying her. "I spoke with George earlier today," he continued, grabbing his jacket from the coat tree in the corner of Jack's office and sliding his arms into the sleeves. "He has the paperwork all written up for your massive promotion." He grinned, shrugging his jacket into proper fit before grabbing his briefcase by the handle and walking over to her. "Congratulations, Ashton," he said, leaning over and leaving a kiss on her cheek. "Much deserved inheritance."

"Thank you, Larry." Still in shock, she stared at him. "So, are you my lawyer now?"

He burst into laughter, shaking his head. "Nope. I made the deal with my wife that after Jack either passed or fired me, I was retiring. I can, however, recommend an incredible attorney. She can start fresh with you as head of the family." He reached into the inside pocket of his suit jacket and produced a business card. "My daughter. She's just as good, yet has the touch of you younger people."

Ashton took the card and nodded. "Thanks, Larry. I appreciate it. I'll give her a call first thing tomorrow."

"Listen, Ashton," the older attorney said, a hand on her arm and his voice serious. "Your father has bestowed quite a well-deserved honor upon you. My advice to you? Surround yourself with smart people. People you can trust and keep in the fold for years. Loyalty and trust will be the greatest gift you can get from the folks in your orbit."

She nodded, realizing the full weight of the burden that had been placed upon her shoulders. "Okay. Thank you."

She walked Larry to the door, accepted an awkward hug from him, then closed the door after he'd stepped out onto the portico. Eyes closed, she leaned back against the doors and let out a slow breath. Though she knew she had a whole new type of weight on her shoulders, she felt a whole other type lifted off, leaving her feeling freer than she had...ever.

With a whoop and cry of a banshee, Ashton took off running through the massive house channeling her inner Kevin McCallister. She was a kid home alone, reveling in her new freedom. She ended up in the library, out of breath and feeling happy and excited.

Running a hand through her hair, she wandered around the massive room, two full floors of books, thousands of tomes collected over many, many decades. On the main floor, where she stood, were leather chairs placed here and there for reading. If perhaps a game of chess was on the docket, a board sat on a table by the massive fireplace, the pieces representing characters from Greek mythology, one side gold, the other silver, on an elm chessboard.

"Tristan would love this," she murmured, noting the bronze bust of Shakespeare that was on a marble column at the center of the massive room.

She'd have to deal with that later. For now, she realized it was time to be an adult again. She had work to do. She headed back to the office to grab her phone. Opening her contacts list, she dialed the number she'd added a few days before.

"Good afternoon. I'd like to be connected to your billing department, please."

Ashton watched with bated breath as Tristan seemed to contemplate what she was tasting. Even behind the white hairnet cap and clear goggles that matched those she herself wore, she could see those wheels turning. One thing she loved about Tristan was that very rarely did she just blurt out something she was thinking or feeling. It seemed with her, everything was carefully analyzed and filtered, well thought out before it passed her lips.

"The smoothness is incredible," Tristan finally said. She popped the last of the chocolate square into her mouth. "So. Good."

Ashton grinned and turned to the woman running the machine they were at. "Thanks so much," she said to her. "And your name is?"

"Debra, ma'am," the woman replied, dressed in the same protective wear as Ashton and Tristan.

"Ashton King. An absolute pleasure to meet you. Thanks for all you do for us, Debra."

The woman's smile could brighten an entire room. "Thank you, Miss King. Nice to officially meet you."

Ashton turned to Tristan. "Ready for more?"

"Let's do it." Tristan smiled warmly at Debra and thanked her as they moved on.

Ashton hadn't been in the production room in a long time, at least not in the Denver location. It was loud from all the machines working, spitting out the best chocolate in the world. Yes, it had been a while, but Ashton had seen it over her lifetime a million times. To see it through the wide eyes of Tristan was liking seeing it for the first time.

Tristan talked to everyone, peppering them with questions, asking if she could press the button or pull the lever. Her interest and curiosity in everything, the ability to truly listen and converse with the workers intelligently on something she'd just learned about, and her mind at large, astounded Ashton. She stood back and watched, impressed by the range of questions Tristan had, things she never would have considered—

and she'd been in the chocolate and dessert business her entire life.

"Good afternoon, ladies."

Ashton looked to see Brian walking up to them. She smiled and held out her hand in greeting, which he took. "Good afternoon, Brian. Nice to see you."

"Who's your friend?"

Ashton and Tristan had had this discussion before coming in. To her surprise, Tristan had given her full permission to use her given name. "This is Tristan O'Toole. Tristan, Brian Lewis. At the moment, he's our man in charge of this division."

"Nice to meet you, Mr. Lewis," Tristan greeted, extending her hand.

Brian studied her for a moment before giving her his usual polite yet boyish smile. "Nice to meet you again as well, Miss O'Toole." He looked to Ashton, heavy, blond eyebrows drawn. "'At the moment'?"

Ashton grinned and slapped him on the back. "I need to talk to you." She turned to Tristan. "Mind if Brian and I go talk for a second?"

"Please, do what you need to." Tristan waved her off. "I'm fascinated by all this."

It took everything inside her not to lean over and leave a kiss on inviting lips, but she resisted, instead reaching out and lightly squeezing Tristan's arm before leading Brian away to the offices.

"Feelin' a bit like I'm in the principal's office," Brian said, watching as Ashton closed the door after he'd entered.

She smiled at him, walking around to the business side of the desk. "Why, what did you do wrong?" she teased.

"Tristan, huh?" He crossed an ankle over the

opposite knee, jiggling his wingtip. "She's beautiful."

"She is."

"Must be something special if you brought her here…" he prodded.

"Maybe. So, I want to make some changes," she began, lacing her fingers and placing them on the desktop. He met her gaze, his a bit guarded. "I'll be leaving the King-Kraft Creations division to come back home."

A confused smile was frozen on Brian's lips. "Here?" he asked, indicating the room where they sat. "In Chocolate division?"

Ashton shook her head. "To take my father's place."

He looked surprised, sitting back in his chair a bit. "Well, damn." He pushed to his feet and stretched his hand across the desk. "Congratulations, Ashton!"

She took his hand, which she held for a moment before releasing it. "Thank you. There's a lot I want to do, a ton of improvements I think we can make that my father wasn't on board for. But what I want to propose to you, Brian, is you taking my place in London." She sat back in the chair, relaxing into the conversation. "Now, I know you have Pam and the kids to consider, so, I don't need an answer today."

Brian looked stunned as he stared at her, bringing up a hand to rub the back of his neck. "Well," he said. "That is not what I expected to hear when I came to work this morning."

"I understand that. Let me tell you where I'm coming from with this," Ashton explained. "I want someone over there who knows the company, knows the product, and knows our values as a company. It's a hell of a lot easier for me to hold somebody's hand by heading down the hall when there's a problem than to hop a plane across the Atlantic."

He nodded. "I can appreciate that." He was quiet for a moment before he said. "Okay. Let me talk to Pam about it. And the kids."

"I can live with that." Ashton pushed to her feet. "I'm headed over there this week to work out a few things, so how about I give you until the end of the week, by time I get back?"

He nodded again, also getting to his feet. "Okay. I can do that."

Just like at the factory, Ashton watched Tristan's awe as she looked at every detail, lightly brushing her fingers over fabric wallpaper that was from another era. She touched antique furniture, marveled at the coffered ceilings and crown molding.

She looked at Aston, eyes wide and sparkling. "This house is incredible," she said. "I've always wanted to tour it."

"Well, I have one more room to share," Ashton said, taking Tristan's hand and leading her out of the north dining room. "Saved the best for last."

Bringing the pale hand within her own to her lips, she left a kiss on her knuckles before releasing the hand. With a side glance to the woman standing in anticipation next to her, Ashton grabbed the handles to the double door and, with a flourish, pushed them open.

She wasn't disappointed by Tristan's reaction as she gasped, eyes wide as she took in the seemingly endless supply of books, shelf upon shelf upon shelf filled to the brim.

"Oh my god," she whispered, hands coming up to cover her mouth. She looked at Ashton as if she were silently asking, *Are you seeing this, too?* "Can I…?"

"Go ahead," Ashton said, waving her on. "Look around."

Like a bee pollinating flowers, Tristan buzzed to this bookshelf then to that bookshelf, stopping to admire a sculpture before buzzing on up to the second floor. Ashton stood down by Shakespeare watching, amused, enamored, and enchanted.

"This is absolutely my *Beauty and the Beast* moment," Tristan called down from the second-floor railing.

Ashton grinned up at her. "Would that make me the Beast?"

Tristan's face transformed into the little vixen that turned Ashton on in a heartbeat. "You certainly were when we got back from the factory."

Later that night, Ashton sighed in contentment as she lay in Tristan's arms. They'd had one of the most amazing evenings Ashton had ever had with a woman. The family cook had made them an incredible dinner, then they'd headed to the library where Tristan had chosen a couple books, as had Ashton, then they'd retired to Ashton's bedroom. A fire in the fireplace, they'd recreated their nest of pillows and blankets on the floor and had cuddled as Tristan read aloud.

Eventually reading had led to kissing, which had led to making love in the pillows. Finally, they'd worked their way to the bed for more. Sated, for the moment, Ashton reveled in the feel of Tristan's breast beneath her cheek and her stomach beneath her hand. If she were a cat, she'd be purring.

"Thank you for a really wonderful day," Tristan said softly, running the fingers of one hand through Ashton's hair.

Ashton smiled. "You didn't mind coming to work with me then, huh?"

"No, not at all. And hey, you've been to work with me," Tristan said, amusement in her voice.

"So very true." Ashton chuckled.

"Which," Tristan murmured. "You can surprise me there any time. But no, I loved it. I found it so fascinating, seeing what you do. I had no idea chocolate was so complex."

"*Good* chocolate is," Ashton corrected, smiling when she felt a kiss to the top of her head. "I have a question for you."

"And I'm sure I have an answer for you," Tristan replied, fingertips trailing along Ashton's shoulder before escaping back into her hair.

"Do you have a passport?"

There was a pause then, "A passport? Yes, I do. Why?"

Ashton raised her head, moving so she could plant her elbow in the pillow beside Tristan's head, her own head resting in an upturned palm. "Well, I need to head to London to deal with some things and get them ready for transition in leadership," she began, looking down into Tristan's eyes. *So lovely.* "I thought maybe you'd like to come with me." She brought up her other hand and lightly ran her fingers alone pronounced collarbones. "I need to be there for about a week, but I can get you back whenever you need it."

Tristan looked at her with such excitement in her eyes, but then that enthusiasm dimmed and she looked away. "I'd love that, Ashton."

"But?" Ashton prodded gently.

Tristan let out a soft sigh. "I can't afford that, Ashton."

"Baby," Ashton murmured. "Tristan, look at me." When she had the other woman's attention, she smiled. "I know that. I'm not worried about it, and neither should you be."

Looking very troubled, Tristan said, "I pay my own way, Ashton. You can't buy me."

Stung, Ashton was taken aback for a moment. She swallowed and pulled a bit away from her but still maintained skin contact. "Tristan," she began. "I'd never do that. In the beginning, yes, that was our relationship." She shook her head. "This isn't the beginning anymore." Tristan looked over at her. "I want you to come with me. Please?"

Tristan looked deeply into Ashton's eyes, almost as though looking for something buried inside Ashton's own psyche. Finally, she nodded. "Okay."

# Chapter Sixteen

After a nine-hour flight, another hour to get through customs, and now the hour drive from Heathrow to Laddingford, Ashton was tired, but not Tristan. She was all eyes, taking in everything as Ashton drove them in her little car. One of Ashton's staff had dropped it off for her at the airport with the understanding that if it got hurt, crashed, or smashed, she had three acres in which to bury a body.

Ashton was amused, glancing over at her passenger from time to time as Tristan pointed out this or that, or squealed at the hairpin curves in the narrow roads as they got out farther into the country.

As they drove through the small hamlet of Yalding, Ashton pulled to a stop at the head of a long stone bridge that was only wide enough for one car to pass at a time. They had to wait their turn as a lorry rumbled across.

"You see this bridge that we're about to cross?"

"I do," Tristan said with a nod, glancing over at Ashton for explanation.

"That bridge is a medieval bridge," she explained, meeting Tristan's wide gaze.

"Are you serious?" She gasped, looking back to the bridge. "As in, horses and peasants and knights and an earl walked or trotted across it?"

Ashton chuckled, getting her car going as the lorry passed with a wave from the driver. "Absolutely."

"This. Is. Incredible."

Ashton pointed things out to her as they went, anxious to get to the house. She knew Tristan would love it. She'd yet to have anyone there who truly appreciated it and the history as much as she did. Bella had been the closest.

The little Mark II slowed down as Ashton neared the entrance to her property, which she knew would suddenly appear out of nowhere in the break in the hedge wall. As she turned right onto the paved road leading up to the house proper, Tristan gasped.

"It's like a whole other world on the other side of the hedge!"

Ashton grinned, loving the absolute vibration coming from the woman sitting to her left. "It's magic."

"Seriously."

"So," Ashton announced, pulling up in front of the manor house. "Welcome to The Ashes."

"Do all your houses have names?" Tristan drawled playfully.

Ashton nodded. "Yup!"

She pulled the car to a stop in front of the grand home and killed the ignition. Looking over at Tristan, she saw that her eyes were everywhere, ducking her head to see as much as possible through the windows of the car.

"Ready?"

"God yes," Tristan murmured. "The history is just oozing from the walls."

"Sounds very Stephen King." Ashton laughed, climbing out of the car.

The front door opened and Lucy, wife of the groundskeeper, emerged, the older woman hurrying down the stairs to meet them. "'Ello, luv!" The longtime employee greeted Ashton with a kiss to the cheek. "Me husband and I got everythin' ready fer ya," she said. "Beds washed and made, pantry fulla good eatin', just like always."

"Thank you so much, Mrs. Hill," Ashton said, genuinely grateful.

"And, who's this lovely?" Lucy asked, turning to Tristan, who had joined them on the driver's side of the car.

"This is Tristan," Ashton introduced. "Tristan, this is Mrs. Hill. She and her husband Henry have worked for me here since I bought the house."

"It's an absolute pleasure, Mrs. Hill," Tristan greeted with a brilliant smile.

Lucy's eyes grew wide as the fifty-something-year-old woman glanced at Ashton. "Look at that lovely face and smile," she said. "So much better than that bloody mug usually here with ya."

Ashton cleared her throat, feeling a bit uncomfortable as the new woman in her life looked on.

"Sod off with that one," Lucy Hill continued. She smiled at Tristan, taking her hands in her own. "This little bird can stay."

Tristan glanced over at Ashton, clearly not sure what to say. Just as it had been for Ashton when she'd first arrived there, she figured Tristan had no idea what was meant by much of what the older woman had said. "Um," she managed, looking back at the housekeeper. "It's so nice to meet you."

Mrs. Hill chuckled. "Henry!" she belted, startling Ashton. She turned back to the women and gave them an excited smile and patted Tristan's hands before letting them go. An older man appeared from the house wearing his ever-present flat cap. He hurried to the car, tilting the cap in honor of the newcomers before hurrying to the boot to gather their luggage.

Ashton met Tristan's wide gaze, looking a bit overwhelmed. Ashton smiled in understanding. "Come on, let me show you around."

Inside the manor, Ashton was explaining the history behind the mantel over the fireplace in the dining room when Tristan gasped and hurried from that room to the room's twin, darting back into the dining room. She looked at Ashton.

"This is a Georgian, isn't it?" she asked, excitement in her voice.

Ashton stared at her, stunned and deeply impressed. "It is. Wow."

Tristan's smile was huge. "I've always wanted to see one. I taught an entire lesson on these to my juniors," she explained.

Ashton shook her head, hands on hips. "You never cease to amaze me."

Tristan's smile morphed into a sexy little grin. "Hey now," she purred. "This woman is good for more than just orgasms."

As though the proverbial record scratched to a halt, the two women looked to see Henry, loaded down with luggage, at the foot of the staircase, foot frozen in midair as it was about to land on the bottom step. He stared at them, they blinked at him, and he scurried up the staircase as quickly as his haul would allow.

"Oh, shit," Tristan murmured, face buried in her hands.

Ashton burst into laughter and reached up to grab one of the redhead's hands. "Come on," she said, tugging her to follow. "I want to show you something." She took them to the kitchen, stepping into the room while holding Tristan just outside by the shoulders. "Okay," she said, pointing down at the small space that ran along the doorway. "Step over that."

Tristan looked down at it then back up at Ashton with a bit of confusion, but did it, standing in front of Ashton in the kitchen.

Ashton smiled. "Congratulations," she said, placing her hands on Tristan's hips and pulling her close. "You just stepped back in time from the eighteenth century to the sixteenth century."

Tristan snaked her arms up around her neck, one hand cupping the back of Ashton's head as she urged the taller woman down for a kiss. "It's incredible," she whispered against waiting lips.

Ashton sighed into the kiss. *I'm in trouble*, she thought. *I'm in deep, deep trouble.*

Showered and dressed for her day, Ashton wasn't at all surprised to see that Tristan was still sound asleep in bed. The jet lag was terrible, especially the first time. It didn't help that they'd left Denver in the afternoon only to arrive the next day in the morning, due to distance and time change. She knew it would take the lion's share of their trip for Tristan to feel somewhat leveled out, by which time they'd be headed back the other way.

"Baby," she said softly, crawling up behind the beautiful woman in her bed whose naked body was wrapped in the covers. She lowered her lips to a warm neck, inhaling the sleepy scent. "Baby?"

"Hmm?" Tristan murmured, eyes still closed.

"I have to go to work now," Ashton said, brushing back auburn strands over a pale shoulder.

"Mm-hmm..."

Ashton smiled, running her hand over that exposed shoulder. "What time is your Facetime call with Tanisha?" she asked. "I'll set an alarm for you."

"Seven," Tristan murmured. "Morning."

Understanding that was Denver time, Ashton reached over Tristan and grabbed her alarm clock from the bedside table. She quickly set the alarm for one thirty, which would give Tristan thirty minutes to wake up, as it was entirely possible she'd still be asleep. The first time Ashton had flown in, she'd slept for thirteen hours straight.

The one contingency of Tristan coming along was that Tanisha felt it was okay and if she did, she'd Facetime Tristan twice to update her on Christine and let her see her sister.

Replacing the alarm clock, Ashton allowed herself a moment to spoon up behind Tristan, absorbing her scent and the feel of her warmth. Though she did have legitimate and important work to do during their trip, she was excited to have five full days with the woman she held. It would be so hard to let her go when they got back to the States.

"I don't know how you did it," she whispered into Tristan's hair as she slept on. "It's too soon, damn it," she continued, eyes falling closed. "It's too soon for that, and I'm scared." She left a kiss where her words had fallen and climbed off the bed.

Hands braced on the long conference table, Ashton looked from one member of management to another, eight pairs of eyes on her, her top people from HR to Production to the Kitchen. She could feel dark eyes boring into her but ignored them.

"These people here look to you," she said, her voice deceptively calm. "They look to you to tell them the truth, to honor them, and to honor this company." Standing erect to her full height again, she crossed her arms over her chest. "There's a full-on investigation happening as we speak," she continued. "I'm not involved in it, told them I don't want to be. I have nothing to hide, but whoever has a problem with me, who tried to smear me and my standing with this company and with my father before he died, will get found out."

With those damning words, she left the room, heading down the hallway to her office.

"Ash, wait!"

Ashton slowed and turned, not surprised to see Katherine hurrying after her in her kitchen whites. She waited for her to catch up.

"I'm sorry about your father," Katherine said, reaching her.

"Thank you." Ashton kept her voice flat.

"I don't know what's going on," Katherine said, hitching her thumb back toward the conference room. "But it sounds pretty shitty. I hope they can get to the bottom of it."

"Me, too."

"I didn't know you were back. How long are you staying?"

Ashton glanced over to a few of the managers who had left the conference room and were passing them on their way back to their respective departments. "Few days," she said nonchalantly. "Just long enough to take care of some things, then I have to head back, take care of more things back in Denver."

Katherine nodded. "Okay. Well, I have to get back to the kitchen, but..." She took a few steps backward, looking at Ashton. "Good to see you." With that, she turned and headed off.

Ashton watched her go before continuing on to her office.

The drive home was an interesting one. It had begun with a pensive, anxious Ashton. Though it had been good to see her people again, she'd had to go through her day knowing that somewhere, one of them at least was against her and she had no idea why. It was maddening to not be able to take each person in that building by the shirtfront and demand if they'd sent that letter to her father.

Ashton's entire career had been made up of building blocks to build both her knowledge of the product and their business, but also to build a reputation as a woman of integrity and honesty. More than twenty years dedicated to that, so for somebody to question that or make baseless accusations pained her soul.

However, on this particular drive home, it hit her that, at the end of the road and difficult day, she had an amazing woman waiting for her. She and Tristan had swapped texts a few times—when Ashton could—and they'd been light, flirtatious, and frankly, loving and warm. She looked forward to a long, comforting hug from the woman she was becoming frighteningly addicted to.

Pulling the little car onto the property, she saw Tristan standing outside with Henry Hill, the older man gesticulating wildly as he seemed to be telling her one of his whoppers. He loved to tell a good tale, and from the delight on Tristan's face, she was enjoying every word.

Ashton slowed her car before braking to a full stop. The two standing just off to the side of the main steps to the house glanced her way, Tristan's smile growing and Henry offering a hand in greeting.

"Hey there," Ashton said, climbing out of the car. She walked over to the pair.

"Hey, you," Tristan greeted, earning her a smile from Ashton.

"Evenin' to ya, Ashton," Henry said. "Been here chattin' up yer lady," he said, indicating Tristan. "I'm chuffed to bits with this one."

Ashton grinned. "Well, I'm glad you've enjoyed your conversation."

"I'll leave ya to it, then," Henry said. "Ye had a minor pipe leak today, Ashton. The last fella ye had here bodged the whole thing." He straightened his stance with a big, cheeky grin. "Good now."

"Thanks so much, Henry. I truly appreciate it."

Tipping his hat to both women, the groundskeeper left them alone.

Tristan turned to Ashton, hand on her arm. "Hungry?"

Ashton nodded. "Yes." She followed Tristan inside the house, and as soon as the front door was closed, she stopped Tristan's forward momentum by grabbing her hand, pulling her back to her and wrapping her in a hug. She needed the warmth and comfort of the other woman in that moment.

Tristan said nothing, asked no questions, simply gave Ashton what she needed. She held them together, one of her hands moving up into Ashton's hair, the other rubbing random, gentle patterns on Ashton's back.

Ashton's eyes closed as she buried her face in Tristan's warm neck. She felt all her stress and anxiety begin to drain away. How was it possible that one person could make everything okay? She'd never known that, never felt that or understood it when she'd heard others talk that way, or the message conveyed in music and movies. Now, in this moment, she was beginning to understand.

"Okay," Ashton said, slightly out of breath after the climb up the winding staircase after parking her car at the top of the narrow streets in the village of Sutton Valence to see the ruins of the castle of the same name. They reached the top and Ashton took in the rugged hillside and vegetation. "Let's see here." She took her phone out of her coat pocket and began to read what she'd brought up from the internet about their location.

As she began to read, Tristan walked up to the massively thick walls of—according to what Ashton was reading—what had once been the keep. It was all that was left of a castle thought to be built in the middle of the twelfth century, owned by a succession of ruling families in the area.

Once Ashton had finished reading, she tucked

her phone away, walking over to where Tristan stood in the middle of the ruins, hands in the pocket of her jacket as she looked around, an expression of absolute awe on her beautiful face.

"What do you think?" Ashton asked softly. From the time she'd told Tristan where they were going that morning, the other woman had been buzzing with excitement.

"This is extraordinary. I know this is a small piece of the puzzle, but it's easy to see how likely the rest of the castle went back that way," Tristan said, pointing toward the trees beyond the ruins. "And of course, that way," she added, pointing up.

Ashton stepped up beside her. Though it wasn't her first time there, it was the best one. It got even better when Tristan moved in behind her, wrapping her arms around her waist and resting her head against Ashton's shoulder. Smiling, Ashton covered Tristan's gloved hands with her own.

"It's incredible to me," Tristan murmured. "How many people lived here over the centuries? How many hopes and dreams were made here, how many babies born, and made?" she added with a chuckle. "How many died?"

"You know," Ashton responded. "You're the first person I've ever brought to something like this who truly gets it. You can feel it, can't you?"

"What?" Tristan asked. "The energy? The past, alive and breathing?"

Ashton smiled. "Exactly. These people," she said, indicating the castle ruins around them. "All that lived and died here, long gone, but still felt."

Tristan let out a long, contented sigh. "Yeah. You have no idea how much I'd love to share this experience with the Medieval Europe class I used to teach."

Ashton considered for a moment, then said, "I think you should go back to teaching." She leaned her head against Tristan's. "Would it take much? Since you've been out for a bit?"

"Well," Tristan began with a sigh, though not content like the previous one, but sad. "I didn't want to have to retake the Praxis test to get a new license, so I kept mine up to date just in case. You know, to keep the dream alive that someday I'd be able to go back. So, it would just be to see if I could get hired somewhere. A lot has changed in the classroom, even just in six years."

"Yeah, but you're brilliant," Ashton argued. "You're young."

After a moment, Tristan asked. "How old are you, Ashton?"

Ashton grinned. "Worried I'm being a cougar?"

Tristan smacked her playfully on the arm. "No."

"I'll be forty-one this summer. How about you?"

"Thirty-five this fall."

"Well, my baby cub," Ashton teased. "Let's go look around."

# *Chapter Seventeen*

With hooded eyes, Ashton looked down the length of her own body, watching as Tristan, who knelt at the vee of her spread legs, slowly pushed the dildo inside Ashton's depths. The longer, thicker end was now inside Ashton, but the shorter, angled portion was inside Tristan, a strapless strap-on, as it were. Each thrust made into Ashton was one made into Tristan, as well.

Tristan met her gaze, filled with the fiery passion Ashton had come to expect and crave. Warm tingles ran down the insides of Ashton's thighs along the trail Tristan created with her nails along the sensitive skin, pooling between her spread legs. One of Tristan's hands moved down, the pad of her thumb rubbing slow circles over Ashton's clit.

"Baby," Ashton whispered, her eyes falling closed.

"You rang?" Tristan murmured, using catlike grace as she stretched herself out atop Ashton, the phallus fully inside Ashton, their hips flush. She initiated a sensual kiss as she ran her hand down along Ashton's side and over her hip. She cupped the underside of Ashton's thigh and urged it up higher on Tristan's side as she began a slow, easy thrust.

Ashton sighed into the kiss, her hips moving with Tristan's as she buried the fingers of one hand into soft, auburn hair. It felt amazing to have Tristan on top of and inside her. She loved the feeling of their breasts pressed together, Tristan's hair and skin against her own. She loved the taste of her mouth, which tasted like Ashton's desire as Tristan had already made Ashton come with said mouth. Just so Ashton would be nice and wet to accept Tristan's cock, of course, so stated Tristan.

Tristan rested on a forearm, bringing the other hand up to caress the side of Ashton's face as she pulled out of the kiss. She looked down into Ashton's eyes, seeming to study her very essence as she gracefully moved her hips, pleasuring them both with each stroke and counterstroke.

"Does it feel good?" Ashton whispered, as she'd never been on the receiving end of this type of phallus.

"Amazing," Tristan murmured, lowering her mouth to Ashton's neck where she left wet, hot kisses that trailed up to Ashton's ear, then said, "I love being inside you,"

Ashton smiled, turning her head so she could whisper against Tristan's lips. "That makes two of us."

Tristan smiled into their kiss. Allowing herself to get lost in all that was the woman above her, Ashton returned the kiss, her hands wandering over the expanse of Tristan's back, muscles moving beneath the soft skin with Tristan's gentle thrusts. Something, somewhere in the back of her mind, told her that something was amiss.

Pulling out of the kiss, she lightly squeezed Tristan's shoulders. "Wait," she said, lifting her head and looking absently at the large bedroom as she concentrated on what she thought she'd heard.

"What is it?" Tristan asked, stilling her movements.

Hearing it again, Ashton gasped. "Somebody's

in the house."

Tristan pulled out and moved off her. "What?"

"Ashton?" came a female voice from down below.

"Oh, for fuck's sake!" Ashton hissed, scurrying off the bed and grabbing her robe from the floor where it had been shed. She was just getting the robe belted fully when she reached the top of the stairs, Katherine looking up at her from the bottom, her hand on the rail and foot raised as though she'd been about to head up. "What are you doing here?"

Katherine's gaze fell over Ashton's wardrobe and mussed hair, taking a step backward from the stairs, hand dropping from the rail as Ashton made her way down. "I tried to call, but it went to voicemail."

"So, you thought that was the perfect reason to drive all the way out here?" Ashton accused, eyebrow raised in obvious irritation.

Katherine stammered for a moment before recovering. "I know you turn your phone off when you read when you're here. I figured that sort of quiet time was the perfect time to talk to you about work." Again she eyed Ashton's appearance. "Clearly you were engaged in a very different type of quiet time." Her gaze snapped up to something behind and above Ashton. Her next words explained exactly what she was seeing, or rather, who. "Hello. I'm Katherine. Who are you?"

"The woman Ashton was spending 'quiet time' with," Tristan responded, stopping on the step just up from Ashton's. Ashton could just barely feel Tristan's leg against her behind.

Katherine's gaze returned to Ashton. "Is this who you walked out on me for?"

"I didn't walk out on you at all," Ashton said,

voice flat, her irritation oozing from her pores. "We broke up."

"None too soon it would seem." She looked up at Tristan again. "Don't get too comfortable. She likes 'em young, beautiful, and willing." She smirked, crossing her arms over her chest. "From the looks of your largely matching outfits, guessing you fill the bill, sweetheart." She looked from Tristan to Ashton then back again. "'Fuck me' hair and everything."

"Katherine, you need to leave," Ashton said, her voice deceptively calm as she was furious inside.

The slow smile that spread across the chef's lips made Ashton's blood go cold. "Oh, I don't know," she said, sauntering over toward the stairs, her hand back on the banister. "Why not take advantage." She reached out, a finger playfully tugging at the belt that cinched Ashton's robe closed. "It's what you're good at, right?"

Ashton's anger bubbled to the surface. Her hand snapped up and grabbed Katherine's wrist in a viselike grip. "I said, you need to leave."

Katherine's already-dark eyes darkened further as she whipped her hand away, her glare boring into Ashton. That gaze swept up to Tristan again as she backed away. "Get out now," she advised. "I assure you, you're nothing special and she'll get bored."

"Meeting you Katherine," Tristan said, her voice its normal soft cadence. "I can see why she came looking for me."

Katherine's glare landed on Tristan. "Fuck you both," she murmured, backing nearly to the door.

"Exactly what we were doing when you barged in," Tristan quipped.

Managing to keep her smile hidden, Ashton

hurried after Katherine. "Give me my key," she said, angry at herself that Katherine still had it.

Katherine turned to face her. For a moment it was a battle of wills, and Ashton wasn't entirely certain she was going to get it back without a fight. But, finally, Katherine reached into the pocket of her jeans and withdrew the key, dropping it into Ashton's outstretched palm. Without another word the chef turned and left, slamming the door behind her, the loud *crack* startling Ashton.

Shaken, she looked down at the key before wrapping her fingers around it and sliding the little piece of metal into the pocket of her robe. Taking a deep breath, she turned to see Tristan standing at the top of the stairs, hand on the rail as she studied Ashton. She was in her own robe, and she looked troubled.

"I shouldn't have said anything," she said at length. "That was none of my business, and I was incredibly rude. I apologize for that." Though her words sounded genuine, it was obvious that Tristan was bothered by more than simply her exchange with a difficult woman.

"You have nothing to apologize for," Ashton said, walking back to the stairs, hand resting on the banister where Katherine's had moments before. "She deserved it."

Tristan tightened the belt on her robe, seeming uncomfortable. "Are you still with her?" she asked.

Ashton shook her head. "No."

"Were you with her when we met?" Tristan asked, seeming to fold into herself a bit.

Feeling the air between them cool about thirty degrees, Ashton hugged herself. "Technically, yes."

"What does that mean, 'technically'?"

Ashton nodded toward the stairs. "Let's go back to the bedroom," she suggested. "At least we have the fire going and we can be comfortable. Okay?"

Without a word, Tristan turned on the stair she stood on and headed up, Ashton making sure the front door was locked, then following. In the bedroom, Tristan made herself comfortable in one of the two wingback chairs set by the fire in the seating area in the large bedroom.

It made Ashton's heart sad, as she'd hoped they could get back in bed and cuddle as they talked about everything. But, that obviously wasn't what Tristan wanted, so she said nothing, simply sat in the twin chair.

Ashton cleared her throat and straightened out her robe covering her legs as she crossed them at the knee. "I told you a bit about our relationship," she began, not forgetting about Tristan's question, but instead deciding to give her more information to explain what she'd meant. "The entirety of our relationship was difficult. Katherine was so unpredictable. What happened tonight," she explained, meeting Tristan's steady gaze. "Could happen on any random Tuesday. It made me uncomfortable, it left me unsettled, and frankly," she added, "I got sick of it."

"But you stayed with her?"

"Off and on. The longest we were apart was about eight months, then she'd wander back into my life, or we'd have to work together closely on a project and it would just start up all over again."

Tristan nodded, looking into the flames. "So, where were you in things when we met? Initially."

"That's where the 'technically' comes in," Ashton

explained. "Had I broken it off? No. Was I done? Yes. I had to go to the States, as I did every holiday rush to work out any kinks for holiday production. Buck had gone to my father for his idea with the club—that was why I was there, Tristan. I wasn't there looking for anything. Or anyone."

"So, what then?" Tristan asked, eyeing Ashton.

"I ended up having to stay in Denver for a couple months instead of the planned two weeks as we worked on Top Shelf, and you and I began to..." She wasn't sure what to say. "Get to know each other." She looked into the flames herself, wondering what Tristan was thinking, then added, "Things between you and me ended somewhat awkwardly that very unexpected night at the club, so I came back home here and buried myself back into my life."

"With Katherine?" Tristan asked, a simple question, no bitterness of jealousy in her voice.

"No, actually." Ashton shook her head. She recalled the weeks they hadn't spoken, those calm, quiet weeks. "One day, after weeks not of talking, she popped over demanding answers, like she did tonight, and I had had enough. I'd decided I wanted out. For good."

Tristan glanced over at her, that seeming to grab her attention.

"I was literally in the middle of breaking up with her when the phone rang," Ashton said quietly, remembering that day like it was yesterday. "Martin. He told me about my father." She met Tristan's gaze. "Katherine was nice enough to give me a ride to the airport, and that was it."

"You haven't seen her or spoken to her in all the time you've been back in Denver? Not even about work?"

Ashton shook her head. "Nope."

"How'd she know you were back?" Tristan asked, running a hand through her hair.

"At work I had a meeting with my department heads." Ashton shrugged. "She's a department head. After, she gave her condolences for my father's death and asked how long I'd be there. That was it. I left and came home to you."

Realizing what she'd just said, the presumptive audacity of it, she looked away. Her stomach was in knots as she couldn't read or feel Tristan. It was like the other woman had shut her out, raised impenetrable walls, just like in the beginning.

"Well," Tristan said at length, uncurling herself from the wingback and getting to her feet. "We have to be at the airport early tomorrow." She stretched, arms high overhead before letting out a yawn. She looked down at Ashton, who still sat. "Thank you for explaining all of it."

Ashton nodded, meeting her gaze, her own guarded. "Of course."

Half an hour later, after brushing teeth and nighttime routines, they lay in bed. For the first time since they'd ever shared a bed, they each wore their own version of pajamas. Ashton hated it but wasn't going to push Tristan. She honestly wasn't sure what was going through the younger woman's mind. She wasn't sure if Katherine's sudden appearance had destroyed their burgeoning…whatever it was they were building.

Lying on her back on her side of the bed, Ashton stared up at the ceiling, hands tucked behind her head. She was thinking about the next day. They'd be flying back to Denver, her business finished for the time being in London. Tristan also needed to get back, both for her job and for her sister.

"We met in high school."

Surprised at the sudden sound of Tristan's voice, no matter how soft it had been, Ashton glanced over at her. Tristan was lying on her side, facing Ashton. Her hands were curled up just under her chin.

"She was a senior when I was a sophomore," she continued. She met Ashton's gaze. "We broke up after she graduated. She was going to college in New Mexico and I still had two years of high school left." A soft smile touched her lips. "I was so angry with her. Hurt."

"Sophie?" Ashton asked. At Tristan's nod, she asked, "How did you two end up together again?"

"Got hired at the same school." She smiled. "We'd lost contact. She'd met someone in New Mexico, and I was figuring out this thing called life. We lost touch."

"How long did it take for you two to get back together after reuniting?" Ashton was curious about Tristan's past, but she was also a little jealous, knowing Sophie had held her heart.

"By spring break," Tristan said with a snort.

Ashton smiled. "Do you still love her?" she asked, her voice not much above a whisper. She was terrified to hear the answer but needed to know.

"I'm not in love with her anymore," Tristan said softly. "Time has taken care of that. Years. But," she added. "Part of me will always love her. At one time we were happy. That part of her will live on inside me." She was silent for a long moment, studying Ashton's eyes. "Does that make sense?"

Ashton nodded. “It does. What was she like?”

“Smart. She had a goofy side to her. Made her a great elementary school teacher.” She grew quiet, her gaze taking on a distant look, as though she were looking back to a place where Ashton could never join her. A smile touched her lips for just a moment, as though she’d hit upon a good memory, before the smile disappeared. “She was good with Christine, too. Patient.”

“Why is there such an age difference between you and your sister?” Ashton asked.

“My parents decided to suddenly get along again when I was twelve.” She grinned. “No, just an unexpected life bonus.”

Ashton smiled. “Interesting way to put it. You know,” she added. “It’s crazy the things we have in common, our family tragedies.”

Tristan met her gaze and stared into it for a long time. “We fly home in the morning,” she murmured.

Ashton nodded. “I know.” She dreaded it, so worried that the past week had been nothing more than a fantasy, a mirage.

“Ashton?”

“Yes?”

“Don’t hurt me,” Tristan whispered. “My heart can’t take it.”

# Chapter Eighteen

The plane touched down gracefully on the runway at Denver International Airport. Luckily, being up front in business class, Ashton and Tristan were able to gather their carry-ons and leave the plane quickly once the door was opened. She'd gotten a text message from Dekayas letting her know Leonard had sent him to pick them up so he could get some experience with this aspect of his job.

Tristan had been largely quiet the entire day so far, sleeping through a lot of the long flight. Ashton had an uneasy feeling and wasn't entirely sure where it was coming from. Yes, Tristan's wall was still a bit in place after a night of restless sleep for Ashton, but it was more than that. She wasn't sure what was bothering her.

Now, sitting in the back seat of the town car, their luggage piled into the trunk, she wanted to reach over and take Tristan's hand but didn't dare. She felt so alone, even as the one person she so badly wanted to reach out to was sitting less than two feet from her.

"Did you need me to make any stops before we hit your place, ma'am?" Dekayas asked, glancing back at Tristan through the rearview mirror.

"No, thank you."

Ashton turned to her. "Do you need anything? Groceries or anything? I'm only asking because we've been gone for a week," she added when Tristan gave her a strange look.

Shaking her head, Tristan gave her a small smile. "No. I'm okay, thank you."

The sleek black car pulled up to Tristan's apartment building. Dekayas turned off the ignition and climbed out of the car, pulling open Tristan's door for her before heading to the trunk to unload her luggage.

Ashton climbed out of the car on her side, not quite ready to say goodbye just yet. "Dekayas," she said, walking to the rear of the car. "I'll help her with her luggage."

The young man glanced at her, surprise in his dark eyes. "Oh. Okay, Miss King. Are you sure?"

She smiled. "Positive. Thanks."

"Yes, ma'am. I'll wait down here for you." He looked to Tristan, who stood nearby, her carry-on bag slung over her shoulder by the strap. "Nice to see you again, ma'am."

She gave him a warm smile. "Thank you, Dekayas. Thanks so much for picking us up."

He smiled shyly, then made his way quickly back to the driver's side door, slipping into the car. Ashton was amused. She looked at Tristan, taking hold of the handle to Tristan's roller bag.

"I can take that," Tristan said, nodding down at the bag.

"So can I," Ashton retorted with a smile.

The two headed toward the building in silence. As they climbed the stairs, Ashton careful not to bang the bag against each upcoming step, Tristan pulled her keys out of her bag, sorting through them until she got to the correct one.

"Oh my god," she said suddenly.

Ashton, who had been focused on the bag,

looked up and around, trying to figure out what was wrong. The door to Tristan's apartment was ajar. She felt a sense of panic and grabbed Tristan by the hand, pulling her away from the door.

"Come on. Let's get back to the car and call the police," she said.

Dekayas stepped out of the car when he saw them coming back. "What's wrong?" Concern laced his voice.

"I think somebody broke in," Ashton said, shaken. Tristan was literally trembling beside her. She released the handle of the luggage and wrapped her arms around her. "We should call the police."

Dekayas reached behind him, beneath his suit jacket, and produced a handgun that seemed to have been tucked into his waistband at his lower back. Ashton was shocked and met his gaze with a question in hers. "Be right back," he said.

Ashton watched him go, holding on to Tristan. "I had no idea I had Rambo working for me," she murmured. She heard a small chuckle from Tristan. "Everything's going to be okay," she assured, leaving a kiss in soft hair. "I promise."

They waited as finally Dekayas trotted back to the car, tucking his gun away as he did. "Nobody in there, but looks like they tore stuff up, ma'am."

Tristan pulled out of the embrace and ran a hand through her hair. She looked as though she were trying to hold back tears. "I need to see if they took anything."

"Dekayas," Ashton said softly. "Please put her bag back in the car."

He did so without a word.

"Come on," Ashton said, a hand on Tristan's

back. They headed back to the stairs and the apartment, where Dekayas had left the door open. "Try not to touch anything," she said. "Just in case police can find fingerprints or anything."

"Okay," Tristan said, her voice small. "Good call."

Many of the books had been wiped from the bookshelves, as though somebody had taken their arm and just shoved. One bookshelf had been knocked over atop the paper contents on the floor. The TV was present but the Blu-ray player was missing, connecting cables left behind. The bedding was thrown to the floor in the bedroom and all the drawers in the dresser were pulled out, some contents scattered on the bare mattress and the floor.

In the second bedroom, the dresses had all been ripped from their hangers, some torn and tossed. It also looked as though one of the dresses, a black one, had been used in some way, as Ashton spied a very suspicious white discoloration was on the material. She felt nauseated by her guess of what it was.

"Jesus," she whispered.

"Hello?"

Ashton and Tristan looked at each other before turning to the doorway of the second bedroom where a uniformed police officer appeared. He looked at the two women.

"One of you lives here?"

"I do," Tristan said, stepping over the soiled dress to the officer.

"Somebody broke in?" he asked, looking around. "When?"

"I don't know," Tristan said, voice shaky. "I've been out of the country for the last week. I literally just got home."

"Do you live here, too?" he asked Ashton.

She shook her head. "No, sir."

"All right. Let's get a statement."

---

Later that afternoon, after going down to the station so the two women and Dekayas could give a statement, they were finally released to go home. Sitting in the back of the car in the police station parking lot, Ashton looked at Tristan, who was still shaken.

"What do you want to do?" Ashton asked softly. "We can take you home—"

"No," Tristan said, shaking her head and meeting Ashton's gaze. "No. I don't feel safe."

Ashton smiled. "I'm glad you said that. I don't want you going back there either, but it's your call." When Tristan said nothing more, biting her bottom lip as though uncertain, Ashton spoke again. "I can get you a room or," she added with a nonchalant shrug, trying not to sound pushy. "You can just come home with me."

Tristan blew out a breath and met her gaze. Finally, she nodded.

"Let's go home, Dekayas," Ashton said, reaching up and placing her hand lightly on the young man's shoulder.

The house staff carried luggage upstairs as Ashton and Tristan followed. Tristan said nothing, but her demeanor seemed to be changing from the tight, pensive woman of earlier to someone who seemed so much younger. She was quiet, almost timid.

Once they reached Ashton's suite, she saw their luggage in the bedroom area and immediately felt exhausted. "I am so tired," she said, shrugging out of her jacket.

"Me, too," Tristan said. "I need to call Buck. He'd wanted me to go in tonight, but I'm just not in the right headspace."

"Of course," Ashton said, looking at her. She wanted to go hug her again but kept her distance. "I'm going to jump in the shower while you do that." She gave her a warm smile and headed to the bathroom.

The bathroom in her suite was large and a mixture of yesterday and modern. Like her home in England, this one also had a huge claw-footed tub, a favorite way for her to relax, as she often liked to read in the tub. But this one had a large walk-in shower that was more like showering in a cave than anything else.

No doors were required as the enclosure was more like a small room entered from a short hallway, sloped just enough for any water to stay corralled in the shower area. Walls made of natural stone, it kept it nice and warm while bathing beneath the large, high-powered rain showerhead. Numerous alcoves held bathing products and a bench made of the same stone was tucked into the corner for shaving or other such activities.

Stripping out of her clothes, she stepped over the ledge at the entrance to the shower that would stop any wayward water and made her way deeper until she reached the back wall where she turned the water spigot to her preferred temperature and then stepped underneath the spray. Mood lighting shone down on her, a sensor turning the lighting on as soon as she stepped over the ledge.

She raised her face to the spray, hands coming up to push her hair back as the water began to saturate it.

"Can I join you?"

Ashton looked over her shoulder, surprised to see Tristan entering the chamber, naked and beautiful, but looking as though she were about to crumble. Ashton waited for the other woman to reach her, glad to have her near. She reached up and lightly ran her fingers down the side of Tristan's face.

"What did Buck say?"

Tristan leaned into the touch, her eyes closing. "He told me to take my time," she responded. "Figure out what I'm going to do." Ashton took a step back, urging Tristan to follow, the wide spray falling over them both. "God, that feels amazing," Tristan whispered, raising her face to the water.

Ashton smiled, watching a bit of the tension seem to melt off Tristan's shoulders under the warm spray. She reached up and gently smoothed back the long, auburn strands. Tristan's eyes opened. "Let me do this," Ashton murmured.

Relaxing, Tristan's eyes closed again as Ashton continued what she was doing. Tristan's hair completely saturated, Ashton glanced at the shampoo options in the little nook.

"Rose petal or lavender?"

Tristan smiled, eyes still closed. "Rose petal. I love roses."

"Good choice." Ashton reached over and grabbed the appropriate bottle. She squeezed a good amount of the fragrant shampoo into her palm and replaced the bottle before she began to gently lather the goop into the wet strands, using fingertips to massage Tristan's scalp.

A long sigh escaped Tristan's lips. "You can stop that in about four days."

Amused, Ashton continued her ministrations. "You have the most beautiful hair."

"Thank you," Tristan said. "I have my grandmother's hair." She smiled as she continued. "It was the running joke in my family that my mom got left out. I look exactly like her mother—my grandmother—and Chrissy looks exactly like our dad."

Ashton chuckled. "I look like my mom," she explained, reaching to the wall to grab the handheld sprayer. "Put your head back, baby," she murmured, Tristan complying. "I got her Persian features."

"You have such beautiful, exotic features," Tristan murmured as Ashton used the sprayer to rinse the shampoo out of her hair. "I wondered what your ethnicity was."

"My mom's parents came to the United States from Iran in the sixties when Mom was about nine. She used to speak Farsi to Jackson and me when we were little."

"Really?" Tristan asked, bringing up her hands to clear the water out of her eyes. She blinked a few times at Ashton. "Do you still speak it?"

Ashton snorted. "Not really. Was never good at languages. Jackson, though, he was damn near fluent." She set the handheld aside. "Conditioner?" At Tristan's nod, she retrieved a small amount of the goop and began to apply it evenly through the long strands. "My mother spoke seven languages," she continued. "Farsi obviously being her native language, but she also spoke French, Italian, and some others I don't remember. I do, however," she said proudly, "remember something in Aramaic she used to always say."

"Aramaic?" Tristan asked, surprise in her voice. "Wow. That's an ancient language."

"It is. My mom's father, who I didn't know well, was a professor. Brilliant man, from what she used to tell me."

"What do you remember from Aramaic?" Tristan asked, her voice having more life in it than it had since Katherine had shown up.

Ashton hesitated, then finally said, "Rikhmith-eykh."

"Say it again," Tristan requested. When Ashton repeated the word, Tristan was quiet, almost as though turning it around in her head and on her tongue as she muttered the foreign word. "What does it mean?"

Finished with the conditioner, Ashton grabbed the handheld again. "It means, 'I love you,'" she said softly.

Tristan said nothing for a moment as she raised her face again as Ashton rinsed her hair. "Want me to wash yours?" she asked at length.

"Nope," Ashton said, setting aside the handheld. "This is just for you." She made a last-minute decision. She was absolutely loving catering to the beautiful woman that she was finding herself wanting to do more and more for. Grabbing the bath loofah, she brought it in front of Tristan so she could see it. "Is it okay if I use this on you?"

"Of course." Tristan chuckled. "I hadn't realized I'd paid for full service."

Ashton smiled, grabbing the bottle of body wash

and squirting a generous amount on the loofah. "Oh yes," she said. "You certainly did."

Standing behind the other woman, she began at her back, reaching up to move the rope of freshly washed hair over a shoulder to Tristan's front as she used gentle strokes of the bath tool to lather the soap across smooth skin. She watched as the soapy water flowed down her back and over the swell of her gorgeous behind, along shapely hamstrings and muscular calves before pooling at her feet before it was washed away to the floor drain.

She could hear soft sighs of pleasure coming from Tristan as she dropped her head when Ashton brought up her other hand, smoothing over the slick skin as her other washed. She ran the loofah down to Tristan's behind, her other hand following. She felt the glutes flexing with each pass.

She retrieved the handheld and took her time spraying off the back of Tristan's body before setting it aside again to focus on her front. Moving up a bit closer, she gasped softly when her nipples brushed against Tristan's back before her breasts lightly pressed against it.

With her free hand, she brought Tristan's hair back behind her shoulder so it wouldn't be in the way. She slid that hand down along Tristan's side until it rested on her hip, the hand with the loofah working over her upper chest. Glancing at her profile, Ashton saw that Tristan's eyes were closed and her lips just slightly open.

The loofah moved down between perfect breasts, then under each before lightly grazing over hard, sensitive nipples with the textured material. Tristan gasped, one of her hands reaching back and resting on the side of Ashton's thigh.

Ashton lowered her head to Tristan's neck, leaving a trail of kisses all the way up to her ear, flicking the lobe with her tongue. Tristan's head tilted, giving her more access. The hand that had been on Tristan's hip glided up to cover Tristan's left breast, the skin slick from the soapy residue left by the loofah, which traveled down over her taut stomach, across from hip to hip. Finally, she dropped the loofah, using her soapy hand to carefully roam down between her legs. She massaged her outer lips.

She continued to kiss Tristan's neck as she reached over blindly for the handheld. Pressing the button that would turn the pressure down, she held the head close to Tristan's skin, the soft spray breezing away the soap, washing it away in a wave of white suds. She took her time when it came to those beautiful breasts, aiming the spray directly at her nipples.

Tristan was getting restless, her behind pressing back into Ashton, who pushed back into her. She ran the water down along her torso, using her thumb to switch the pressure, increasing it as well as narrowing the spray to a more focused, pulsating, and intense stream.

A small cry slipped from Tristan's lips as her head fell back against Ashton's shoulder. Ashton brought her free hand back to the left breast, lightly rolling and tugging on the nipple as her other hand kept the spray steady against Tristan's clit.

Finally, breasts heaving as her breathing increased, Tristan let out a loud cry and fell back against Ashton, who wrapped her arm around her waist to hold her steady. To her surprise, the other woman began to cry. It didn't seem like tears from pain or fear, but more like her body did more than just release physically. The emotional energy flowed out of her like the water that sluiced off her body.

Ashton released the trigger on the handheld and reached over to place it in its holder before turning Tristan around and pulling her into a tight hug. "I've got you, baby," she whispered. "It's all going to be okay."

# *Chapter Nineteen*

Standing in bra and panties, Ashton studied her reflection as she brushed her hair out after her morning shower. She winced when the brush caught a tangle. She worked at it when she heard someone enter the bedroom suite. A glance at the clock she kept in the bathroom to keep her on track for getting ready told her that it was six thirty-two.

Smiling as Tristan's reflection came into view, she met her tired gaze. "Good morning," she said, turning and walking over to where Tristan stood in the bathroom doorway. She leaned in and left a lingering kiss on her lips. "You smell like a cinnamon roll."

Tristan grinned. "Can't imagine why."

Ashton playfully nibbled at her neck. "Can I eat you for breakfast?"

Tristen left a quick kiss on her lips before moving away, entering the bathroom to head into the small water closet where the toilet was and closed the door. "I've been thinking about something," she said, voice muffled behind the door.

Ashton returned to the counter and grabbed her toothbrush. "Okay, what's that?" she called out, squeezing some toothpaste on the bristles.

"I need to stop being a chicken shit," Tristan said. "I need to go back to my apartment."

Ashton felt her stomach fall at the words she'd been dreading, but knew she'd hear. She put the toothbrush into her mouth and began her task so as not to say anything that might get her into trouble like, *No, no, just move in and stay here forever. Yes, I know we've known each other for like four months, but who's counting?*

Moments later, the toilet flushed and the door opened again as Tristan stepped out, still buttoning her jeans. She walked over to the sink and washed her hands, glancing over at Ashton's reflection in the mirror. Ashton could feel her eyes on her but couldn't make herself meet that gaze, as she was afraid Tristan, so very perceptive, would read right through her.

"It's been nearly two weeks," she said softly. "And, other than to go back and grab some clothes and a few things, I haven't been back there. The police said I could a week ago." Drying her hands on a towel, she looked over at Ashton the person, Ashton finally looking back at her. "What do you think?"

Ashton held up a finger as she grabbed the small tumbler filled with water, taking a drink to rinse her mouth, spitting the frothy water into the sink and swishing again before rinsing both glass and sink with fresh water from the tap.

"I'm not real comfortable with you going back there," Ashton said quietly, wiping her mouth with a tissue. "They don't even have a suspect yet."

"I know." Tristan sighed, resting her shoulder against the wall along with her head. "I just can't mooch off you like this, Ashton."

"You're hardly mooching, Tristan." She tossed the soiled tissue into the trash and walked over to her. "Have I done something wrong?" she asked, feeling self-conscious and uncertain. "Do you not like being here? And I'm not asking because I'm trying to manipulate you or get you to say or do anything. Just want to understand where you sit."

"No," Tristan said, meeting her gaze and shaking her head, the end of her ponytail flopping from side to side of her neck. "You've done nothing wrong. And, that's part of the problem," she added with a small smile. "I like being here a bit too much."

That made Ashton feel better, but she could see that Tristan was uneasy about staying at the house, at least as things were. Perhaps too soon, too fast. She could understand that.

"Can I ask you a question?"

"Of course."

"What do you want?" Ashton asked. "As in, realistically, what do you want?"

Tristan leaned her back against the wall, hooking her thumbs into her belt loops as she seemed to be considering the question. "Well," she began. "For the moment, circumstances being what they are, I want to feel safe where I live. I'd say I'd love to change Chrissy's situation, but you said realistically." She smirked. "So, it's that simple. This apartment situation has put a huge kink in what was a relatively well-working life."

"What if I can help?"

Tristan shook her head, pushing away from the wall. "I don't want your money—"

"No," Ashton said, stepping over to her and resting her hands on her hips. "I'm not offering you money, not offering to get you a place. I would if you wanted that, but I respect your independence and want and need to be an adult. Honestly," she added with a smile. "It's one of the things I love most about you." She shrugged a shoulder, nonchalant. "So, how about I offer you something else."

"Like what?" Tristan asked, absently running her fingers over Ashton's forearms.

"This house is massive," Ashton said. "No," she said, holding up a hand when she saw Tristan opening her mouth to speak, likely to object. "I'm not asking you to move in with me, not in the traditional way, anyway. This house has a number of suites and a handful of regular bedrooms. Tons of bathrooms. Hell," she added with a flourish. "There's even another wing from this one, where my parents' suites were."

Tristan's head fell to the side a bit as she eyed Ashton. "What about rent? Utilities?"

"We can work that out. But," she added, bringing up a hand and running a thumb beneath Tristan's left eye, puffy from exhaustion. "I want you to be able to simplify your life. Maybe quit the bakery? Go back to teaching?"

Tristan's small smile was visible just before she lowered her head, letting out a long sigh. "I'd love that, Ashton, but as I've told you, I can't afford it. I have responsibilities now," she added, looking up once more. "Promises to keep."

Ashton nodded. "I understand. Please let me help you," she said. "At least with this." She was a little nervous inside when it came out what else she'd been up to already. "I know that rent has gone up exponentially in Denver. Since the legalization of marijuana, people are being gouged, and no doubt you were, too. So, let us settle on something reasonable, sane. That way you can pay all your bills and take care of Christine without killing yourself."

Tristan chewed on her bottom lip as she studied Ashton, as though weighing her words. "Would I have access to the library?"

Ashton grinned. "You'd have access to the entire house." Her grin turned lecherous. "And me."

"Well, that goes without saying." Tristan smiled. A yawn nearly split her jaw, hand coming up to cover her mouth. "Sorry." She shook her head as if trying to wake herself up.

"Okay, I need to get ready for work. You," Ashton said, leaning over and leaving a lingering kiss on soft lips. "Get some sleep."

She grabbed her hand and led her to the bedroom. She hadn't made the bed yet, as she knew Tristan would be coming home from her two a.m. shift at the bakery, and pulled the blankets back on Tristan's side. She removed Tristan's clothing, piece by piece, doing her level best not to ogle the beauty before her.

With Tristan in just her jeans, socks, and boots, Ashton softly ordered her to sit on the bed. When she complied, Ashton lowered herself to a knee, placing each booted foot on her thigh to unlace and pull off, setting them aside before removing her socks. She rose and tugged Tristan back to her feet and, with a quick kiss to her lips, reached down and unbuttoned her jeans, sliding her hands down past Tristan's waist and pushing both denim and panties down together.

Tristan stepped out of the clothing, leaving her naked. Ashton reached up and as gently as possible tugged her hair free of its ponytail. She tossed the hairband to the bedside table and returned her hands to the long, soft auburn locks, gingerly fingering them as they fell down around Tristan's shoulders.

She had truly never seen a woman so beautiful in all her life. It didn't matter what she was doing—playing the vixen Pearl, doing laundry, just waking up or making love—Tristan was stunning.

Forcing herself to behave, Ashton guided Tristan to climb into the large bed so she could tuck her in. Tristan clearly had other ideas as she wrapped her arms around Ashton's neck and pulled her down with her.

Ashton's hands flew out to brace herself so she didn't crush the other woman, who grinned up at her. Before she could say anything, she was taken in a deep kiss, which was so easy to fall into, even as she knew she needed to pull away and let Tristan sleep so she could get ready for work.

Those thoughts were pushed clear out of her head as Tristan's hands shoved at Ashton's panties, pushing them down as far as she could before murmuring, "Off," into the kiss. Using their feet, together they got her panties off and Tristan spread her thighs as Ashton settled her hips between them.

Eyes closing as Ashton broke from the kiss and raised herself to her hands, she began to move against Tristan in short, quick, focused thrusts that sent intense pleasure straight from her clit to blossom throughout her entire body. From Tristan's heavy breathing and little whimpers, she knew she was feeling the same. The intensity of the pleasure as well as intimacy brought from the position had made it a favorite for them.

It didn't take long before they were both taken over the edge, seemingly simultaneously from the way Tristan gripped Ashton with painful talons for fingers right as Ashton orgasmed. Panting heavily, she lowered herself down to Tristan, who wrapped her up in a tight hug.

"Would this be that access to you that you mentioned?" Tristan murmured into the hug, her voice breathy.

Ashton chuckled and nodded. "Yes, yes it would."

Lifting her head, Ashton expected to see a smile on Tristan's lips from her comment, but instead she was very serious, though her expression was soft. There was something in her eyes that Ashton had not seen before. Tristan brought up a hand, fingers soft as they caressed Ashton's face, before the expression was gone and her hand dropped away.

"You better get going," Tristan murmured. "It's Thursday, and I know you have meetings today."

Ashton nodded, leaving a lingering kiss on soft lips. "I do." One last kiss and she moved off Tristan, her body still buzzing from the unexpected experience. She also realized she needed another shower. She didn't think it was a wise idea waltzing into a meeting smelling like sex.

"I work tonight," Tristan said, her voice growing soft and dreamy. "So, I won't be here when you get home."

"Okay," Ashton said, reaching down and pulling the covers up to cover Tristan, who rolled onto her side and curled up into her favorite sleeping position. "You be safe."

"I will," Tristan promised, her eyes growing hooded. "I'll make sure something's waiting for you to eat when you get home," she slurred, eyes finally drifting shut. "Promise you'll eat."

"I promise," Ashton whispered, leaning down and leaving a lingering kiss to her forehead. "Good night, baby."

"Can I see that one, please?" Ashton asked. "No, the one to the right. Yes, that one."

She watched as the sales lady retrieved her requested item, carefully removing it from the display case. The chain was delicate gold, and the length would allow the small apple, made of ruby and tiny diamonds for the stem, to hit the wearer at the hollow of the throat.

"This is really beautiful," Ashton murmured, leaning over the glass case to get a better look. It was easy to imagine that on a certain former teacher's neck. She glanced up at the saleslady. "I'll take it."

"Wonderful. Shall I wrap it up as a gift?"

"Please." Ashton reached into the deep pocket of her peacoat and produced her wallet.

Purchase taken care of and wrapped gift in a bag reflecting the jewelry store's logo, Ashton left the store and headed into the wide hallway of the Cherry Creek Mall set in one of the wealthier, high-end parts of Denver. Ashton didn't like being there. Despite her monied roots, those who saw money as their identity turned her off.

The only reason she was in the area at all was that she wanted to meet with the store manager of their newest brick-and-mortar location for King-Kraft Chocolate, except this one was the first to carry Top Shelf products. She wanted to see how sales were and if was a hit outside of the coffee shop and bar atmosphere.

Noting she still had a few minutes to spare before their appointed meeting time, she headed downstairs to get a mocha breve at the Starbucks kiosk. Standing in line, she was about to check her schedule on her phone when she stopped. Looking up, she glanced around to see if she'd accidentally cut in line in front of someone, as she felt she was being watched.

Turning to look around, she saw nobody but random shoppers, a couple women passing by chatting, neither one of them even glancing her way. The hair on her arms began to stand up, a prickly sensation of anxiety finger-walking up her spine. She turned to look the other way, accidentally bumping into the guy standing in line in front of her.

"Sorry," she murmured to him with a small smile before stepping out of line as she suddenly felt very trapped.

Stepping away from the kiosk, Ashton scanned the area again, the large hallway echoing laughter from somewhere above, ambient music piped throughout the mall while other music bled from individual stores.

She gasped when she heard something to her right. A bunch of boxes went tumbling off a shelf at an unmanned cart filled with sunglasses for sale, the pricy eyewear locked in clear cases while boxes and packages of accessories were stacked upon the shelves. Looking around, she didn't see anybody suspicious. Walking over to the kiosk, she knelt down and picked up the boxes, placing them back on the shelf.

From underneath the high-sitting cart she noticed the lower half of a pair of denim-clad legs, a pair of worn, brown cowboy boots on the feet. The pointed toes of the boots denoted the person was looking her way. She was distracted when she heard a loud gaggle of teenage girls getting close.

Pushing to her feet, she expected to see the owner of the legs to be standing there looking at her, but the swarm of girls swept through like locusts, blocking out anything but them. Reaching up, Ashton rubbed the back of her neck, feeling ill at ease. She decided to start heading toward their storefront on the upper level of the mall, hoping that leaving the main level would help calm her nerves. With one final look around, she turned and headed for the escalator.

Feeling a little better once she reached the floor she needed, she headed toward the store when she got a text from the manager letting her know she was stuck in traffic and running a few minutes late. Deciding to hit the ladies' room then, Ashton turned off into a hallway where the public restrooms were.

The stall doors were those that swung closed on their own once opened, so it looked as though each stall was in use. Looking down under the length of stalls, she realized she was alone, so picked the farthest stall from the door and closed and locked it behind her.

She'd reached down to unfasten her trousers when her hands froze. The door to the bathroom was slowly being pushed open, hinges squeaking, then a thud as the heavy door was released to shut on its own. She stood there, listening. It wasn't remotely an unusual thing for a woman to enter the ladies' room, but Ashton felt her hair stand up again.

She tried to look between the crack between the door and stall frame, but it was too narrow, so she slowly bent down, silently cursing when her knees popped. Old car accident injury from her twenties. Looking under the stall door, she nearly gasped when she saw the cowboy boots that she'd seen downstairs.

Hand going to her mouth, her nerves returned tenfold. She slowly pushed to her feet as quietly as possible. She looked down at the lock, considering disengaging it and stepping out, but that same feeling she'd had downstairs told her to stay put. So, she listened, nearly holding her breath.

With slow precision, the boots walked along the row of stall doors, the boot heels thudding dully against the tile. Ashton started when she heard a stall door shoved open, the door banging against the wall behind it. More steps, then the next door was shoved open.

As silently as possible, Ashton pulled her phone out of her pocket, looking down at the black screen as she considered calling the police. But then it occurred to her, to say what? *I have a weird feeling about some person wearing cowboy boots, can you please come save me?* Rolling her eyes at her own predicament, she lifted her hand to reach for the lock when, again, something told her not to.

Her phone chirped to life, alerting her to an incoming text message, the sudden sound nearly giving her a heart attack. She pressed the button to silence the phone, but it was too late. The booted steps slowly made their way to her stall, the person stopping just on the other side of the closed door. She could see only the tips of the cowboy boots before they disappeared, the footfalls leading back toward the bathroom door, which opened and slowly closed again.

# Chapter Twenty

Brian stared at her, mouth open and, though it seemed he was trying, nothing was coming out. Ashton grinned. "There's a sentence in there just dying to get out."

He burst into laughter, which seemed partially a valve release. "Wow, Ashton," he finally said, a hand resting against his stomach. "I knew taking the London job was a promotion of sorts that would come with perks, but I honestly didn't realize that being named President of the entire company would be one of those."

She grinned from where she sat on the other side of the desk that had once belonged to her father but now she had claimed at the King-Kraft headquarters in their Denver offices. "Yes, well, I've taken the time to really look into your numbers and performance during your time here," she explained. "Stellar, Brian. Truly stellar. Plus, the face you've given our brand, your dedication and loyalty to it. And," she added, pulling open a drawer in the desk and retrieving a pile of handwritten pages that had been found among her father's files after his death. She slapped the stack onto the desk. "All notes about you from my father."

Brian's eyes widened as he took in the pile.

Ashton set her elbows on the desk and laced her fingers before resting her chin on them. "My father may have lacked in parental skills, but he had a hell of an eye for talent, and I trust that." She indicated the lavish praise Jack King had felt the need to commit to paper. "He saw you as the son he lost twenty years ago. So..." She shrugged, dropping her hands and sitting back in the comfortable leather chair, which creaked as she shifted. "I thought it was only right to give you the position I think he would have liked to see you in."

He nodded, clearing his throat as he ran a hand over his closely cropped blond hair. "That means a lot, Ashton. Thank you."

"There will be a ton of traveling for you, so get your bags ready," she said with a smile, getting to her feet and extending her hand across the desk. "Congratulations, Brian."

He also stood, taking her hand in a firm grip. "Thank you, Ashton. This is something else."

After they shook hands, she came from around the desk and walked him to the door, resting her hand on his back. "It's a new adventure, my friend," she said. "I'll get all the contracts and everything drawn up both for King-Kraft Creations and for your new position in the Ivory Tower." She smiled.

"Hey, now," he said, hand on the door handle of her office. "I was upset that day and didn't think upper management was hearing me."

She raised her eyebrow. "And what do you think now?"

"Don't know," he hedged. "Tell you once I get my office up there."

She chuckled. "Promises, promises." She took the door from him when he pulled it open, holding it open for him to leave. "Talk to you soon," she said, then closed the door behind him.

She was returning to her desk when her phone rang Tristan's ringtone. A smile instantly came to her lips. She picked up the cell from the desk. "Hey, you," she said into the phone, smiling at the greeting she got. She listened and Tristan explained her issue. "Of course. I can cut out of her in just a few minutes. Good timing, actually. Just finished up with Brian..." Her eyebrows fell. "Are you okay?" She opened the desk drawer and gathered her wallet and keys. "Absolutely. I'll stop at the house to change clothes and pick you up, okay?...Martin found you boxes? Wonderful. Okay, see you soon." She smiled. "Nowhere else I'd rather be...Okay, yes, I'd rather be there, and since you're not working tonight, I imagine I will be. But, for the time being...See you soon. Bye."

Using her teeth to remove the Sharpie cap from the marker, Ashton held it in place as she wrote on the taped box what was inside. Recapping it, she got to her feet. Hands on hips, she looked around the small living room and dining nook area. It was filled with boxes. They'd worked together to take the bookcases, a few of them damaged from the break-in, to the dumpster, the others left nearby for a resident of the complex to utilize.

The only furniture remaining was the couch and the bedroom furniture. She headed into the bedroom where Tristan was finishing up boxing her belongings, more books, knickknacks, and other odds and ends that had been in the closet.

"How goes it?" she asked, looking around. The bed had been taken apart, the mattress, bedframe, and headboard leaning up against the wall. All of Tristan's clothing and personal items had been taken to the house once it was determined that Tristan would be staying, even if for a short time, before she'd made the decision to move into one of the suites.

"Well," Tristan said, also looking around before meeting Ashton's gaze. "Just about done. The movers should be here any minute." She let out a slow, nervous sigh. "How about out there?" she asked, nodding toward the living room.

"Good news is, everything is packed. Bad news is, three books were destroyed when whoever trashed the bookcase. Broken spines."

"Bastard," she muttered.

"Sorry, baby." Ashton walked over to her and hugged her from behind. She nuzzled the side of Tristan's neck, left bare and totally tempting with the long, auburn hair pulled back into a ponytail. Tristan covered her hands, clasped at her waist, with her own. "Still okay with everything?"

Tristan nodded. "I am. I'm not sad leaving this place, to be honest." She turned in the circle of Ashton's arms and snaked her arms up around her neck, hands playing lightly in her hair. "I only came here to sleep." She shook her head. "No heart here."

Ashton's hands settled on Tristan's shapely, denim-clad behind. She'd never known anyone who could wear jeans quite like her little fireball. She had a body made for sin. And jeans.

"How are you feeling about everything?" Ashton asked softly, making a point to check in every so often to make sure Tristan was okay with the massive changes happening in her life. She didn't want anything to sneak up on either of them.

"I'm okay," she said, a soft smile on her lips. "I'm nervous, won't lie about that." She looked up into Ashton's eyes, her own a bit guarded. "I'm grateful that you're giving me time to ease into things. I like you, Ashton. I really, really do."

Ashton studied her face, her eyes, and she could swear she saw something in those eyes that matched what was in her own heart, something she dared not put words to. "I like you, too."

Something passed between them in that moment, something deep and terrifyingly beautiful. Tristan looked away, clearing her throat as she stepped out of Ashton's personal space. Hugging herself, she moved to the other side of the stack of boxes, effectively placing them between them.

"It's been nice not having to work at the bakery anymore, I have to admit," she said with a small laugh.

"Oh, I bet." Ashton shoved her hands into the back pockets of her jeans to quell her temptation to reach for the other woman. "Listen, I know you're working at the club because there you can make the money for your sister's care," Ashton began slowly. "But you don't have to do that. I can help—"

"No." Tristan walked back over to her, looking sternly into her eyes. "No." She took Ashton's hand like she was trying to remove the sting from her tone. "Listen, I know that I essentially came into your life because you…" She shrugged with a rueful grin. "You basically bought me. But I don't want that now. Your money is your money, Ashton. It's not why I'm here, and I never want it to be why I'm here."

Ashton wanted to dispute Tristan's thoughts on her intentions, and had opened her mouth to do so, when a man's voice interrupted them.

"Tristan O'Toole?" he asked, glancing at the clipboard he held, the logo stitched on his work shirt indicating he was from the moving company.

"Yes, that's me," Tristan said stepping away from Ashton.

"Great. Let's get started."

---

"Here you are, my dear," he said, placing a crystal tumbler in front of her. "My latest batch. Tell me what you think."

Ashton set her mask aside on the desk and took the glass. The aroma from the liquid inside was so strong, she could smell it from where she sat. Blinking rapidly, she felt it in her nostrils. "That is strong, Buck."

He chuckled, raising his own glass. "It is. This is just a sample of what I'm looking to do. Some more ideas for Top Shelf." He studied her. "Tell me what you smell."

"Butane?" she said, sparing him a glance. She smiled at the burst of laughter that erupted from his mouth.

"Being a bit dramatic, aren't we?" he quipped.

She grinned, getting serious as she brought it to her nose. "Peppermint." She glanced up at him. "Right?"

He nodded. "Yes. Peppermint and chocolate are divine together, so I figured…" He shrugged. "What the hell?" He held out his glass, which she clinked hers against. "Cheers."

She brought the glass to her lips and took a sip. After the initial burn passed from the strong liquor, she was pleasantly surprised. "It's a hell of a lot smoother than I expected."

"See?" he exclaimed, raising a bushy eyebrow. "This could make a wonderful Saint Paddy's Day treat."

Ashton took another small sip, just enough to get the taste on her tongue again. She plugged in his suggestion while tasting and definitely could see it. She nodded. "That's a great idea. Perhaps some sort of snack size that melts in your mouth or something."

"Love that. This one, of course, isn't aged like our normal barrels, but I wanted to see what you thought." Buck finished his drink, placed the tumbler on the desk, and stared at her. "This is one reason I called you to come down, but I also wanted to give you my congratulations, Ashton. Personally, though I had my doubts, I think Jack made the right decision."

"Thank you, Buck. What were your doubts about?" she asked, setting her tumbler on the desk, two fingers of liquid still in it.

"That your father would actually *make* the right decision," he clarified.

"You mean, leaving everything to me?"

He nodded. "He tossed around a few ideas over the last year or so. Though that stroke hit him fast and hard, I think somewhere inside he knew it was coming."

Though not terribly surprised, it didn't mean it didn't hurt that she, his only living child, wasn't the first and obvious choice. But then, what else was new? "Who did he consider?" she asked. "Besides me."

Buck shrugged, reaching for the bottle and pouring himself some more. He glanced over at her glass with a raised eyebrow.

"I have to drive home," she said with a grin.

He nodded. "True, true." He recorked the bottle and set it aside. "The usual suspects," he said. "Bart Hinton, Mesa Cragg, Brian Lewis, hell, even Judith Winslow."

She shook her head. "What was he thinking with that one? Judith Winslow doesn't know her ass from a hole in the ground."

He chuckled, sipping his bourbon. "I know many people I can say that about."

"Amen," Ashton agreed. "So, you said you already spoke with Brian about this?"

"I did. He's on board as well, so the three of us are in agreement, and I say let's get some workups. Brian has all my recipes and access so he can get things started here before he heads abroad. Make it a lot easier on whoever takes his place."

"Excellent." Ashton pushed to her feet, grabbing her mask. "Well, I need to get going, Buck. I have an early start tomorrow."

Buck set his glass down and stood. He met her next to his desk and gave her a tight hug. "I'm proud of you," he said, business forgotten for a moment as the longtime friend of her father emerged. He smiled at her, squeezing her shoulder. "Jack made the right choice," he said once again.

Ashton felt her heart swell at his sincere words. "Thank you," she murmured. His confidence in her felt good, a warm ray of respect and approval, hard-won and nary a hint of it from the man she'd needed it from while he was alive.

Ashton walked to the door of the lavish office, pausing to put her mask in place before pulling the door open and leaving. She could hear the muted voices of the members chatting among themselves as well as the soft underlying tones of the music coming from the baby grand in the corner, a tuxedoed man sitting behind the Steinway.

She knew Tristan was working that night and had weighed whether she should bother her at work or not. She'd love any opportunity to spend time with her, but the woman had a job to do. Which, by what Ashton spotted, was exactly what she was doing.

Standing near a grouping of chairs, Tristan chatted easily with the three men there, two seated and one standing next to her, his hand almost possessive as it rested at her lower back, just at the start of the swell of her behind. She was amicable with the men, the lilt of her laughter flowing through the space and straight to Ashton's heart.

As their discussion continued, Tristan turned to the man she stood next to, laughing anew at something he said as she placed her hand on his chest, quite comfortable with him. His hand fell to her ass, giving it a little pat.

Ashton felt her body grow warm, then downright hot. Her heart raced, the throb increasing in her temples and throat. She knew she had zero right to say anything nor feel the way she was feeling. Even so, she began to feel nauseous. Turning, she hurried toward the curtain and stairs, making her way down them as quickly as her high heels would allow her to go.

Bursting out into the cool spring night, she reached up and yanked off her mask, feeling the night air on her face as she sucked it into her lungs. Her heated skin felt like it had been splashed with ice water, jarring her back into reality.

She took several deep breaths as she reached

into her jacket and retrieved her keys. She was about to pick her car key out of the collection on the ring when something caught her attention.

Looking across the street, she saw movement in the darkened alley between two three-story brick buildings. She felt the same feeling as at the mall—she was being watched. Still feeling out of sorts from experience inside, this time she didn't feel afraid: she was pissed.

"Who's there?" she called out.

She saw someone peek out of the shadows and recognized him as the man she'd seen months ago in that very place. As he stepped farther into view, she saw the same shaggy hair, though now his beard had grown out more. He wore an ill-fitted sweater, jeans, and worn cowboy boots, which made her heart stop.

"Hey!" she exclaimed, hurrying across the street. "What's your deal?"

He stared at her for a moment longer, then ducked into the shadows.

"Hey! Come back here, you son of a bitch!" she yelled, reaching the sidewalk. He'd vanished, though she could hear movement down the alley by the trash bin.

"What do you want?" a man's voice said from the shadows.

"Why were you following me?" she responded, taking a step into the darkness. "What's your problem? You get off on stalking women?"

"Fuck you," he said, though his voice was farther away now.

She stopped, realizing he could be trying to lead her deeper into the shadows where she'd be in a tremendous amount of trouble. Looking around with a quick glance over her shoulder to the street beyond, she knew she needed to leave. Turning back to where the man had disappeared, she scanned the shadows to see if she could see him. He was gone.

"Bastard," she muttered, then hurried back the way she'd come.

# Chapter Twenty-one

"Okay, sorry to keep you waiting, ladies," the detective said as he stepped into the small interrogation room where Ashton and Tristan had been directed by a uniformed officer. The man sat down in a dress shirt and tie, which he smoothed down as he sat across from the two women. He glanced at both and nodded a greeting. "I'm Detective Weiss, and I called you in to give you an update on your case, Miss O'Toole," he said to Tristan.

"Okay," Tristan said, reaching under the table to grab Ashton's hand, who laced their fingers together.

"Now, first I have to ask," he said, tossing a folder onto the table. "Do you know a man by the name of Albert Vallejo?"

"No," Tristan said, shaking her head. "Never heard of him."

Ashton said nothing, as it wasn't her case, but she, too, had never heard of him. So, she remained quiet, simply there for moral support.

"Okay," he said, flipping open the folder, which held several pages and a color mug shot. He took the picture and tossed it out onto the table in front of Tristan. "Ever seen this guy before?"

Ashton leaned over to get a look and gasped, garnering the attention of both the others. She stared into the cold, empty dark eyes that stared back at her. He was younger, with no facial hair, and his hair was slicked back from his face, but it was him. "I've seen him before," she said, tapping the picture with a finger. She glanced up at the detective. "Twice. But I suspect he also may have been following me one day at the Cherry Creek Mall."

"Ashton." Tristan gasped. "Why didn't you tell me?"

"I didn't want to scare you," Ashton responded.

"Where did you see him, ma'am?" Weiss asked.

Ashton turned her focus back to him. "Outside of The Black Pussy Cat club."

"Do you have a connection to that club, Miss O'Toole?"

Looking stricken at the information she'd learned, Tristan nodded. "I work there."

"And, do you work there as well?" he asked Ashton.

"No, but I've been there because the owner has business with my company." She tapped the picture again before pushing it back across the table toward him. "Who is this guy?"

"Bad news," Detective Weiss said, grabbing the picture and placing it back inside the folder. "He's no stranger to us. Drugs, domestic violence, indecent exposure, assault, you name it." He looked at Tristan. "He's also involved in the break-in of your apartment. His DNA and his fingerprints were found there." He looked to Ashton, pulling a pen from his shirt pocket and clicking it to life. "When did you last see him?"

"Thursday, around nine, nine fifteen at night," Ashton responded. She could feel Tristan's gaze on her, no doubt confused as to why she'd been there. "I chased him into the alleyway across the street."

The detective stopped jotting down notes, pen

still poised over the paper. "You did what?"

"Not wise, I understand that. I was angry at him for scaring me."

He finished his notes, then dropped the pen on the pad of paper and sat back in the chair, eyeing them. "We're looking for this guy. Do you have somewhere else you can stay until we get this taken care of, ma'am?" he asked Tristan.

"I've already moved out," she said. "My lease isn't up until May, but I no longer live there."

"Excellent." He slapped the folder closed and gathered it and his notepad as he shoved away from the table. "And you," he said, pointing at Ashton. "No more chasing this guy. Call us to do the heavy lifting."

Ashton gave him a sheepish grin. "Yes, sir."

In silence, the two women made their way out of the police station and to Tristan's car. It wasn't until they were securely belted that Tristan looked over at her, Ashton meeting her gaze.

"Why didn't you tell me? I know you said you didn't want to scare me, but Ashton…"

Letting out a sigh, Ashton nodded. "I'm sorry," she said, leaning her head back against the head rest. "The first time I figured he was just a homeless guy or something. He was across the street from the club. Both times, actually."

"And, stalking you?" Tristan asked, eyes wide, a tremble in her voice.

Ashton cursed herself as she could tell the other woman was not only upset at the facts, but also with her for not saying anything. She reached over and took Tristan's hand. "The day I told you I had to meet Becky at the mall. He, well, I *think* it was him, was following me."

Tristan stared out the windshield for a long moment before she started the SUV and got them on the road. "You were at the club Thursday?"

"I had a meeting with Buck."

"Did you try and find me?" Tristan asked, confused hurt in her voice.

Ashton glanced out the window, a sting of the jealousy she'd felt coming back. "I did," she said. "But you were talking to some of the members, so I just left."

"What did I do wrong?" Tristan asked. "I can hear it in your voice, what didn't you like?"

Ashton glanced over at her, angry at herself for not hiding it better in her tone. She cleared her throat and reached up to adjust her sunglasses. "Nothing, Tristan. It was just strange seeing that guy there with his hand on your ass."

"Hand on my ass?" Tristan muttered as though trying to recall. "Oh! Shawn?"

Ashton shrugged. "I have no idea."

"Gray sport coat?"

"Yes. I believe so, yes."

"Yeah, that's his thing. He does it with all of us, baby," Tristan said, briefly glancing over at her passenger. "It's nothing personal toward me, and certainly not *to* me."

Ashton didn't respond, afraid she'd say something really stupid and deeply unfair. So, she just glanced over at Tristan and gave her a smile. She should have known it wouldn't fool nor placate Tristan.

"This is my job, Ashton," she said, slowing as they neared a yellow traffic light, which turned red as the SUV came to a stop. "Of anyone, you know that."

Ashton glanced over at her. "What is that

supposed to mean?"

"It means that you know what my job is, we *met* at my job, for crying out loud." She studied Ashton as they sat at the red light. "Why are you acting like this? I mean, honestly, if it weren't for my job, me accepting the job *from* you, we wouldn't be here now."

Ashton looked away, feeling like a complete asshole. Angry at herself, she blindly reached over to find Tristan's hand, wrapping her fingers around it and resting their joined hands on her thigh. Nodding, she met Tristan's gaze. "Yes. I'm sorry. That was the first time I'd been in there since we've been together. It was hard."

"Are we?"

The question confused Ashton, but then she realized what she'd said. "Is that what you want?"

Tristan grinned and shook her head. "That's not what I asked."

"Fine," Ashton blew out dramatically. "Yes. That's what I'd like." She studied Tristan's profile as the redhead got the Rav4 moving again when the light turned green. "What about you?"

Tristan was quiet for so long, it began to make Ashton nervous. She was just chastising herself for being so vulnerable when Tristan finally spoke. "I have to be honest with you," she said softly, her voice faraway and almost wistful. "I never thought I'd want to get involved again." She shook her head, not looking at Ashton. "Never thought I'd be able to. But yes." She finally met Ashton's gaze. "Yes, I want that, too. With you." She gave her a brilliant smile, which Ashton returned.

Ashton studied the machine that wrapped individual pieces in foil stamped with the company logo. Instead of processing thousands of candies per hour, it sat silent and still. Tapping her chin with her finger, she shook her head. "Damn." Turning to the man waiting for instructions, she said, "Okay. I guess we've nickel and dimed this bad boy long enough. I'll authorize a new machine."

"Excellent. Great news, Miss King."

"Get with Carmen in Acquisitions and cc me on everything," she instructed.

He nodded, jotting down what she'd said. "Yes, ma'am. Will do." With a curt nod, he scurried off to work on his given task.

She also turned and began to walk away from the dead machine when she got a text alert. Slowing her pace, she brought up her phone and looked down at the incoming message:

*Tristan: We need to talk. Meet me at the house.*

Ashton's stomach dropped to her feet and her heart jumped up into her throat. It was the first of the month, and she knew this would be coming. Not for the first time, she hated herself for being such a coward. Taking a deep breath, she replied simply:

*Ashton: On my way.*

The drive home seemed to take forever. Her heart was racing and she went over and over again in her head how to deal with what she assumed was about to happen. If it wasn't, she was coming up with a way to talk to Tristan about what she'd done. Either way, it was time to come clean.

The Rav4 was parked out front, so Ashton brought her car to a stop and cut the engine. Unbuckling herself, she grabbed her keys and phone and, with a deep breath, headed inside. Martin informed her that Tristan said she'd meet her in Ashton's bedroom.

Making her way to her suite, she saw that the sitting room door had been left ajar. Shrugging out of her winter coat, she unbuttoned her blazer as she continued into the bedroom.

Tristan stood at the window, looking out. She was in yoga pants and a long-sleeved T-shirt, hair back in a ponytail. Her casual attire made Ashton's stomach drop again, as she knew that's how she dressed on her days spent with Christine, so she could be comfortable to help Tanisha and the other staff with her sister.

Ashton tossed the blazer to the bed when she heard Tristan's voice break the painful silence.

"Why is it not important to you what I think? What I feel? What I say?"

Ashton stood by the two wingback chairs near the cold fireplace, keeping distance between them. "It is. Very important."

Tristan whirled away from the window, eyes on fire. "Then why did you do it?"

"I wanted to help you," Ashton said simply.

"Help me? Helping somebody is handing them the coffee cup from the cabinet by your head. Throwing a load of laundry in while I'm at work. Not paying for an entire fucking year of care for my sister!" She paced away from the window, her agitation clear as day. Ashton could feel it rolling off her in waves. "And, after we talked about this, Ashton," she continued, turning to look at the silent woman. "We fucking *talked* about this!"

"I did it before we had that conversation, Tristan," Ashton said, attempting, as lame as it was, to defend herself.

"When did you pay it?" Tristan demanded.

"Not long after we got back from England."

"What? And you didn't tell me?"

"I know," Ashton said, running a hand through her hair. "I'm sorry. I should have, and I understand why you're upset." She looked at Tristan, hoping against hope she'd understand. "My heart was in the right place, Tristan."

"And, what's that?" Tristan asked, hands on her hips, head slightly cocked to the side. "To find another way to buy me? Pay for services rendered?" She stared Ashton down. "How am I supposed to repay this?"

Stunned, Ashton could only stare at her. She was shocked and deeply hurt that that was what Tristan took from her actions. "I..." Utterly lost for words, she turned, needing to put a bit more distance between them, but Tristan was going to have none of it.

"If that's what you want," she said between clenched teeth as she reached Ashton. "Then that's what you'll get."

"Tristan, what are you doing?"

Before she could stop her, Tristan had Ashton pushed up against a wall, her body holding Ashton there while one of her hands tore at the clasp and zipper of her pants.

"Tristan—"

Ashton's words were cut off by the savage kiss Tristan delivered as she shoved her hand down inside the pants and panties. Ashton reeled as those deft fingers found their way to her most sensitive place, Tristan knowing exactly what to do to get her wet and ready, which was happening even as she willed it not to. This wasn't the way she wanted to be with Tristan, not in the middle of an argument, but her body was conditioned to respond to anything Tristan did, and she was helpless to derail it. She gasped as two fingers entered her, thrusting with firm, deep strokes while her thumb rubbed her clit with every thrust.

Both breathing hard, the kiss ended but Tristan didn't move away, the two sharing breath as finally, Ashton cried out as the orgasm was ripped from her body. With tears in her eyes, Tristan removed her hand and stepped back from Ashton.

"Consider this the first repayment remitted," she whispered, then turned and left the room, closing the door softly behind her.

Ashton slowly slid to the floor, the tears coming quick and hard just like her release had, which her body still rocked from. She buried her face in her hands, unable to control her emotions as they seeped between her fingers.

After what seemed like an hour but was likely only ten minutes or so, the tears slowed and finally stopped. Her face felt tight, eyes burning. On shaky legs, she got to her feet, feeling dirty, guilty, and so afraid that she'd lost Tristan. Pushing her hair back with her hands, she walked over to the table between the chairs and grabbed a tissue from the box, wiping at her eyes and face before grabbing a second to blow her nose.

Later that night, Ashton lay in bed alone. Her stomach had given her fits all evening from anxiety and upset. After their week together in England and then the weeks they'd been back, this was her first night without Tristan by her side. Though Tristan had wanted her own suite of rooms in the house, somehow they'd always managed to find their way together into one or the other's bed at night.

Used to a solitary life, Ashton wasn't one who often felt lonely, but in that moment, she felt like she was the only living person left on the planet. She had no best friend to talk it out with. No family to speak of to get advice from. The one person she craved wanted nothing to do with her, and she was profoundly angry at herself for how she'd handled herself. She was profoundly sorry that she'd not just been honest from the start.

Yet again, the tears came. As she stared up at the ceiling, she allowed them to flow down the sides of her face, saturating the hair at her temples.

# *Chapter Twenty-two*

Ashton stood at the Keurig coffeemaker, waiting for her cup to finish brewing, the large kitchen scented with chocolate-covered cherry coffee. She braced her hands against the counter, waiting.

"Hey."

Glancing over her shoulder, she was surprised to see Tristan standing there. A smile spread over her lips, She hadn't spoken to nor seen her since the day of the ugly confrontation, which was three days before.

"Hi," she responded, angry at herself for the hope she couldn't quite keep out of her voice. "Want a cup?" she asked, tapping the coffeemaker.

Tristan glanced at it, then back to Ashton from where she stood across the room. "No, I have to go. I have an appointment."

Ashton nodded, noting her casual dress. She hoped like hell it wasn't to look at another place to live, but she said nothing.

"Um, I usually don't work Mondays, as you know, but Lisa asked me to switch with her, so I just wanted to let you know." She shrugged, looking a bit uncomfortable. "Didn't want you to worry or anything."

Ashton nodded in acknowledgment. "Okay. Thanks for telling me. Supposed to snow tonight. Want me to ask Dekayas to pick you up? The bad weather doesn't bother him."

"No, but thank you, though." She gave her a small smile then turned as if to leave but stopped, turning back to Ashton. "Why aren't you at work today?"

Ashton looked down for a moment before glancing back up. "Not feeling very well," she said quietly.

Tristan met and held her gaze for a moment before nodding and turning away. "I hope you feel better," she said softly.

"Tristan?" Ashton said. "I'm sorry."

The redhead met her gaze for a long moment, her own looking sad and tired. "We'll talk another day," she murmured, then hurried out of the room.

Ashton watched her go, wanting so badly to run after her and beg her to stay or let her go, too. Instead, she remained where she was, turning to fix her cup of coffee.

Ashton started, eyes blinking several times. Looking around, she realized she'd fallen asleep with the TV on as she was slumped over on the couch in the second-floor entertainment room. Pushing herself up from where her head rested against the arm of the couch, she winced, her neck and back arguing with her life choices. It was then that she saw what had woken her.

On the TV screen was a scene of hellish proportions. It was the local news and the night was filled with police and fire sirens. The night sky was ablaze. She was wide awake as she looked at the screen. She was startled when her cell phone began to ring.

It was Brian. "Hello?" She was surprised by the panic in his voice. "Wait, wait. What?" She nearly flew off the couch as she stared at the screen. It was then that she recognized it. "Jesus Christ! I gotta go."

She ended the call as she ran to her bedroom suite, tugging on a pair of tennis shoes, not caring that she was wearing flannel pajama pants. She threw on her jacket, grabbed her car keys, and was gone.

The entire block was filled with emergency vehicles, from police cars to ambulances to fire trucks. A few news vans peppered the side streets, reporters out with their microphones and cameras to document what was happening.

As she pulled up to the barricade that had been erected, an ambulance raced from the scene, lights flashing and sirens screaming. It was apocalyptic, the brick building an inferno. She opened her door and stepped out of the car, unable to take her eyes off the building she'd come to know so well.

She stood at the open car door, crying out in surprise, as did many on site, as there was an explosion from the second floor. Her heart racing, Ashton moved away from her car to look for Tristan, praying to anything upstairs that she'd escaped.

Among the emergency personnel, she saw a few of the people who worked in the club, though it was strange to see many of them without their masks. However, the man she was headed toward, a bartender judging by his clothing, wore a mask in reverse. His face was covered in soot except for the area his mask had covered before being removed. He had a few scraps on his face, and his tuxedo jacket was torn along the left side.

"Have you seen Tristan?" she asked him,

hollering over the horrific roar of the blaze.

He met her gaze. “Who?”

“Pearl! Have you seen Pearl?”

He shook his head.

Moving on, Ashton took in the woman lying on the ground and the firefighter who was desperately trying to save her life with CPR. It was clear the woman wasn’t Tristan. She saw people from neighboring buildings huddled together watching the carnage from the sidewalk on the opposite side of the street.

Noticing a couple women who were holding each other, both dressed in torn, soot-streaked evening gowns, she hurried over to them, startling them when she grabbed one by the arm that she could have sworn was Tristan. It wasn’t.

“Pearl?” she asked, beginning to feel panicked as she was seeing fewer and fewer of the people who worked at the club.

“I don’t know,” one said, tears leaving a skin-tone trail through the soot. “Last I saw her she was upstairs.” The other woman held her tighter as the tears began anew.

Too panicked to stay and offer her comfort, Ashton moved on, looking at every face she passed, even if she knew it couldn’t be who she was desperately trying to find. What was disconcerting was, every time she’d been at the club, there were at least two dozen employees between waitstaff and the ladies, as well as anywhere from twenty to fifty members. She could only count perhaps a dozen recognizable employees based upon their dress, and perhaps a handful of members.

“Ma’am, you need to leave,” a police officer said, stopping Ashton in her frantic search. “This is not safe."

"I'm looking for Tristan O'Toole," she said to him. "Have you seen—" She interrupted her own question when she looked over his shoulder.

Squatting next to a huddled figure sitting on the ground was a paramedic, their back to Ashton. Her heart was telling her to go over there. Pushing past the officer, she ran to the two figures.

"Tristan?"

The paramedic glanced up at her over her shoulder, nearly pushed backward on her butt when the figure she'd been tending to popped up, throwing herself at Ashton. She was trembling, holding on to Ashton as though her life depended on it.

"Oh my god," Ashton whispered into her hair, which was all over the place and smelled of smoke. "Thank god." She pushed Tristan away enough to look her over, her hands cupping Tristan's tear-, soot-, and blood-streaked face. "Oh baby. Are you okay?" She could see a cut up near the hairline that didn't look like it needed stitches but was bleeding pretty good, as all head wounds did.

"You can take her home, miss," the paramedic said, standing and stepping over to them. "She doesn't need to be checked at the hospital but is really shaken up."

Ashton spared a glance at the woman before nodding and looking back to Tristan. "Okay." She gently ran her hand over Tristan's hair. "Okay."

They headed to the car, an officer stopping them, letting Tristan know that she needed to stop by the police department when she could to give a statement. Agreeing, they continued on, reaching the car.

Ashton used gentle touches as she wiped off the blood as well as the silent tears that continued to roll down Tristan's cheeks. The warm spray of the overhead shower washed it all away. "I'm sorry, baby," she whispered when Tristan winced as Ashton apparently passed over a sensitive spot.

As she continued to gently clean Tristan's wounds, she felt Tristan's gaze on her. The damage seemed to be mostly superficial, though from the sorrow in her eyes, Ashton suspected they'd only just touched the surface of her wounds.

Meeting her gaze, Ashton asked softly, "What is it?"

"I love you, Ashton," Tristan whispered, never looking away from Ashton's eyes. "I really do. And, no, I'm not saying this because of what happened tonight," she added. "What happened tonight was a bitter reminder that life is so short, and it's imperative that we speak our truth."

Ashton's eyes closed as she leaned her head forward, resting her forehead against Tristan's, her hands cupping her beautiful face. She'd been fighting her own emotions since she'd arrived at the scene of the fire. But, hearing those sweet words, her heart threatened to burst.

"I love you, too."

Tristan let out a relieved breath, smiling before placing a lingering kiss on Ashton's lips. She took her in a long, full-body hug, the warm water falling over them.

Ashton awoke to the bed vibrating. Confused, she opened her eyes and took in the darkened bedroom. She had no idea what time it was, but it felt like early morning, two or three. After a moment, she realized that it was the woman who lay a foot away, her body shaking with her quiet sobs.

Rolling over to her side from her back, Ashton scooted over to Tristan, spooning her body to Tristan's warm nakedness. She held her close, saying nothing as Tristan continued to cry. She left a kiss on a pale shoulder.

Finally, Tristan began to calm. "I'm sorry if I woke you," she whispered, her voice nasally from the upset.

"Don't you dare apologize," Ashton said, pulling Tristan back even closer into her, their bodies nearly becoming one. She swore after a while, even their heartbeats began to sync.

"It started downstairs," Tristan said after a few minutes of silence. "I was on the third floor and the whole building was shaken. Such a loud boom."

"Was it a fire that hit the gas line or something?" Ashton asked softly, not sure how much Tristan would want to talk about such a traumatizing situation.

"I don't know," she responded. "It sounded like a bomb. Glasses fell off the tables, a clock fell off the wall." She pulled away from Ashton so she could turn over, pushing Ashton to her back and half lying on top of her. Ashton could sense her need to be as close as possible, so she wrapped her up in her arms and pulled the covers up. "I didn't know what had happened, so I went to head downstairs to the bar."

Ashton ran her fingers absently through Tristan's

hair, leaning her cheek against Tristan's forehead. "Then what?"

"It happened again," she whispered. "Nearly fell down the stairs." She readjusted her head on Ashton's shoulder, her hand resting on Ashton's rib cage, tucked up against the bottom of her left breast. "By the time I got to the second floor, the fire was horrible. So hot." She was silent for a long time. Finally, she continued, her voice even softer. "People were screaming. I turned around and ran back up the stairs. Lost my shoes," she said with a small laugh. "Cinderella. I told everyone upstairs what was happening, and the guys broke out a window."

They lay there in silence for a long moment, Ashton working out what she'd been told. Images of what she'd seen flashed before her mind's eye as she tried to imagine what it had been like from inside.

"Do you think it's that Vallejo guy?" Tristan asked, her voice soft in the quiet darkness.

Ashton was quiet for a long time, considering. She hadn't even thought of that, too caught up in the fact that she could have lost Tristan. "I don't know," she said at length. "I hope not. I hope he's not that crazy."

"Can I ask you something?" Tristan asked.

"Of course you can."

"Why did you pay that?" Tristan asked. There was no anger in her voice, no accusation, just a woman wanting to understand.

"Christine?" Ashton asked, to make sure they were on the same page.

"Yes."

"Because you'd been through enough. You've lost everything, including, it seemed to me, though correct me if I'm wrong, your own identity in a lot of ways. Then, after all that, you have to take on this horrible burden. I don't mean your sister, but the burden of trying to figure out how to keep you both above water." She left a kiss on her forehead. "You've been through enough,' she whispered against the soft skin.

Ashton padded into the kitchen after her morning shower, dressed in a robe with her hair wrapped in a towel. Tristan was making coffee. "Good morning," she said, stepping up behind the other woman and hugging her back against her. "I missed you this morning," she whispered into her hair.

"Good morning, baby," Tristan said, turning her head so they could share a morning kiss. "I'm sorry. I just couldn't sleep. I didn't want to bother you, so I went to my room to read." They shared a slow, lazy kiss before Tristan left a quick peck to Ashton's lips and turned her head back to focus on her task. "Want some?"

"I do," Ashton responded, moving away from Tristan and to the fridge to grab the coffee creamer. "Have you heard anything?"

"Lisa called me this morning. They're not sure on the death count yet, but Buck is dead, Ashton."

Ashton froze as she reached for the bottle of Irish Cream creamer, her breath stolen from her for a moment. Finally, she took a deep, shaky breath, then closed the fridge door as she removed the bottle.

"I'm sorry," Tristan murmured. "I know he was a family friend, not just a business associate."

Ashton nodded, feeling her insides go numb with shock. "I'm sorry for you, too," she managed. "He was your boss." She carried the creamer over to the massive island where Tristan met her, bringing her arms up around Ashton's neck and hugging her close.

"How did you find out?" Tristan asked into the hug. "How did you know to go down there?"

Ashton held her, burying her face in Tristan's neck. "I was just seeing it on TV when Brian called. He said even in England it was all over the news."

"I have to go down and talk to the police today." Tristan was quiet for a moment. Then, "Can I be a big baby and ask you to come with me?"

Ashton smiled. "You're not a big baby. I'll be happy to."

The Keurig gurgled and growled to a finish, alerting them both. Tristan pulled out of the hug and walked over to the machine, removing the finished cup and setting it on the island in front of Ashton before returning to make a second. "I haven't not had a job since I was fourteen," she murmured.

Ashton opened her mouth to say something then snapped it shut, only to open it again. "Can I make an offer?"

Tristan glanced over her shoulder at her, her eyebrow raised. "I'm listening."

"Why don't you take some time to figure out what you want," Ashton offered. "Let me worry about things for a while." She met Tristan's gaze and held it, giving her a smile.

Tristan turned back to the second cup of coffee, not saying anything for so long, Ashton really worried she'd stepped in it again. But finally, after the cup of coffee was finished brewing, she carried it over to the island and set it down. Hand on the cool marble, Tristan stared down into the black depths of the fresh coffee. Finally, she pushed the coffee cup over toward Ashton, who held the bottle of creamer.

Ashton glanced at her, a question in her eyes. "Can I help you?" she teased.

Tristan gave her a teasing look in return. "I guess we'll see, won't we?"

# Chapter Twenty-three

It was their third funeral that week, but by far the largest. Buck Reynolds was well-known in the community, as his many businesses hired hundreds in the Denver metro area. The nave of the church was filled with young people who worked as bus boys and waitresses, older people who had been cooking in his restaurants for years, and filled with what was left of the staff of The Black Pussy Cat. All of them still bore their scars from the incident, but the biggest scar—and hardest to see—was inside, reflected in the flat affect of their eyes.

Ashton had tried to give Tristan her space to deal with everything, but Tristan had been interested in none of it. She'd clung to Ashton, often crying in her arms at night. She'd not gone back to her own suite after that first morning. Ashton had done her level best to be there, even working shorter days to spend time with Tristan.

In all of the grief Tristan was experiencing, Ashton had yet to truly deal with her own. She knew it was coming and dreaded it when it crashed over her. For now, she sat next to Tristan in the pew, holding her right hand as Lisa, Tristan's friend and former coworker at the club, held her left.

It was a strange thing seeing the guys and gals of the club in the light of day dressed like normal people in mourning, no masks, no dark and dangerous makeup meant to seduce. These were everyday, average women and men, all of whom were now out of work.

They'd lost seven of their coworkers: five the night of, including Buck, and two more in the hospital later, as well as four of the members. The event had become a story of heroism and scandal. The members and employees were lauded as heroes for their actions that night, saving lives, yet the scandal raced across the nation when the type of business it was and the names of the rich and powerful men involved were revealed.

Buck had crossed all his T's and dotted his I's, so the club wasn't illegal on paper, though some of the ladies and male staff had taken their fortunes into their own hands. None of that was provable on the books, so no arrests were made.

The service ended and mourners began to meander and chat. Ashton stood with Tristan as the redhead talked to her former coworkers and friends, all of which Ashton found were wonderful women and men.

Glancing around, she noticed Brian and Pam, who were talking to some of those put on the Top Shelf team. "Baby," she said softly to Tristan. "Sorry to interrupt," she added to the group. "I'll be right back. I need to talk to Brian for a minute, okay?"

Tristan nodded. The two shared a quick kiss, then Ashton left her to join Brian's group. Pam met her with a warm hug and kind words. "Thanks, Pam. Pretty shocking situation."

"No kidding. Do the police know anything? What happened?"

Ashton shook her head. "Tristan went in and

gave her statement the next day, but beyond that…" She shrugged. "Nothing. Just a horrible, tragic night. I was so surprised to hear that it made the BBC news," she added.

Pam looked surprised. "Really? I hadn't heard or seen that. My goodness!"

"Really? Oh wow. Yeah, when Brian called to tell me, he'd seen it on the news," Ashton said.

"I heard my name. What did I do?" Brian stepped up to them, putting his arm around Pam's waist. "How are you doing?" he asked quietly, reaching out with his other hand and lightly squeezing Ashton's arm.

She nodded with a shrug. "I still can't really believe it happened, to be honest."

"Just terrible," Brian agreed. "From what the news showed, it's amazing anybody got out alive."

Ashton nodded. "How long are you going to be in town before heading back to England?"

"Well, I figured you and I could meet up and figure out what to do while I'm here," he said. "Pam is flying back tomorrow. We left the kids with the nanny since we had to leave on such short notice and they've got school. But I can stick around if you need me to."

"Good thinking." She turned to Pam. "Are you sure you don't mind, Pam? I know it's a long flight alone."

Pam waved her off. "You two have business to deal with. I understand." She smirked and glanced lovingly at him. "Besides, I won't have to listen to him snore on the plane."

Ashton chuckled. "Okay." She met Brian's gaze again. "I'll give you a call tomorrow and we'll work it out, okay?"

He nodded, leaning over and giving her a one-armed hug. "Again, so sorry for your loss."

"Thank you," she said, touched. "I appreciate that."

⁂

Hands on hips, Ashton looked around the room. The hospital bed and equipment had all been returned to the medical supply company they'd rented from, leaving the room largely empty. The pictures and art hadn't been returned to the walls nor had the bed been brought back in. The chairs and tables that were placed at the perimeter of the room was all that was there.

She walked across the expanse of the room to the smaller room where her father's nurse had stayed. They'd fitted the room, which was the size of a large bedroom in a normal house, with a kitchenette including hot plate, microwave, small fridge, and a cabinet for storage above and beyond the walk-in closet. The queen-sized bed remained as well.

Chewing on her bottom lip, she allowed an idea to pickle as she turned and left the room. Tristan wasn't in their bedroom, so she went to the one Tristan had used briefly. After the fire they hadn't discussed it, but it became a silent understanding that Tristan was going to move into the suite.

The bed in the suite was covered by dresses and a smattering of masks, all the same "cat" style but different colors, though mostly black, which was all Ashton had seen. She walked over to the bed and scanned everything before glancing to the walk-in closet where she could hear Tristan moving around. They nearly ran headlong into each other as Tristan headed out, her arms full of more dresses.

"Oh my god!" she cried out. "You scared the crap out of me, Ashton."

Ashton grinned. "Sorry." She stepped aside to allow the other woman to pass with her heavy load. "What are you doing?"

Tristan stopped at Ashton on her way back to the closet. She left a lingering kiss on her lips before continuing back to her task. Ashton followed. Tristan's regular clothing was hung up or folded neatly on the built-in shelving, her handful of regular shoes lined up like little soldiers on the floor beneath as opposed to the arsenal of shoe boxes stacked on the other wall.

"Are these your heels?" Ashton asked, tapping one of the shoeboxes.

Tristan glanced over and nodded. "They are," she said as she grabbed another armful of dresses.

"Are they coming out, too?"

"They are."

Without a word, Ashton began to stack boxes on one arm before hugging the pile to keep them stable as she followed Tristan out of the closet. She carefully set the boxes on the floor so they wouldn't tumble over, avalanche style.

"Today," Tristan explained as they headed back. "I'm shedding the woman I had to become. But I think I'll hang on to these." She looked at the three dresses that remained hanging in the closet. One was an emerald-green evening gown that Ashton recognized as the dress Tristan was wearing the night they first met. Another was also long but ruby red, while the third was much shorter, the proverbial "little black dress."

"They're beautiful," Ashton said. "And I happen

to know from personal experience how ungodly gorgeous you look in a dress."

Tristan glanced over at her, the softest smile spreading across her lips. She cupped Ashton's cheek. "I love you."

Never getting tired of hearing it, Ashton reached up and covered her hand, turning her head so she could plant a kiss in the palm. "I love you," she murmured against it. "What's brought this on?"

Tristan was quiet for a long moment, her hand released after a second kiss. She turned to face Ashton, hooking her fingers in Ashton's beltloops, and said, "Am I a horrible person to say that, despite how completely terrible the fire was, tragic, and no matter how devastated I am by what happened, I feel free?"

Ashton brought her hands up and smoothed Tristan's hair back from her face as she shook her head. "No," she said softly. "Not a horrible person at all." She felt so much love for her in that moment. "I know you'd never want anything bad to happen to any of those people, or the building."

Tristan tugged playfully on the beltloops. "How about we finish up here, then go soak? I want to talk to you about some things I've been turning over in my head."

"Absolutely. Just let me know what you want me to do," Ashton said.

"I want to donate the dresses," Tristan explained. "I found a site for prom dresses, bridesmaid dresses, that sort of thing, for underprivileged women and girls." She looked down at the ground. "I'm not sad I no longer have to do what I did for those years," she said softly, still refusing to meet Ashton's gaze. "But I don't want to just throw them away." She glanced up, her gaze shy. "Can't act like it just didn't happen."

Ashton gave her a reassuring smile. "Those years working there served their purpose," she said. "It wasn't all for naught. You were able to provide you and your sister with the safety and care you needed. And hey," she added with a big grin. "You got to meet me, right?"

Tristan's head tilted to the side slightly as she studied Ashton's face. Her fingers came up to trail along Ashton's jaw. "The best thing that's happened to me in…ever."

Ashton's smile grew. She felt the exact same way. "Then don't look at the club as a mistake or with any regrets," she said. "It served its purpose, and now you're ready for something different. Time to start over."

Tristan buried her fingers in Ashton's hair and urged her to meet her for a long, sensual kiss. They hadn't made love since the horrible argument over the bill for Christine's care. Tristan had been too distraught in the week and a half since the fire at the club, wanting nothing more than for Ashton to hold her and stay close. Her body was waking up from its situation-imposed exile as Tristan's tongue caressed her own, garnering a soft moan from Ashton's throat.

Tristan ended the kiss, both women breathing hard. "I think the dresses can wait until morning," she whispered, her hand leaving Ashton's hair and grabbing her hand, leading her out of the closet.

"That's right," Brian said, sitting back in the chair across from Ashton's desk. "We never really got that last batch of contracts signed and settled."

"Nope." Ashton sipped from her water bottle as she eyed her president. "I spoke with George for a long time today, and he'd already spoken to Burk's lawyer. The way the contracts were written, Top Shelf reverts totally back to us." She tapped the large desk that had once belonged to her father in the home office.

"Including the rights to use BR Bourbon?" he asked, looking skeptical.

"Yup." Ashton finished her water and set the empty bottle on the desk. "But not only use rights for food products. The lawyer said he recently amended a provision that states that King-Kraft assumes total control of the BR Bourbon product. Not just for our Top Shelf line."

"How is that possible?" Brian asked. "He had the company before we came along with our chocolate combo."

"I know. George thinks it may have been because Buck had bigger plans for everything. I mean, think about it. He was pushing hard to get contracts reworked, after the three of us, plus attorneys, had worked hard to work them out in the first damn place."

Brian rolled his eyes, bringing an ankle up to rest on the opposite knee, dangling foot jiggling. "So true."

"But then, my father died and things just kind of got pushed aside."

"Can it be fought in court?" Brian asked. "I mean, Top Shelf is proving to be incredibly lucrative, Ash. And it would be an equally incredible bummer if we made a business plan based around this, then have some relative come and swoop it out from underneath us."

"Yes," Ashton agreed. "Real bummer." She shrugged again. "But, from what George said, that thing is airtight."

Brian glanced at his Rolex. "Shit, I better get going." He placed both feet on the floor and pushed to his feet. "You can still get me to the airport, right?"

"Of course." Ashton reached to the desk and grabbed her phone, sending off a quick text to Dekayas, who'd been alerted earlier to what she needed him to do. Response in the positive, Ashton set the phone back down and got to her feet, walking around the big desk to her friend and subordinate.

Together they walked out onto the massive portico, Dekayas already parked at the bottom of the stairs in the newly washed and polished town car.

"Didn't you have another guy that was the driver?" Brian asked as they made their way down the stairs.

"Leonard," Ashton said. "He wants to retire, so has been teaching Dekayas the ropes."

"Send in the new guard, huh?" Brian chuckled.

As they reached the car, Dekayas standing at the back passenger side, Tristan's Rav4 pulled into the circular drive, well out of the way of the town car. The small SUV came to a stop and the engine was cut off before a gorgeous Tristan stepped out, dressed to kill. She wore a skirt suit in deep blue, her hair pulled up in a chignon.

It absolutely astonished Ashton the natural grace and elegance Tristan possessed. As she walked toward them, she looked like she should be walking to the Resolute Desk in the Oval Office rather than a driveway at a private residence in Highlands Ranch, Colorado.

She was breathtaking.

She hadn't told Ashton where she'd been off to that morning but said she'd explain when she got home. Now, as the woman who had so quickly owned her heart walked toward them, Ashton could see an excitement in her blue/green eyes that she hadn't seen in the entirety of the time she'd known her.

An instant smile coming to her face, Ashton stretched out her arm, Tristan stepping into it. "Hey, sweetheart," Ashton greeted, the two women sharing a quick kiss in greeting.

"Hello," Tristan responded and gave a polite smile in greeting to Brian. "Hello, Brian. Nice to see you."

"Good afternoon, Tristan," Brian said, extending a hand, which she took. He kissed her knuckles before releasing her hand and turning to Ashton. "I'll get with you soon."

"Sounds good. Safe travels, Brian, and tell Pam and the kids hello for me."

"Will do!" Brian nodded at Dekayas, who held the door open for him, then disappeared within the confines of the luxury vehicle.

Ashton watched the car leave then turned to Tristan, who was nearly vibrating next to her. "Okay, *now* are you going to tell me what's going on?"

Tristan reached up and grabbed the lapels of Ashton's suit jacket. "You have anywhere you need to be just now?"

"I do not," Ashton said, hands going to Tristan's hips.

"Good. Then come with me."

Ashton's mouth swallowed Tristan's cries as she came, Ashton's fingers buried deep inside of her. After several moments, Tristan finally calmed and floated back down to earth. She brought up her hands, water dripping from them as she cupped Ashton's face.

"That was amazing," she whispered against Ashton's lips before leaving a lingering kiss there. Tristan lifted herself so Ashton could slip her fingers out before Tristan settled back down, straddling her hips in the warm, bubbly cocoon they'd created for themselves in the claw-foot tub.

Ashton basked in the affection and love she felt as Tristan hugged her head to her, running her hand down the long rope of wet hair. "So," Ashton finally said, half wanting to fall asleep. "What's going on?" she asked, meaning whatever Tristan had wanted to talk about. They'd barely gotten undressed before Ashton had found herself lying on the bathroom floor with Tristan's mouth buried between her legs.

Tristan sat back a bit so she could look into Ashton's upraised face. "I went for an interview today," she said, tracing her fingers down along Ashton's cheek to her jaw. "With Highlands Ranch High School." She kissed Ashton's lips, Ashton staring up at her in wonder. "And," she continued softly. "I'll be subbing for Douglas County for the remainder of the school year." Tristan looked down for a moment before meeting Ashton's gaze again. "I thought it would be a good idea to ease back in."

Ashton ran her hands down the slick skin of Tristan's back before settling them on her hips. "Why didn't you tell me?" she asked gently.

"I didn't want to say anything until I had

concrete information," Tristan responded. "I didn't want to disappoint you." She gave her a shy smile and a shrug. "In case things didn't work out."

"Baby," Ashton said softly, reaching up to cup Tristan's cheek. Tristan leaned into the gesture. "You are the most amazing woman I've ever known. Your mind, your heart, your ingenuity, your utter brilliance in every way." She shook her head, in awe of the woman before her. "I admire you like I've never admired anyone. You could never disappoint me. I love you."

Tristan hugged her again. "What did I do right to deserve you?" she whispered.

# Chapter Twenty-four

To say she felt awkward was an understatement. She held the bouquet of roses she'd bought, the plastic wrapped around them crinkling in the crook of her arm. She inserted the key into the door that was shorter than the average door but wider, solid oak, painted black. It was a heavy, thick door.

Door unlocked, she pushed it open, the door squeaking a bit on its hinges. As soon as it was opened, the stylized lighting inside was engaged, and embedded lights, long and narrow inlaid in the marble walls, came to life. The inside was a circular design with nooks carved out in the walls, just large enough to fit the metal burial vault containing the casket of a King. There was one nook left, and it literally had her name on it.

At the center of the crypt was a pedestal made of the same marble as the building with a brass vase for flowers. Empty. Walking over to it, Ashton unwrapped the roses and set them inside, arranging them just so. She removed the bottle of water she'd tucked into her pocket and twisted off the cap, pouring the contents into the vase, adding the packet of plant food included inside the plastic wrapping.

A set of marble benches were set in a circular pattern around the pedestal, a mourner able to sit upon any one to face whichever family member they wished, the crypt equipped to house the four of them. Like a Pharaoh, Jack King had his own death monument built after the birth of Jackson, the last of the Kings to come from his loins. Little did he know, Jackson would also be the first to fill it.

Blowing out a breath, she took a seat on the bench facing her mother's casket. In that moment, the once-empty flower vase behind her, she realized she hadn't been facing her mother's death. She sat there for a long while, thinking back to when she'd been alive, back before Jackson had died.

Her mother had been full of life and knowledge. She'd been beautiful and a light in the dark world created by Jack King. A talented painter, she'd painted portraits of both her children. She'd told a wide-eyed eight-year-old Ashton tales of Simurgh and other ancient Persian fairytales.

Once Jackson had been killed, the final bit of light that had been left in her had gone out, squeezed by her tyrant of a husband and extinguished by the death of the one right thing she'd ever done in his eyes. It didn't matter that her daughter still needed her, it was the only thing she had. Her mother gave up and ultimately drank herself to death.

Ashton was surprised to feel emotion beginning to rise as she sat there, emotions that she truly hadn't realized she'd been holding down in all the years since she'd died. Her face crumbled as the tears came, hard and fast. She mourned the woman her mother had been, and she mourned the woman she'd become.

Her hands came up as her body shook with her unleashed grief. She cried for herself, she cried for her mother, and she cried for her brother. She had no tears left, certainly not for her father. The well had dried up.

Her emotions spent, Ashton took several cleansing breaths, reaching into the pocket of her jacket to retrieve a tissue. She wiped her eyes and cheeks before blowing her nose. Pushing to her feet, she walked over to her brother. Placing a hand atop the burial vault, she sent a silent prayer for him.

"I love you, Jackson," she said softly. "I'm in the place now that Father always wanted for you. I hope I do you proud." Moving to her mother, she sent the same prayer before, saying, "Mom, I've come to realize that I've merely existed for so many years, going from one ambition to the next, trying to outrun my father's disappointment in my gender. Now, I'm living for me. I'm working toward the love you so desperately wanted and hoped for but were never given from him." She brought her fingers to her lips and kissed them before laying them on her mother's burial vault. "I love you, Mom. I promise to allow myself to be happy and free."

Walking over to her father, she stared down at it for a long time, allowing the anger and hatred she felt for him to surface, if just for a few moments. Finally, she felt a weight lifted off her shoulders and she swore she heard her mother's voice say, *Be proud of who you are.*

She squared her shoulders, hardened her jaw, and steeled her resolve. "You're dead, you bastard," she muttered. "It's my turn."

With that, she headed to the door, looking back at her family one last time before walking out of the crypt, closing and locking the door behind her.

"Turkey, sharp cheddar with mayo, mustard, and extra tomato with lettuce, just like you like it," Ashton said, meeting Tristan's gaze before placing the sandwich she'd made herself back into the lunch bag. "Baby carrots," she continued, holding up the clear baggie of Tristan's favorite food to nibble on. They joined the sandwich in the bag.

Tristan looked on, an amused smile on her face.

"Applesauce," she previewed, placing the snack cup into the bag. "And," she added with eyebrows raised. "A sweet for my sweet, a Cadbury Creme Egg for dessert."

Tristan moved into Ashton's personal space, taking the colorful foil-wrapped chocolate treat from her fingers. "Mmm," she purred, full-on Pearl in her eyes as she looked up into Ashton's. "You had me at creme."

Ashton grinned, her stomach doing the little flop that it always did when her little vixen came out to play. "And here I thought I had you at nice ass."

Erotic spell broken, Tristan burst into laughter, making Ashton grin. "God, I love you for this," Tristan said, the look of absolute adoration melting Ashton where she stood. They shared a kiss. "Thank you for this," she murmured against Ashton's lips.

"Of course. My girl doesn't have a first day back as a teacher every day, ya know," Ashton said, feeling a bit nervous as she was ready to give Tristan her final gift.

"Well, I'm not a teacher yet, just a subbing gig right now," Tristan said, using her hands to smooth out some non-existent wrinkles in Ashton's blouse.

"Not 'just' anything. It's a wonderful thing. But," Ashton said, taking a deep breath. "I have one more thing to add to that lunch."

"Good lord, woman." Tristan laughed. "How much do you think I can eat?"

Ashton smirked, receiving a smack to the ass. She pulled out a long, velvet jewelry box, the necklace she'd purchased weeks ago from the Cherry Creek Mall inside. "I bought this on a whim one day, hoping that someday it would be relevant," she explained, handing it over to Tristan.

"What is this?" she asked softly, almost more to herself than to Ashton. She opened the box, which squeaked slightly from the tiny hinges, revealing the gold chain and dainty apple pendant made of ruby and diamonds. She gasped.

"Apple for teacher," Ashton said softly. "I know you're a pearl, but I thought this called for a ruby."

"This is absolutely beautiful." She looked at Ashton with tears in her eyes. "Thank you. Put it on?"

With a nod, Ashton took the box, gently removing the necklace before she urged Tristan to turn her back to her. The redhead lifted her hair out of the way as Ashton placed the necklace then fastened the lobster clasp at the nape of her neck, where she left a kiss.

"Let's see," she said, a hand on Tristan's shoulder to nudge her to turn back around. When Tristan did, Ashton's smile was immediate. She wore a women's-cut button-up blouse, tasteful yet feminine. The necklace was visible through the vee where the top two buttons were left undone. "Beautiful."

Tristan took her in a long, full-body hug, Ashton's favorite. They held each other for a long moment before Tristan left a kiss on Ashton's neck. "Thank you. I love it."

"And, I love you."

Tristan smiled. "I love you, too." She initiated a long, slow kiss, meant to convey passion, yes, but mostly love and connection. She reached up and cupped Ashton's face as she pulled out of the kiss, studying her eyes for a moment before smiling, content and peace in her eyes. "I need to go. Walk me out?"

"Of course." Ashton zipped the insulated lunch sack closed and handed it to her, as well as two quarters. When Tristan looked at the coins with confusion, Ashton said, "Milk money."

Ashton looked up from her desk where she was working from home. She had a personal business appointment, which had just arrived. "Thank you, Martin," she said, standing from her chair and walking around the massive desk to greet her guest. "Mrs. Tillman, so grateful you took my case."

The woman, who looked to be in her mid-fifties, was tall and big boned. Her shorter brown hair was streaked with gray, and her face showed the stress of her pre-retirement life as an NYPD homicide detective before she and her husband had swapped the hard streets of New York for the picturesque views of Colorado Springs. Once there, they'd opened up their own private investigation firm.

The woman waved away her words before taking Ashton's extended hand in greeting. "None of that missus stuff. I love my hubby, but I'm Lee Ann."

Ashton smiled. "Then you can call me Ashton."

"I wouldn't dream of calling you anything else," Lee Ann said, her New York accent and attitude on full display.

Amused, Ashton offered her a seat as she walked back around to sit behind the desk. "I'm glad Burton was able to connect us," she said, speaking of an old friend, who had been a reporter in Denver once upon a time and had done many stories on the company. The ambitious young reporter had been her kind of people.

"As am I," Lee Ann said, slapping the leather file satchel she had with her. "I know I coulda just sent you a file over email with an explanation, but I'm old school," she explained, unclasping the brass fittings before opening it and reaching inside to remove a manila folder. She met Ashton's gaze. "Prefer to talk face-to-face with my clients."

"Thank you for that," Ashton said, nodding in approval. "I certainly appreciate it."

"Okay, now that we got that outta the way," Lee Ann said, opening the folder. "This Vallejo guy is a stinker. I can see why the Denver PD is having a hard time pinning this one down."

"Why's that?" Ashton asked, intrigued.

"Because they're cops, so they're going at it like a cop," she said, as though that explained it all. "But," she added, holding up a finger for emphasis. "I'm a *retired* cop, so I can go at it from the point of view of a cranky, tired housewife."

A bark of laughter escaped Ashton's throat, a hand slapping across her mouth. "Sorry," she muttered.

"So, Albert Joseph Vallejo's criminal record is open for any Tom, Dick, and Harry to find, no big deal there. But where the coppers around here failed to be creative was looking at his work history."

Confused, Ashton's eyebrows fell. She accepted

the pages she was being handed. "Work history?"

"Yep. You see, this guy is the worst kind of criminal."

"Violent?" Ashton asked, looking over the pages.

"Nah. Tall, dark, and violent are a dime a dozen," She met Ashton's confused gaze. "He's smart. And a planner. Now, I don't mean planner as in the guy goes to Home Depot and buys a fifty-gallon drum before he goes on a killing spree. I mean, a planner like you."

"Me?" Ashton asked, baffled.

"Yeah. An Ivy League kid like you plans which school carefully, makes the right connections, makes the right grades, all the right internships, all that jazz. Am I right?"

Ashton nodded. "Sure, okay."

"Hey, seemed to work pretty good for you, huh?" Lee Ann said, indicating the room around them. "Be proud. Anyhoo, lookie here." She reached across and took the top page she'd presented to Ashton. "What's the common denominator in this entire list of jobs this guy's had?"

Ashton scanned the job titles, based all over the country: plumber, bus driver, phone company, construction worker, school maintenance...

"Well," she said. "All very blue collar. Decent, honest work." She shrugged. "I don't follow."

"Every one of those are union jobs," Lee Ann said. "And, if there's one thing I know, those union guys stick together. And then look at this," she said, taking that page away to reveal the page beneath it. "The ultimate union."

Ashton met her gaze. "He's a Mason. Son-of-a-bitch. My father was a Mason. I know those guys will keep any secret for anyone." She smirked. "Who's a

Mason?"

"Bingo. So," she said, flipping to another page, giving Ashton her very own old-school PowerPoint. "I started going this route, unions, Masons, all that. This dude doesn't have his own address, just a PO Box. Well, more accurately, twenty-three of 'em in fourteen different cities across the country. This dude is always on the move, staying with this one and that one."

"Damn," Ashton whispered.

"So, I started looking into these crimes here," she said, holding up a hand as she began to tick off on her fingers. "The break-in of your girl, Tristan O'Toole's apartment, your sightings of creepo near the club, both linked via DNA and witness identification," she said, indicating Ashton. "And," she added, palms resting flat on the desk as she sat forward in her chair. "Cops got security video of Vallejo in the general vicinity the night of the fire, which has been ruled arson." She sat back, eyeing Ashton.

"Okay," Ashton said again. "So, we all know this guy is likely responsible for this. That's already known and alleged." She met Lee Ann's gaze. "But I see in your eyes you've got more to say."

"That I do. The thing is, if you look back at his arrest record," she said, reaching across the desk and placing that page back on the top of the pile for Ashton to look over. "Look at all that. Bullshit stuff. Yes, some violence and even assault that he did a little time for. But mostly petty shit. Not to say he's a nice guy by anyone's description, but H.H. Holmes he is not."

"Agreed."

"So," Lee Ann continued. "That got me thinking.

Most criminals, as in lifelong criminals, *career* criminals, like this yahoo"—she indicated the file on the desk—"start small and escalate. This guy, he's been doing the same crap for thirty years. So, why now? Why this massive escalation of a chain crime?"

"What's a chain crime?" Ashton asked.

"A cluster of crimes that are all connected for some reason, some purpose. Or," she added cryptically. "Someone."

"Someone," Ashton said slowly, her blood beginning to grow cold. "As in, Tristan? They all seem to revolve around her."

"Or do they?" Lee Ann hedged. "So, I started doing some research into you."

"Me?" Ashton gasped, baffled and feeling a bit annoyed.

"Yes, you. I have to tell you, Ashton, I rarely come across somebody so clean," she said with a small chuckle. "Not even a parking ticket? Jesus, Snow White. But a birdy did tell me that you had a complaint against you, some anonymous letter to your late father, God rest his soul, regarding embezzlement. Nothing came of it, but why was it sent? Who has the beef? What would have happened had your dad read that before he got dead?"

"I'm still furious about that," Ashton muttered.

"You've got every right to be pissed about that. You're a good kid, worked your ass off. So, I started thinking, who's got a grudge? Here's the thing," she continued. "What happened in Tristan's apartment, that wasn't some lovesick weirdo with a penchant for pretty girls in the service industry. The amount of damage done, and him jacking off in one of her dresses...I can sit here and say with surety that if she'd been home, that man has enough ickiness in his background to prove he'd be capable of enough that we'd be sitting here having a very different conversation."

Ashton felt nauseous at the thought of Tristan being touched, let alone anything more, by that monster. She nodded, rubbing the back of her neck. "Yeah."

"Ashton," Lee Ann continued. "Our buddy, Big Al, was told to leave a message."

"By who?" Ashton asked, her voice small.

"Well, I wondered that, too, so I got to thinking yet again. Who got this schmo into the Masons?"

Not seeing any correlation to any of this, Ashton stared at her. "What?"

"You don't just waltz in and say, 'Hey, give me a fuzzy hat and let me chant with you.' You gotta have a sponsor," Lee Ann said, as though Ashton hadn't spoken at all.

"Okay."

"What's the chain of custody here?" she said. "How did our grudge-holder find this guy?"

Ashton nodded. "So, who knew who, that knew who, knew this guy?"

"Exactamundo. So, back to who got him in. Who sponsored his application." Lee Ann reached over and peeled away a few pages, setting them aside before tapping the page revealed, which had a hand-drawn tree chart.

Ashton studied it, eyes panning across the page filled with a sea of names before Lee Ann got her attention directed to the top as she began to explain.

"This fella, Nicholas Tennison. Who's Nicholas Tennison, you ask? Well, I'll tell you."

Ashton chuckled, all ears.

"He was a higherup in SMART, the International Association of Sheet Metal, Air, Rail, and Transportation Workers back in the late eighties in Pittsburgh, when our boy Big Al was a new member. Tennison was also a higher-up in the Masonic Lodge, as well as," she added, glancing at Ashton. "Busy boy Mr. Tennison, the grandfather of Janice Tennison, who became Janice Vallejo, wouldn't ya know it."

"She married Alberto?" Ashton asked.

"You got it. Unfortunately, Janice dies in childbirth three years later. But Janice has a brother, Alec. He marries a woman named Francis, and Francis has a sister and that sister's name is Pamela. Back in twenty-oh-five, Pamela marries a fella by the name of Brian Lewis."

# *Chapter Twenty-five*

Ashton turned down the bed, glancing over at Tristan from time to time. The redhead sat in one of the wingback chairs removing her shoes. She'd been quiet and moody since the conversation had begun.

Folding the heavy comforter at the foot of the bed, she finally asked, "What are you thinking?" Bed finished, she began to work on unbuttoning her blouse.

Tristan sat there for a moment, shoes set aside. Finally, she glanced over at Ashton, who looked at her expectantly. "Why you?"

"Because I'm the target," Ashton said honestly, shrugging out of the silky material.

"All the more reason it shouldn't be you," Tristan reasoned. She placed her hands on her thighs and pushed to her feet, reaching down to grab her flats and carrying them to the closet.

"It has to be me, baby," Ashton said, following. Her closet had been reformatted to accommodate both their everyday clothing. With both having extensive wardrobes for their professional positions, the closet in their bedroom as well as the one from Tristan's former room were needed to accommodate them both.

"But, why?" Tristan asked, angrily pushing hung clothing aside on the bar to free an empty hanger for her skirt. "Why can't they just get a confession from the Vallejo guy?" she demanded. "He's part of this, anyway."

"He's dead," Ashton said softly, tossing her blouse into the dry-cleaning basket. Leaning back against the wall in her slacks and bra, she crossed her arms over her chest, letting out a heavy sigh. "They found his body Sunday in Estes Park. They believe a self-inflicted gunshot wound."

Ashton would have found it amusing had the situation not been so serious as Tristan literally seemed to deflate right before her eyes. She leaned back against the opposite wall where Ashton stood and chewed on her bottom lip for a moment before looking away, but not before Ashton saw the tears welling in her eyes.

"Talk to me," Ashton said gently.

Finally, Tristan met her troubled gaze. "It was early January, I think," she began. "It was after you'd gone back to England after our early encounters." She gave her a small smile, no doubt remembering the same thing Ashton was. "So, one night Brian came in."

"To the club?" Ashton clarified.

"Yes, the club. I knew who he was from all of you coming in during the talks with Buck and all that. He requested some time with me, so we went upstairs to the little room."

Ashton instantly felt rage threaten inside her, born out of anger and jealousy. *How dare he?* She shoved it down and listened, doing her damndest to keep her face expressionless.

"We chatted, no big deal, really. He was interesting, can definitely see why you have him in the position he's in at the company. Smart guy, kind of funny in a dorky sort of way," she said with a bemused smile. "But then, he changed. Everything about him changed."

"Changed how?" Ashton asked, afraid to hear the answer.

"He propositioned me," Tristan responded. "Not entirely unusual working there. Happened all the time, honestly. But the members learned quickly that, when we said no, it meant no. And either they came back like good little boys, respecting us and our rules, or they didn't return at all. No big deal."

"But, not with Brian," Ashton said quietly.

"No. Not with Brian." Tristan was quiet for a moment, as though lost back in time for a moment before she let out a sigh and met Ashton's gaze again. "I told him no, I don't meet with members outside the club." She smirked. "Unless your name is Ashton King, apparently."

Ashton gave her a weak smile, though what she wanted to do was throw up.

"Anyway, he got angry. Tried again, said he'd double the payment. Again, I told him no, that wasn't what I do."

"What did he do?"

"He called me some horrible names, which is fine. You learn over the years that men with mommy issues tend to take them out on women who they feel can't fight back or argue." She smiled. "But what got me, though, and what I didn't really understand it until now was, as he was leaving he muttered, 'Fucking bitch has it all.' I thought he was talking about me, or perhaps someone else in the club." She shook her head. "I wasn't sure. But I think he was talking about you, Ashton." She held Ashton's stunned gaze. "Did you tell Brian about us? Our time together prior to that?" she asked, no accusation, simply trying to understand, as Ashton was.

"No," Ashton said, shaking her head. "Nobody. I never did." Ashton ran her hands through her hair, feeling uncomfortable and angry. "How would he know about us, though? I hadn't brought you here yet."

"No, but even Lisa told me it was obvious you and I had a connection. She asked me about it after the first night we met. If she saw it..."

"Maybe he did, too."

"Exactly. And," Tristan added. "When you introduced me to him at the factory here, he recognized me."

Ashton stared at her. "How do you know?"

"He said it was nice to see me again, or something like that."

Ashton felt her blood go cold. She hugged herself tighter, so many emotions fighting within her. She felt everything from anger to fear to disgust to downright terror. The woman she loved had been targeted twice, both times a potential death trap.

"Baby?" Tristan said softly, garnering Ashton's attention. "Can you send in an undercover cop or something? Why does it have to be you?"

"With the evidence that Lee Ann found, the police think this is the only way. And, with Vallejo gone, they need a confession from Brian, if he did this," Ashton explained.

Tristan nodded. "You think he did?"

"I do."

"And the police feel you're the one who can get it out of him?"

Ashton shrugged. She walked over to Tristan and wrapped her arms around her, needing to touch her. "We'll get past this," she murmured into Tristan's neck. "Then we can move on with our lives."

❧❧❧❧

Ashton met Tristan's eyes as with trembling fingers, Tristan placed the listening apparatus where the female cop, who stood in the bedroom with her back turned to a topless Ashton, had told her to.

"Is that okay?" Tristan asked quietly, taping the little Bluetooth device, no bigger than a Bic lighter, between Ashton's breasts. According to Officer Lance, her bra would help secure it further, and the placement wasn't somewhere likely to be felt during a hug or where she was likely to be checked should Brian pat her down for some reason.

"Yeah, it's okay. It won't bother me," Ashton said, adjusting her shoulders, moving her arms, and wiggling a bit to make sure it was stable.

"Okay, it's taped on, Officer Lance," Tristan said, looking over Ashton's shoulder to the woman standing across the room. "Now what?"

"There's a little blue switch on the bottom, Tristan," the officer said over her shoulder, eyes downcast. "Switch it on, will ya?"

"Yes, ma'am." Tristan's fingers were gentle as she felt for the switch, Ashton watching her. "There it is."

"Okay, Paul," Officer Lance said into her phone to the officer stationed outside the house. "It's in place and switched on." After a moment, she said, "Ashton, recite your ABCs, would you? He wants to make sure it's a clear connection."

"Sure," Ashton said, then began her recitation. She got to the letter F when she was asked to get dressed so they could try another run with clothing on.

More than capable of doing this part herself, Ashton said nothing, simply let Tristan dress her, her touch so loving. She knew Tristan needed to be needed and involved in this, no matter how small the involvement. Their gazes met often, no doubt the trepidation Ashton felt was reflected in her eyes as it was in Tristan's.

Ashton lifted her arms through the straps of the bra, sliding the cups in place as Tristan moved behind her and clasped the garment, Ashton making adjustments as needed.

"Okay?" Tristan murmured.

"Yeah," Ashton said, nodding.

Next came the blouse Ashton would be wearing for the dinner she'd be having shortly with Brian, who was flying in. She and Dekayas would be picking him up from the swanky hotel she'd booked for him that was connected to Denver International Airport. He'd been told there was some movement with Top Shelf, and as president of the company, including that LLC, she wanted his input. Speaking to his ego had seemed the best path to get him stateside.

She began to button her blouse as Tristan went to get her jacket, the final piece of the suit that the officers had told them was the main garment they needed to make sure wouldn't disrupt the signal.

"Ready?" Tristan asked, standing behind her, holding the jacket for her.

Ashton shrugged into it, pulling it to fit correctly

and buttoning it. “Okay, Officer Lance,” she called out, turning now to face the officer. “I’m dressed, jacket in place.”

The heavyset woman turned to face her. “Okay, Ashton, go ahead and recite your ABCs again, please.” Ashton began and got to Q this time. “Okay, ma’am, you can stop. We’re good.”

Tristan held Ashton’s hand as they headed downstairs where Dekayas had been working with another officer. He was also being outfitted with a wire, though not as hidden as Ashton’s was. No need for it. He was purely backup in case her device malfunctioned if Brian decided to say anything in the car.

They reached the front doors to the house and Dekayas and the officers stepped out into the early evening, the horizon steel blue. Ashton glanced out the door before looking to Tristan, who stood in front of her and looked incredibly worried.

“I don’t have a good feeling about this, Ashton.”

“It’ll be okay, baby. Officer Lance and Officer Sanchez will be at the restaurant when we get there.” She took Tristan into a long hug. “I promise I’ll text once we drop him off after dinner, okay?”

Tristan nodded into the hug. “Don’t do anything crazy, Ashton. If you can’t get it, let it go. Promise me.”

Ashton left a lingering kiss on Tristan’s lips as she pulled out of the hug. “I promise you.” Another kiss. “And, I love you.”

“I love you, too,” Tristan said softly. She took a deep breath, then stepped away.

Ashton gave her a smile and a small wave, then headed out of the house. The police were gone, already headed to the location downtown, where a couple undercover officers had been planted as waitstaff.

Dekayas pulled open the car door for her. The two shared a quick look of concern before she stepped into the town car. The ride was silent toward the airport and hotel. Ashton's heart was racing in her chest. In the three days that she knew she'd be doing this, she'd gone over and over in her mind what she'd say, what she *could* say to get him to talk. Officer Lance had come over the previous day to work with her on ideas and given her advice.

Now, as she watched the scenery whiz by, she wondered if perhaps she'd bitten off more than she could chew. Nancy Drew, she was not. As the night began to fall, it got dark outside the windows of the car, as the airport and hotel were out in the middle of nowhere.

She saw the lights of the massive, modern-style glass building that housed the Westin. The building, and its insides, looked more like something out of a sci-fi movie than a high-priced hotel of convenience.

Dekayas pulled into the large parking lot. "Go ahead and park," Ashton instructed. "I'll go up and get him. Sometimes he likes to have a drink and chat before we leave."

"Yes, ma'am." The young man found a parking spot up close to the hotel and pulled in. He began to unbuckle his seat belt to get out and open her door, but she stopped him with a hand to his shoulder.

"It's okay, Dekayas," she said. "I shouldn't be long."

"Yes, ma'am." He stayed put.

Ashton went to tug the door pull but the door wouldn't budge and the door lock wouldn't open when she hit it. "Dekayas?"

"Yes?" he asked, looking back at her through the rearview mirror.

"The child safety lock?"

"Ah, shoot, ma'am. I'm sorry." He gave her a sheepish grin and hit the button on his driver's control panel. The lock clicked and disengaged.

Taking a deep breath, Ashton opened her door and stepped out of the car. "Okay," she said, loud enough to be heard in her listening device. "I'm heading to the hotel now."

Ashton made a beeline to the front desk to find out what room Brian was in when she spotted him in the elevator as the doors opened. He wore a suit, his overcoat folded over an arm. She forced a smile on her face, her heart nearly jumping out of her mouth as she called out to him to get his attention.

"There you are," he said, greeting her with a polite peck on the cheek.

"Here I am. Good flight?" she asked, the two heading back the way she'd come.

"It was. Long, as you know."

"Well, I hope you're rested, I know you came in last night, and I sure as hell hope you're hungry," Ashton said with a laugh, ribbing him with her elbow, behavior she would have done before.

"Yes, I am," he exclaimed with his boyish smile. "My mom spoiled me last night with her homemade potato soup, so tonight I'm more than excited about some good steak at Bastien's."

Ashton began to panic, hoping like hell her team was listening. "Really? I thought you wanted to go to Luca?" she asked, trying to sound casual.

"Eh," he said with a shrug. "Not in the mood for

Italian tonight."

"All right, steak it is," Ashton said, leading the way to the car. "I had Dekayas park because usually you like to have a drink before dinner," she explained.

"No worries. So, how are things here in town?"

"Good, good," she said. "Jude has really caught on quickly. Quite impressed with her. I do miss the hands-on with the creative process, I admit."

He snorted as they reached the car, Dekayas immediately jumping out and hurrying around to the back passenger side to open the door. "Admit it," Brian said to Ashton. "You just miss the tasting."

She grinned and nodded. "I do." She spared a glance at Dekayas, grateful to be back to her ally. "Thank you," she said, trying to convey that her appreciation had a far deeper meaning.

He gave her an almost imperceptible smile. "Anytime, Miss King." He turned from her to Brian. "Nice to see you again, Mr. Lewis. Hope your flight was pleasant."

Ashton was about to step into the car when she heard something that caught her attention. Turning back to the two men, she was only able to register that Brian had pulled a handgun out from beneath his overcoat, and he'd just fired it at Dekayas's head.

Time went from super slow-motion to super warp speed. She screamed, horrified as she watched her employee and co-conspirator crumble to the asphalt. Eyes wide as saucers, she turned to look at Brian, only to see the gun aimed at her.

"Get in," he said, slamming the back car door closed. "You're driving."

# Chapter Twenty-six

Ashton's gaze was drawn to the muzzle of the gun, the small, round hole to the barrel appearing like it was the size of the Grand Canyon. "Brian," she said, swallowing hard, fear gripping her heart in a tight fist. "You don't need to do this."

She cried out in fear and surprise when she heard the gun go off again. It took a moment before she realized she'd been shot. Suddenly, white-hot pain sliced through her left biceps. Immediately she felt the thick, warm blood coursing down her arm.

"Any further instructions needed?" he asked, his eyes no longer the light blue they'd always been but somehow impossibly black as tar.

She shook her head in shock. She couldn't bring herself to look at Dekayas as she headed to the other side of the car and to the driver's-side door, which she opened, then climbed inside.

She was shaky as she reached for the key that was still in the ignition and turned the car on, Brian settling into the passenger seat next to her. He held the gun in his lap, resting on his thigh.

She backed out of the space, hoping like hell she'd hear the SWAT team making an entrance any moment, and turned the car in the direction of the long aisle that would lead out of the parking lot.

"Where am I going?"

"Just drive," he said.

"Brian," she said, able to feel the sleeve of her jacket becoming saturated with blood. "I need a hospital, Brian."

He snorted, shaking his head. "No. No, you don't."

Ashton felt her blood go cold. In that moment she knew in her bones that if she left the parking lot, she'd never be seen alive again. Looking around, she saw the rows of parking spaces, many filled with cars of hotel guests. Off to the left, she noticed a large bank of snow that had been pushed there by plows after the storm they'd had the night before.

A mental calculation and she pressed her foot to the gas pedal, flooring it. The powerful engine in the sedan roared as the car sped up, flying down the parking lot aisle. She held the wheel, fingers like a vise.

"Slow down, Ashton," Brian said. "Slow the fuck down!"

Ignoring him, Ashton reached the end of the aisle and, tires squealing, took a turn to the right and then another, headed down the other row of parked cars to the right, snowbank all along the left side. Straight ahead she saw a large bus parked at the end of the lot, taking up several parking spaces.

"Stop or I'll fucking shoot you!" Brian yelled.

"You already did, you fucker," she muttered with determination.

Reaching down and hitting the child lock button with her left hand, she took one final look out the window, then swung open her door and launched herself into the snowbank, praying with everything in her that she wouldn't miss and be run over by the unmanned Mercedes.

She cried out in pain as she landed on her left

arm, the pain so fierce she nearly passed out. The breathtaking cold of the snow kept her lucid. Rolling from her left side to her back, she glanced over when she heard a scream and then the sound of the car plowing into the side of the bus.

The crash was horrible and the impact so hard that the back wheels of the town car lifted off the ground for a moment. She couldn't see much of the front of the car, but it looked like it was accordioned. She knew the Mercedes had been modified to protect her father over the years, nicknamed The Little Beast. Unbidden, her thoughts turned to the absurdity of her father's ego that he would name his little car after the vehicle that protected the US president. Because of that, it wasn't in as bad a shape as a regular car would be, but it was ugly.

In a great deal of pain, Ashton managed to get to her feet, wincing and crying out as she collapsed back down to the snowbank as her right leg crumbled beneath her weight, shooting lightning bolts of pain through her entire body. It was surely broken.

Ashton gasped, trying to catch her breath, her world beginning to dim as her body threatened to shut down to deal with the pain. She fought vigorously, trying to sit up, trying to get herself moving.

As though stuck in a horror movie, Ashton heard a car door being pushed open. She looked over in that direction and blinked rapidly, the edges of her vision beginning to close in.

Brian all but fell out of the driver's side, grunting as he hit the pavement as he landed partly on his left shoulder and partly on the back of his neck. He strained, trying to look around. When he spotted Ashton, his face contorted into a grotesque mask of hatred.

Ashton tried again to stand up, but it wasn't going to happen, so she began to crawl, pulling herself along as best she could as she pushed with her uninjured leg. Panic began to overtake the pain as Brian gathered himself up, half his head and face covered in blood, so much so that the white of his eye stood out in stark contrast.

A tempest of emotions filled her as she pulled herself away from him: terror, rage, panic, frustration at not being able to move faster, grief that this was it and that she'd be hurting Tristan so profoundly.

She cried out in pain and surprise when her head was yanked back, a fistful of her hair held tight.

"You fucking bitch," Brian hissed. "Why couldn't you just stay put in England where you belong?"

She flopped over onto her back, looking up at him. His suit jacket was shredded along the right arm, slacks covered in blood, though she wasn't sure if it was from his heavily bleeding head wound or if he was hurt elsewhere as well. He was unsteady on his feet, looking as though he, too, were about to pass out.

"Why are you doing this?" she asked stupidly. What does it matter now? "Why did you have those people murdered?"

"Because Jack went back on his word! It was mine," he roared, pounding his own chest. "I was responsible for building it up. I was responsible for putting together the team for Top Shelf. I was the one who talked Jack into involving you."

She had no idea if he was telling the truth, and in that moment, she didn't care. She was fading fast, shivering from the cold snow beneath her and the loss of blood. "Do it," she said, voice shaky, teeth beginning to chatter. "You won't get the company anyway, you simpleton."

He glared down at her, raising his arm up and pointing the gun down at her. He had to blink several times as the blood was flooding his eye. Finally, he brought the other arm up to wipe at it with the sleeve of his jacket.

Ashton's heart was pounding and, as she stared into his eyes, forcing herself to look at that rather than the damn gun, she felt herself beginning to let go. This was it, her last moments. Tristan's face flashed before her mind's eye and she tried to send all the love she had for the other woman to her, hoping against hope that Tristan would know how much—

*BANG!*

Brian's arm went limp and his eyes became hooded as, like a human waterfall, he seemed to pour down onto the pavement, blood and hair spotting the snow around Ashton. Confused, she looked up to where Brian had once been standing and saw Dekayas standing a couple feet back, his pistol still raised, smoke emanating from the barrel.

She stared, mouth open in shock.

"Asshole," Dekayas muttered, looking down at Brian's body like it was last week's trash. Blood ran down the right side of his face from a wound on his forehead.

"But," Ashton gasped. "He shot you."

"Sucker grazed me," Dekayas said, bending down to set the pistol on the asphalt far from Brian before he bent down, gathering Ashton under her knees and behind her back and lifting her out of the snow. "I gotcha, Miss King," he murmured. He set her down on the pavement, the wail of sirens in the distance. "I spend all my life on the mean streets of

Baton Rouge and manage to stay in one piece," he said with a heavy sigh. "Then I come here and work for Richie Rich, and I get shot."

She couldn't help it as a smile spread across her lips.

He shook his head. "Think it'll leave a scar?" he asked, indicating his head.

"I don't know," she managed, consciousness threatening to disappear. "But you're getting a raise."

Then, all went dark.

Humming. It was soft, ethereal, and was slowly pulling Ashton out of the warm and dark cocoon that she'd been wrapped in. With a little sigh, she tried to open her eyes, which felt so heavy. Finally, she managed to open them just enough to see the light of day shine in. It took a moment, but she realized she was lying in bed in a hospital room. The sweet humming was coming from Tristan, who sat next to the bed, one of Ashton's hands held in her own.

Blinking a few times, her world coming more into focus, she studied Tristan's face. The woman, the love of her life, was staring off into space as she caressed Ashton's fingers while she hummed. She looked tired and pale, and a wrinkle of worry was settled between her eyebrows.

"Hey," Ashton said, her throat dry, so the simple word came out as a hoarse whisper.

The humming immediately stopped and wide, hopeful eyes were focused on Ashton. The smile and look of total relief were palpable on Tristan's face. "Hi." She gasped, her other hand joining her first, holding Ashton's. "How are you feeling?"

Ashton took a moment to consider the question. "Tired. Sore." She slowly moved her head to look around the small, private hospital room. Clearly not an ER cubical. "How long have I been here?"

"Three days," Tristan said. "First day was full of surgeries, then these last two have been quiet, letting you heal."

"Am I done?" Ashton murmured. She was happy with the smile that earned her.

"I wish. Dr. Britton is due in here soon." She pushed up, and with the gentlest of touch left a soft kiss on Ashton's dry lips. "I love you," she whispered against them. "It's so good to see your beautiful eyes open."

Ashton smiled, basking in Tristan's love. "I love you, too. Is it all over?"

Tristan took her seat again, never letting go of Ashton's hand. She nodded. "Yes. Brian is dead, Dekayas is an utter hero and he's okay. Thank god the bullet just grazed his head." She leaned down and kissed Ashton's fingers. "You actually just missed him. He was here to see how you were doing."

"He saved my life, Tristan," Ashton murmured, beginning to feel groggy again.

"I know he did, baby," Tristan responded softly. She brought up one of her hands and caressed the side of Ashton's face. "You get some rest. I'll be here when you wake up."

Ashton's eyes were huge as Tristan's Rav4 drove down the long, winding road to the house. The entire path was lined with people, cheering, clapping, whooping, and holding signs of welcome. She recognized many as people who worked for her at the Denver factory. Several were former employees of the house, some who had left for other opportunities, some who had retired.

"Did you do this?" she asked, looking over to Tristan, who looked just as surprised.

"No," Tristan said, shaking her head. "Martin asked what time we'd be back, and I told him."

As they got closer to the house, the crowd followed them. The circular drive and portico were filled with more former and current employees. Like those lining the way, they cheered and held up massive signs: *Welcome Home!, We've got your back!, We Missed You!,* and, her favorite, *YOUR LAUNDRY IS DONE!*

Ashton laughed at that one. Though tired from a long week, her body still hurting after being put back together again, she was thrilled to be home. Seeing all the friendly faces, many of whom she had genuine affection for, was the icing on the cake, the cherry on top being a grinning Dekayas, who waited for the car's arrival.

When Tristan pulled to a stop, he opened her door and Ashton couldn't unbuckle her seat belt fast enough as she reached for him. She couldn't stand, but he leaned in and hugged her, obviously needing the connection as much as she did. Cheers went up around them as the small SUV was surrounded by those gathered.

Tears instantly came to her eyes as she relived what had happened that night, the nightmare the two of them had shared. But, after a long squeeze, he pulled away, tears in his own eyes.

"Thank you," she said, reaching up to cup his face. "With all my heart, thank you."

He smiled, nodding. "You still owe me that raise, now," he teased.

She burst into laughter. "You got it!"

They shared another hug before Ashton noticed Tristan pushing her wheelchair from where she'd unloaded it out of the SUV. Noticing it, too, Dekayas stepped out of the way, allowing Tommaso, one of her gardeners and a mountain of a man, to take his place.

"You ready?" the large Italian man asked, indicating he was going to lift her out of the Rav4 and into the wheelchair.

"Ready."

A fresh round of cheers went up as she was lifted out of the car, her leg in a cast from mid-thigh down to her toes, her leg crushed by the back tire during her daring jump. The good news was, she hadn't even realized it from the adrenaline of the moment.

Lifted up high, as Tommaso was six foot six, Ashton waved to those gathered to welcome her home. "Hello! Thank you!"

Tommaso carried her up the stairs to the portico where Tristan had staged the wheelchair and gently settled her in the seat.

"Okay?" he murmured.

"Yes, thank you." She gave him a wide smile. It was hard not to keep the dorky smile on her face as Tristan stepped behind the wheelchair, turning her to face out at the large gathering. Ashton felt so much love in that moment, so much relief that it was all over. Tristan told her that police had said they believed the threat had been fully neutralized with Brian's death.

No charges would be filed against Dekayas, as every ounce of evidence proved the whole thing was self-defense.

Feeling Tristan's hand on her shoulder, she reached up and wrapped her fingers around the warm ones of the woman who meant more to her than any one person or thing. Ironically, as she sat there, her leg held together by screws, duct tape, and bubble gum, her arm stitched up from where a bullet had passed straight through the muscle, and covered in bumps in bruises, she had never felt more whole.

# Chapter Twenty-seven

And, we're live in three, two..." The cameraman held up his finger for "one."

"Hello, everyone!"

Ashton waved into the camera. Beside it sat a monitor which showed the audience of her employees in the auditorium at the factory. She felt emotion well in her chest as she received a standing ovation from her people when she appeared on the giant screen there.

Chewing on her bottom lip, she took several deep breaths through her nose trying to settle her emotions. "Okay, now," she said, laughing at herself. "You guys are going to make me cry."

She was glad she'd chosen to go natural, no makeup and her hair pulled back into a ponytail, as otherwise she'd be worrying about running mascara as she dabbed at her watery eyes. After nearly a minute, the crowd began to quiet down, people taking their seats.

"Thank you all," she said softly. "I'm deeply touched. Deeply touched. I'm coming to you today because I wanted you all to hear it from me. No doubt, you've seen news coverage as well as rumors, but I think you need to hear it from a first-person account."

Ashton waited until everyone was still and listening, also wanting to take a moment to get her emotions together. It had been a rough couple of weeks between the pain, learning how to live life in a wheelchair, as temporary as it may be, and the unending nightmares.

"It is true that Brian Lewis is dead," she began. "He was shot by a man who works for me here at the house after that man was shot in the head by Brian. Brian also shot me." She waited as a round of gasps flowed through the crowd. "As you can see, I'm okay," she said, giving them an encouraging smile. "I was shot, yes, but I'm going to be okay. My leg was also broken in the situation, but again, I'll be okay."

The cameraman got her cast and wheelchair in the shot, as she didn't want incorrect rumors to be spread.

"I'll be working from home for a bit," she continued. "But we're all still a team. Jude is there as my eyes and ears to make sure everything runs smoothly. I love you all, and I'll be back soon." With a winning smile to her people, again applauding, the shot ended.

"And, we're off," he said, moving away from the camera.

"Thanks for coming to do this, Max," Ashton said from where she was reclined on the bed she shared with Tristan. It was too difficult for her to get around by herself still, so she thought it better to do the shot from where she spent most of her time when Tristan was at school so she didn't trouble anyone.

"Absolutely." Max was the guy they relied on for all their marketing projects involving a camera from commercials to training videos. Very talented and easy to work with. He gathered up all his gear, then stood next to the bed. "You need anything before I go, Ashton?"

"Nah," she said, waving him off. "It's nap time."

He smirked. "Not a bad idea." He bent down and left a quick peck on her cheek before heading out.

Left alone, she lay back against the pillows, exhausted from the simple task. Definitely nap time.

It was so peaceful and beautiful as the snow fell during a late spring flurry. The true storm was supposed to hit overnight, but for now, they were fat, white, lazy flakes falling to the ground, the kind you could catch on your tongue.

Tristan pushed Ashton's wheelchair along the paths on the property. They ended up where they all converged in a large circle of brick path that had once held a massive fountain at the center. It had been removed years before, so now was just an empty space.

"Stop here please, baby. Cannot wait until this arm heals so I can get myself around," Ashton said. When Tristan complied, Ashton looked around the space. "You know what I think we should do here this summer?"

"What?" Tristan asked, placing her hands on Ashton's shoulders as she stood behind the chair.

"I think we should turn this into memorial gardens." She was quiet for a moment as she imagined what could be done. "Maybe put a gazebo in there at the center, or even a pergola, surrounded by a garden with pathways. Benches along the way denoting those we've lost." She looked back and up at Tristan, who was looking down at her. "What do you think?"

Tristan smiled, her hand moving from Ashton's shoulder up to cup her jaw. "I think it's a wonderful idea. I imagine your mom and brother would be happy about that."

Ashton looked into her eyes, studying her for a long moment before slowly shaking her head. "I'm not the only one who has lost, Tristan," she said softly. "All of them should be remembered."

"Really?" Tristan asked, surprise in her voice.

"Of course."

Ashton knew, like she knew her own name, that Tristan would be with her forever. They'd been close before, deeply in love and certainly in lust, but after the events of the night of Brian's death, their bond had grown to a depth Ashton had never known, almost a connection of souls, not just hearts.

Though long gone, Ashton wanted Tristan's parents, and even Sophie, to be part of their lives, a place where Tristan could go to remember them, love them, and continue to heal from their loss, as well as Ashton and her family.

❧❧❧❧

The early summer rain washed over the grounds, turning the lush lawns emerald green. Ashton pushed herself along the long track of the upstairs hallway, listening to the steady, comforting beat.

❧❧❧❧

"Come on, Ashton. Push a little harder," Jody, the physical therapist, encouraged.

Ashton, who lay on her back on the padded bench, squeezed her eyes shut and growled through clenched teeth as she tried to push against Jody's hand with her foot. The pain was exhausting but necessary, she knew.

"Come on, girl!" Jody exclaimed. "We'll get you up and around in no time. Come on!"

Cries of wonder filled the warm, night air as explosions above the man-made lake on the property signified the independence of a young nation so many years ago. Ashton sat on a bench in the newly created Memory Garden with Tristan sitting next to her, holding her hand. Ashton's walker stood sentinel next to the bench.

Once again, Ashton found herself in her mother's old suite. She stood there, taking in the space, hand braced on the silver-topped cane that had become her best friend. She heard her name called out and responded with her location.

Finally, Tristan found her. "I have to say." Tristan laughed, stepping into the room. "I don't care how long I live here, I'll never get used to how massive this house is."

Ashton grinned. "It was awesome when I was a kid," she said. "Best games of hide-and-seek with the staff ever."

Tristan chuckled. "No kidding. Are you coming, baby? Candy is all ready to be handed out, and from what Martin has told me, kids show up by the carload here."

Ashton grinned and nodded. "Yes. God," she whispered. "It's been so long since I've been here for

Halloween, let alone lived in the house during." She looked at the woman standing next to her, studying her face for a long moment. "You know," she continued. "As we're heading into the holiday season, it's the first time I've celebrated them living here in years." She reached up with her hand that wasn't on her cane head and brushed some of Tristan's hair behind an ear. "This may sound stupid, but I'm so glad you're here with me."

Tristan studied her for a long time, head slightly tilted to the side. Finally, she cupped Ashton's face and brought her in for a lingering kiss, resting their foreheads together. "Me, too," she whispered. "Christmas is coming, and you're the best gift I ever could have gotten, Ashton."

Ashton's eyes closed as Tristan wrapped her arms round her, the two sharing space and a moment in time. No words necessary, simply a shared heartbeat. Finally, she pulled away and left another kiss on Tristan's lips before saying softly, "Come with me."

They took it slow across the expanse of the large room until finally they ended up in the smaller room adjacent.

"Wow," Tristan said, looking around. "It's like a whole little apartment in here. I didn't expect this." She smirked. "Would have loved this in college."

Ashton grinned. "Yes, you see, that room," she said, indicating the larger one they'd just left. "Was my mother's room. This room that we're standing in was the nursery for many, many generations of babies, including Jackson and me. When my father had his stroke, I knew the hospital was absolutely not where he wanted to be. So, we brought him home and put him in Mom's room, brought in whatever medical equipment he needed, and I had this room transformed into a place where his hired nurse could live until either he got better, or he died."

Tristan nodded, walking around, fingering the furnishing and little fridge. "Very cool. Smart."

"Yes. So," Ashton said, taking a deep breath for courage. "You mentioned Christmas. I wondered what your thoughts would be if we had a very special gift delivered here," she said, indicating the space around them. "Put this little apartment to use once again for a round-the-clock nurse."

Tristan eyed her, the wheels clearly turning in her head. "What are you saying, Ashton?" she asked, her voice quiet, almost as though she were holding her breath.

"I'm saying, what would you think about bringing your sister home?"

Tristan looked away, but not before Ashton saw tears in her eyes. She blew out a long, slow breath as she wandered around the space, a hand running through her hair. Finally, she turned back to Ashton. "Are you serious?" she asked, hope in her voice.

"Very serious," Ashton said. "I've been thinking about this for a while, to be honest." She gave her a sheepish grin. "I learned my lesson last time, so I didn't want to push anything on you or make you think I was trying to make any sort of decision."

Tristan gave her a shy smile. "Yes, well," she said, walking back over to Ashton and placing her hands on her hips. "I know you better now and understand your heart." She let out a shaky breath and nodded. "If that's what you really want to do, if you're sure..." Her face broke out into the amazing smile that always left Ashton speechless from its glow and beauty. "You'll make one of my biggest dreams come true."

Ashton stood back out of the way. Though she was more stable on her feet now and only had to use the cane on "bad days," she still wasn't quick enough to move out of the way of the women and men moving such precious cargo.

A wall panel opened, revealing a single-car elevator hidden behind. The mobile bed from the ambulance that Christine was strapped to appeared, along with the paramedic team that was in charge of transferring her safely from the long-term care facility to Pittman House.

Tristan was on Christmas break from her teaching job at the high school and was zooming around coordinating everything, as she had since they'd begun the process with Christine's doctors and the facility. They had even hired Tanisha as Christine's private day nurse.

Tanisha was familiar with Christine, and Tristan believed her sister knew Tanisha's voice and her touch. For Tanisha's part, she was a firm believer that if Christine were ever to awaken, she had a much better chance of doing so at "home" and not in a cold, sterile facility, no matter how much the medical profession tried to warm it up for her.

Truth of the matter was, Tanisha seemed beside herself with excitement at this new phase for her "favorite" patient. She'd come in, and together with Tristan had worked to turn the old bedroom into something that Christine would have once upon a time found comforting, familiar. It was filled with many of her things, which Tristan had kept in storage all these years, such as particular stuffed animals that, even as a teen, Christine had still cherished.

Essence oils in a diffuser had been a staple in the O'Toole house, as their mother had been a spiritual woman, and there had been certain scents that had been Christine's favorites. Those, too, had been brought in. In other words, it was an all-out experiment to see if anything would reach into the recesses of Christine's sleeping mind.

She caught Tristan's gaze across the room as the paramedics worked together to lift Christine from the gurney to the bed. The excitement was nearly vibrating off the beautiful redhead. She mouthed the words, *I love you.* Ashton smiled and mouthed them back.

Later that night, after she'd spent some time with Tristan and Christine, Ashton left the sisters alone, as she sensed Tristan needed it—even if Tristan didn't know it. She made her slow way to the bathroom to get ready for bed. She'd left her cane by the bed, her doctor urging her to go without it when she felt she could.

She washed her face and brushed her teeth and other business before making her way back into the bedroom area. She'd started a fire in the fireplace and turned out the lights, leaving only the fire and Christmas tree lights for illumination. Tristan had insisted they put up a small tree in the bedroom, as she said it was her favorite holiday but hadn't had a reason to celebrate it in far too many years.

Initially Ashton had been a bit dubious about putting a tree up in front of the large windows of the bedroom, but now, as the lights added a beautiful, festive intimacy to the room, she was a convert. She'd never put up a Christmas tree in her life. As a child, the house staff had taken care of it, and as an adult, she'd thought it childish and a waste of time.

Now, she understood all her years of *bah, humbug* had far more to do with an inner unhappiness and emotional void than anything else. Tristan had changed all of that. As Ashton turned down the bed, she marveled at how one woman had changed so much of her life and within her, in just a year's time.

How was it that, during the most perilous moments of her life, the biggest betrayal she'd ever faced, her father's death, and shock of inheriting the company, Tristan had kept her on track, steady and calm? What sort of magic did the woman possess?

She smiled at that thought as she climbed into her side of the bed, getting comfortable before reaching for the book she was currently reading, which awaited her attention on the nightstand. Moments later, the bedroom door opened and Tristan came in, nearly floating, her smile soft and serene.

Ashton grinned. "My, my, somebody's happy."

Tristan took a running jump and launched herself on the bed, grinning like a teenager who just got her first paycheck from work, landing just shy of Ashton. "Very happy."

Ashton accepted the soft kiss she received. "I'm so glad," she said against softer lips.

"Be right back." Tristan gave her a final kiss before hopping off the bed and disappearing into the bathroom.

Ashton set her book aside again and got settled in the bed, ready for Tristan, who she could hear following her nightly routine, not dissimilar to her own. Finally, the bathroom light was switched off and a naked Tristan made her way to the bed, rubbing lotion into her hands and arms from the bottle they had on the counter.

It amazed her how comfortable Tristan was with her nakedness—not that she didn't have a reason to be, as she was beyond gorgeous. But there was a freeness about her, a sense of deeply rooted self-worth and self-awareness that was intoxicating.

Lotion rubbed in, Tristan climbed into bed, scooting over to Ashton, who held out an arm to encircle her as she rested her head on Ashton's shoulder. Ashton's eyes fell closed as she absorbed the woman in her arms, her scent, the feel of her skin and her hair, the gentle touch as Tristan got settled, her hand resting just under Ashton's left breast.

"Know what?" Tristan asked, her voice soft, sounding sleepy.

"Hmm?" Ashton murmured, hands trailing through long, auburn hair.

"Life is perfect. Just perfect."

# *Chapter Twenty-eight*

It was a new year, the holidays behind them, and Ashton would be returning to work full time the following day. She'd taken the previous months to heal completely from her injuries, which had seemed to take forever. But now she was without cane, though she sported a slight limp that her doctors said may or may not be permanent.

Though she hadn't been going into the office, she had been working from home, and she was standing at one of the filing cabinets she'd allowed to stay after purging the home office of her father's wall of filing cabinets. She planned to take some records in with her the following day to give to HR to add to the digital record for the company.

Fingering her way through the files until she found what she was looking for, she was about to pull the folder when the door to her office opened. She glanced over her shoulder to see who it was when she stopped dead in her tracks.

Tristan stepped in, her gaze locked on Ashton's. She closed the door behind her, leaning back against it. She reached behind her, the *click* as the lock was engaged making Ashton's heart jump. Her hair was down, brushed to a shine in fiery waves around her shoulders. She wore an off-the-shoulder dress that didn't even quite reach mid-thigh. It was the proverbial "little black dress" that clung to her body of perfection.

The look on her beautiful face was one of determination, predatory and damn sexy. She pushed away from the door and that was when Ashton realized she held something in her hand. When she realized what it was, she immediately became wet.

Tristan made her way over to Ashton, the sway of her hips, the confidence of her stride, the swell of her cleavage devastating. The drawer of the filing cabinet slowly pushed closed as Ashton leaned back against it, nowhere to go as Tristan reached her. She placed her bundle on top of the filing cabinet behind Ashton, never breaking eye contact with her.

Ashton swallowed.

Without a word, Tristan brought her hands up to Ashton's button-up shirt, deftly undoing one button at a time, sparing a glance into Ashton's face as she did. Shirt unbuttoned, she brushed the two sides apart, revealing the black lace bra that cupped Ashton's breasts. She studied them as her fingers trailed over them, eventually cupping them, squeezing.

Ashton sucked in a quiet breath, her clit jumping with the move, heart racing. Again, sparing a glance up into Ashton's eyes, Tristan's hand trailed down Ashton's stomach, the muscles beneath the skin flexing in sympathy with the light touch until Tristan's fingers reached the button and clasp of Ashton's jeans.

Ashton's breathing was increasing as Tristan reached both hands down into the undone jeans along her ass, pulling her hips away from the filing cabinet as they pushed down the jeans and her panties, the garments gathering at her knees. The look in Tristan's eyes dared Ashton to deny her.

Moving into Ashton's personal space, she

brought up a hand, trailing her fingernail down along Ashton's cheek and jawline, using the other hand to grab the bundle on atop the filing cabinet. She made quick work of the satin drawstring bag, removing the oddly shaped cyberskin-covered item. She reached over Ashton's shoulder again to put the bag back on the filing cabinet, pressing her breasts into Ashton's.

Ashton was so aroused it was painful. She could hardly breathe even as her breasts heaved with her anticipation. A long, slow breath left her lips as Tristan's free hand made its way between her legs. When her fingers came into contact with the immense wetness already gathered there, Ashton saw the first break in Tristan's mask of dominance. Her lips opened slightly and eyes became a bit hooded.

Ashton's eyes fell closed as Tristan initiated a slow, sensuous kiss, controlled yet filled with the passion that was synonymous with Tristan O'Toole. Ashton found herself getting lost in the kiss and gentle strokes of soft fingers. It always amazed her that, no matter how passionate their lovemaking got, how animalistic or primal, there was always an underlying gentleness and awareness to Tristan's touch.

As the kiss continued, Tristan took her fingers away, to the great disappointment of Ashton, only for that disappointment to be replaced by a sigh of satisfaction as Tristan eased the wearer's end of the strapless strap-on inside of Ashton. It was the shorter end, yet curved to give the wearer pleasure as she used it on her partner.

The cock inserted, Tristan pulled up Ashton's panties as much as they'd go to help hold it inside, as clearly she had plans for the business end of that cock. As she nibbled at Ashton's lips, her hand gripped Ashton's cock, slowly rubbing it, each little movement fucking Ashton a bit. She was beginning to worry she'd come before that cock ever got near its intended goal.

Reaching down, she stopped Tristan's hand, grinning as her eyes pleaded for mercy. Tristan gave her a sexy little smile but obliged. One last kiss and she moved away, turning her back to Ashton as she walked the few steps over to the massive desk, bracing her hands on it as she very deliberately bent over to the best effect of her gorgeous ass.

In that position, the hem of the short dress she wore rose to reveal she wasn't wearing any panties, and she was very ready for Ashton. That alone nearly made Ashton come, despite what Tristan had already done to her body. The position Tristan was in brought back that first night at the club, the first moment she'd laid eyes on the stunning woman. Perhaps that was the point.

Taking a deep breath to focus herself off her own body's pre-orgasm buzz, she walked over to Tristan. She brought her hands up, fingers itching to touch her. She thought back to that night, more than a year ago, when she'd stared at the behind she touched now, wondering what it would be like to touch it, hold on to it as she took Pearl from behind. She hadn't even seen Tristan's face at that point but was already drawn to her.

After they'd shared their bodies, shared their dreams and desires, shared their hearts, and now, shared a home, they'd come back full circle. It all began with a deep, powerful connection made of attraction, passion, and desire that had turned to an equally deep, passionate love.

She ran her hands over the material of the dress, up to Tristan's bare shoulders and down her sides to her hips, allowing her fingers to enjoy the tactile bliss before reaching her ass. She brushed the dress up to bunch at Tristan's waist, revealing soft skin to her eyes. Her fingers made their way between Tristan's parted legs. She hissed in appreciation, and sympathy, when she felt the saturated, swollen folds of her pussy.

Tristan's head fell as Ashton used the pads of two fingers to rub slow circles over her engorged clit. Ashton's own excitement grew with the little whimpers coming from the woman before her. Nearly trembling with arousal, Ashton finally removed her hand and used her slick fingers to coat the head and shaft of her cock, not that Tristan being properly lubricated to accept its girth was a problem.

She carefully guided the tip to Tristan's entrance, easily sliding it in, using her hips to ease in the entire length, her hips coming into contact with Tristan's ass. Gripping her hips, Ashton slowly withdrew her hips before pushing back in, beginning a slow rhythm that was comfortable for them both. Her thrusts were long and slow at first, but as she caressed the skin of Tristan's hips, she shortened them a bit, moving her own hips a bit faster, though still keeping it slow for the time being.

As she moved, her unbuttoned shirt began to get in the way, so she shrugged out of it, tossing it to the leather chair close by, leaving her in only in her bra above the waist. Freed from the extra material, she brought her hands back down to Tristan's hips, holding on as she increased her thrusts.

Her eyes closed as the end inside her moved, inciting amazing sensations within her own body, amping up the psychological impact of feeling as though a part of her own body were buried deep inside Tristan's pussy, causing the heavy breathing and rising whimpers from the woman before her.

Soon, the office was filled with the sounds of their breathing, Tristan's soft cries and Ashton's hips slapping against a shapely ass. Tristan had dropped down to her forearms on the desk, forehead against the cool wood.

Ashton felt her orgasm beginning deep inside, like a slow burn that was sparking with every thrust. It didn't take long for that spark to catch her entire body on fire as she bared her teeth, pounding her cock into Tristan's pussy, nearly moving the heavy desk with the impact.

With a guttural cry, Tristan gave in to her own pleasure, her nails trying to find purchase on the smooth wood as she released. That sent Ashton over the edge, her hips stilling as she grinded them against Tristan's ass, milking all she could out of her clit as it was pressed against the flat panel of the cock made for just that purpose. She could swear in that moment, as she came hard, that she came inside Tristan. It felt that close, that intimate.

Exhausted and panting, Ashton gently pulled out of Tristan before removing the cock from her own body and setting it aside. She hugged Tristan from behind, resting the side of her face against her back before leaving a kiss there and standing erect. She stepped away from Tristan so the other woman could push herself away from the desk. She turned around and Ashton immediately took her into her arms.

They held on to each other, both trying to calm their breathing. Ashton allowed herself to absorb

Tristan, her love for her, need for her. It was moments like that that she wondered how she'd survived the first forty years without her.

"So," she finally said, running her fingers through Tristan's hair. "Where did that come from?"

Tristan chuckled, her face buried in Ashton's neck. "You gave me my dream," she murmured. "So, I wanted to return the favor." She lifted her face and looked into Ashton's eyes, her hand coming up to caress Ashton's cheek.

Ashton smiled. "Baby," she said softly. "You *are* my dream."

Tristan returned the smile. "And you're mine."

Ashton placed a lingering kiss on soft lips. "What do ya say we go to bed?"

Tristan grinned. "You don't have to ask me twice."

# *About the Author*

Kim has spent her life in Colorado and can't imagine living anywhere else. She's been writing since she was 9 and stumbled into her first book being published in her mid-20s. She's worked in the film industry as a writer, director and producer, but now enjoys the quiet, happy life of a professional author. She can be reached on Facebook and on her website at, www.kimpritekel.com

## *IF YOU LIKED THIS BOOK...*

Share a review with your friends or post a review on your favorite site like Amazon, Goodreads, Barnes and Noble, or anywhere you purchased the book. Or perhaps share a posting on your social media sites and help spread the word.

Join the Sapphire Newsletter and keep up with all your favorite authors.

Did we mention you get a free book for joining our team?

sign-up at - www.sapphirebooks.com

## ***Check out Kim's other books.***

*Zero Ward* - ISBN - 978-1-943353-19-4

Danny Felts grew up in the heart of the Midwest on a dairy farm, expected to follow in her mother's footsteps and marry a farmer and become a mother. Danny had other ideas. As World War II heats up, she makes a decision that will change her life forever as she becomes a lie, serving with the Seabees in the Navy as Daniel Felts.

Kate Adams is about to graduate high school in her prestigious and elite San Diego neighborhood when she's dragged to the USO for a dance with friends and servicemen. There, she meets the person that will catch her eye and her heart, only for jealousy and vengeance to tear her apart.

Are Danny and Kate strong enough to win the battle within and fight for their love?

*After Shadow* - ISBN - 978-1-939062-10-9

Clara always knew she was different, but just how different she was was to be seen. She will be forced on a journey to places that, though nightmarish to some, make perfect sense to her. While living a life in darkness and shadow, massaging the ghosts we all want to hide from beneth the covers, she will discover her own light of day. But, can she discover her heart?

*Shadow Box* - ISBN - 978-1-939062-07-9

Erin Riggs is an average woman with a normal life, though with decidedly un-common fears of exploring her world or her own truths. One 3 a.m. incident would change everything forever.

Tamson Robard spent a childhood with a weak mother, desperate to land a man in order to escape a horrific secret that Tamson can't even fathom. Tamson ran away as a teenager, but is now a grown woman. Other than drugs, her only friend is a guardial angel, Penny, whom she confides in, sharing feeble hopes and unending pain.

Together, the two will discover buried truths that will lead them through tears and to death's door. Can the cossision of Erin and Tamson's worlds save them both?

*Connection* - ISBN - 978-1-939062-24-6

Julie Wilson lives a charmed life as a beloved teacher and aunt in the small town of Woodland. Close to her brother and guardian of two adorable Yorkies, she loves her life, the only negative being ex-boyfriend, Ray who can't seem to understand the phrase, "We're done." Believing that's her only problem, Julie has no idea what hell awaits her during a normal summer afternoon.

Remmy Foster is the quirky, friendly drifter who has never found roots after a difficult childhood, as well as the difficulties her very special gift brings into her life. Though she may call it exploring, the truth is she's running from ghosts that haunt her every step.

After a chance meeting with Julie while hitchhiking, Remmy will be thrown head first into darkness she could never have foreseen, regardless of her abilities. As the clock ticks, life and death is on her shoulders to make the right connection.

***Warning - Some scenes may be too intense for some readers.***

*1049 Club* - ISBN - 978-1-939062-97-0

Almost two hundred souls, one plane, six survivors, endless heartbreak.

When flight 1049, headed from Buffalo, NY to Italy falls from the sky, a firestorm of drama, pain, angst and sorrow ensues. Can an author, a business owner, a teenager, good ol' boy, veterinarian and ruthless lawyer survive? Better yet, can those left behind?

1049 Club is a story of survival, love, deep regret and miracles. Can the living make peace with the presumed dead? Can the presumed dead make peace with the lives and loves they thought they had before?

*Blinded* – ISBN – 978-1-943353-53-8

After a horrible explosion sends local television news reporter, Burton Blinde reeling both physically and emotionally, she walks away from her life and the dream job she was about to start at a major news network.

For six long years she hides out in a small mountain

town, working at the local library, though is haunted by the life she had, including mysterious messages and gifts she was receiving before her life was turned upside down, a veritable bread crumb trail leading to the unknown.

Unable to resist, Burton begins to follow the clues, which will lead her into the darkest places of human nature that she may not be able to return from.

*Damaged* - ISBN - 978-1-939062-45-1

Family. A group of people you are related to by blood or love.

Nora Schaeffer has come home to her family after twenty years working around the world as a photographer for National Geographic. She's welcomed into the open arms of her father and siblings.

Family. A group of people who support you, lift you up when you fall.

Shannon, the youngest of the four Schaeffer siblings, has vanished, leaving her five-year-old daughter, Bella, terrified and alone. To help find Shannon, Nora has no choice but to turn to the dark-haired specter who has haunted her for twenty years. Along the way, she finds her own long-dead heart and uncovers chilling family secrets beyond imagination.

Family. A group of people who will stick together to hide the rotten soul at its core at any cost.

Who will live? Who will die? Who will be the most damaged? And who will learn to love again?

*The Gift* - ISBN - 978-1-948232-47-0

The dead do speak. You just have to listen. Homicide Detective Catania "Nia" d'Giovanni is the only daughter in a large Italian family of six children. The backbone—a position not applied for nor wanted—she continues to create new glue to hold the dysfunctional group together. For Nia, family time feels more like herding cats than spending time with her brothers and feisty, aging parents.

Her heart has always been in her career with the Pueblo Police Department, especially since it will never be okay with her very Catholic mother to openly give her heart to any woman, until she meets a secretive waitress who has her at, Can I take your order?

And then it begins…

Three murders that are so gruesome, so horrible, they rock the small town to its core. Nia and her partner Oscar are left to piece together a deadly puzzle to find the key to unlock the monster they hunt.

Or, are they the hunted?

As they dissect the murder scenes where not one shred of evidence is left behind, more bodies begin to show up, each cleaner than the last, the shadowy specter that is the killer vanishing without a trace, making the woman Nia loves disappear right along with it.

When there is no evidence to follow, Nia must trust her instincts...or, is she being guided?

*The Plan* – ISBN – 978-1-948232-43-2

As the dark days of the Dust Bowl came to an end, the midsection of the United States tried to rebuild and revitalize. In the small, dusty farming town of, Brooke View, Colorado, teenager, Eleanor Landry and her mother were dealing with her father, a self-appointment fire and brimstone preacher to his congregation of two. A plan to survive.

As the dark era of the robber baron comes to an end, giants of industry and innovation emerged with fabulous fortunes manifested in the mansions that dotted the landscape across the country. Lysette Landon, the teen daughter of the wealthiest family in Brooke View, was everything a good, proper girl of privilege should be. Only problem was, she wasn't dreaming of finding a young man to raise a family with. A plan to be free.

One look, one touch, all plans are off.

Secrets deeper and darker than the grave would bring Eleanor and Lysette together, their families connected by a web of lies and broken promises. A plan to escape.

Be careful because, life has other plans...

*The Traveler Book One: The Hunted* - ISBN - 978-1-948232-91-3

A story so epic one book can't contain it. BOOK ONE:

1977: In the era between flower power and the yuppie, Sonia Lucas is a young wife and mother, just starting out in life. Without warning, a strange presence and dark force enters her life, clouds building...

1917: ...and a storm brewing as the world reeled from the horrific events of World War I just before it was ravaged by a Spanish flu epidemic that would kill millions. Sephora Lloyd is a 16 year old girl lost in the responsibilities of an adult world helping to support herself and her mother. A beautiful young nun-in-training enters her life, bringing love and hope with her. That is, until a force bigger than either of them threatens everything Sephora holds dear.

Four women - three deaths - two words - one house
THE HUNTED

*The Traveler Book Two: The Hunter* - ISBN - 978-1-948232-93-7

A story so epic one book can't contain it. BOOK TWO:

1890: In the dying days of the Old West, Sally Little runs her booming brothel with the passion and tenacity the business of sex requires. Savvy and indulgent, there's one itch Sally can't let herself scratch. Afraid of hurting the woman she loves, she instead unleashes...

Present Day: ...her renovation crew and fixer upper TV show on a dilapidated mansion that has known nothing but death since a murder there in 1977. Samantha Leyton sees ratings gold in bringing the sagging old house to life, but instead she discovers only she has the power to unlock the mystery that hunted four women across time, leaving death and destruction in its wake. Can she release her sisters who came before her and finally be granted the gift of love that is stronger than any evil?

Four women - Three deaths - two words - one house THE HUNTER

*Finding Faith* (Wynter Series Book 1) - ISBN - 978-1-952270-16-1

Faith Fitzgerald thought that if she got an education and became a high-powered attorney in Manhattan, maybe—just maybe—she'd gain the attention and respect of her absentee father. Considering he was the only parent she had left after her mother's suicide when Faith was just a child, she thought that's what it would take.

She was wrong.

What she dreamed would be glamorous and satisfying turned out to be grueling and thankless. Since she wasn't willing to play the game between the sheets, she was forced to stay in the cubicle jungle doing all the heavy lifting while the men got the credit and the rewards.

Deciding she is done, Faith packs up and, with the flip of the bird to the rearview mirror, leaves New York and heads home to Colorado. She has nothing there: no job, nowhere to live, no relationship with her father. Truth is, she barely has a relationship with herself.

On the drive home, she finds herself in Wynter, a tiny mountain town at the foot of the Rockies. Looking more like it belongs in a made-for-TV Christmas movie than on the map, Faith is utterly enchanted. When she tries her luck and buys a raffle ticket at Pop's, Wynter's charming café, her prize is far more than meets the eye—or the heart.

Enter Wyatt, a feisty, sexy southerner and waitress at Pop's, who just happens to be married to a local sheriff's deputy. All is not as it appears with the All-American boy and his Georgia peach.

A colorful cast of unforgettable and charming characters will teach the jaded attorney that sometimes to find yourself all you have to do is go back to the basics...and have a little Faith.

*Taking Liberty* (Wynter Series Book 2) - ISBN- 978-1-952270-24-6

A victim of a massive corporate downsize, Liberty Faulkner suddenly finds herself without a job, without a home, and without a plan. Though certainly not part of her vision, Libby decides that the familiar is the safest path back to her life goals. In this case, the devil she knows is home: the tiny mountain town of Wynter, Colorado, a close-knit place where everybody knows everybody and everybody's business. Seems like the perfect place for the twenty-five-year-old to start over and figure out who she is without being noticed...not.

Sergeant Grace Montez escaped her dead-end job and toxic relationship in New Mexico and moved to Wynter to help build their police department from scratch. Now an established figurehead in the community, she's got her professional life dialed in and even mentors new recruits on the force. After a challenging childhood and lifetime of abandonment and disappointment, Grace hasn't been interested in another relationship—especially because no one has caught her eye since a certain quirky college student who used to make her caramel macchiato at the local coffee shop moved away three years ago.

Now that quirky college student has returned as the beautiful, mature woman Libby has become. Can Grace keep her distance, or will she finally take liberties with what is being offered?

*Justice Won (Wynter Series Book 3)* - ISBN - 978-1-952270-36-9

In 1890, seventeen-year-old Justice Kilkoyne and her mother, Ninny, are one bad decision away from living on the streets of Azrael, Pennsylvania. Ninny's propensity for the bottle has left Justice to play the adult, her androgynous good looks helping her pass as a young man to gain employment and keep them—if just barely—above water.

Determined to find a better life for them, Justice saves every penny to get them on a train headed west to the sunshine of California. Before they can leave, the bigotry of one shopkeeper sends Justice on the run, chased by the police for a crime she didn't commit and straight into the unwitting arms of a stunning young prostitute, who, after an unexpected connection, becomes Justice's Angel.

The day arrives to leave Pennsylvania for good. As Justice and Ninny get settled, they're surprised by the appearance of Angel, also wanting to start anew. When the trip is violently interrupted in Colorado, Angel just may be lost to Justice forever.

Can Justice find a new life when she makes her way to the fledgling mining town of Wynter, Colorado? Can her heart ever be whole again?

*Curtain Call* - ISBN - 978-1-952270-42-0

What do you do when you come from a long line of dancers that spans the globe and generations, yet you can't tell your right foot from your left? You fall in love with a dancer, of course!

Gray Rickman is an awkward seventeen-year-old when she first sets eyes on Christian Scott at the dance studio/theater Gray's parents own and run in Denver, Colorado.

Though only a handful of years older than Gray, Christian carries herself with poise and wisdom far beyond her years. A woman of few words, she speaks volumes with her body.

Before Gray even really knows what her type is,

Christian stars in endless daydreams and even fulfills a couple of her fantasies before vanishing out of thin air, leaving Gray in an empty bed with nothing but bittersweet memories and broken dreams.

With no choice but to move on, Gray attempts love, even moving with her college girlfriend to New York City to pursue a career in journalism. But her standard has been set, the bar way too high for any other woman to reach or clear. It's an unexpected encounter in an obvious place when Gray sets eyes on her dancer again. Will the bright lights of Broadway illuminate the way back to the woman of her dreams? Or will they blind her to any other possibility of happiness?

Break a leg, Gray. The Great White Way calls.

*Encore Performance* - ISBN - 978-1-952270-52-9

Grey Rickman, a journalist for The New York Times, is offered the opportunity of a lifetime and a huge boost to her career—ghostwriting a memoir for one of the world's most beloved actors. She is deeply in love with her girlfriend, dancer Christian Scott, and her world couldn't be better.

Christian, though proud of Grey and all that she's accomplished, is facing her own career dilemma. All she's ever wanted to do is perform and create, her body her kinetic canvas. But, in one of the few industries where youth matters above all else, her time is coming to make decisions that no woman in her mid-thirties should have to make: is it time to retire?

As the career of one begins to explode into the stratosphere and the other's implodes after a career-ending injury that makes any retirement discussion irrelevant, Grey and Christian begin to drift apart. Changing priorities and newly built walls lead to fears and accusations, further tearing at the fabric of the love they've worked years to create.

Will cooler heads prevail to warm up the hearts of the deeply passionate couple in time to create a new dream for their second act?

*Swann Song* - ISBN - 978-1-952270-63-5

Christine Swann is a world-famous singer/songwriter and lesbian icon, known for her edgy style and heart-pounding songs. Gorgeous, rich and miserable. Her music has always been her life, her escape from an unimaginable childhood, and choices no thirteen-year-old should have to make.

Now, pushing thirty, she wants out. From all of it.

Willow Bowman lives in the farmhouse her beloved grandmother left her, with her husband. A pediatric nurse and small-town girl, she relishes in the safety of her marriage that keeps difficult questions at bay and keeps her life quiet and peaceful, because that makes sense to her.

Until one night when Willow is driving home and is about to cross the old, rickety Dittman Bridge not far from the farmhouse, and she sees a figure jump off into the cold waters below.

The moment she jumps in and pulls the woman dressed in leather pants out, both their lives change forever.

*Keeping Hope (Wynter Series Book 4)* - ISBN - 978-1-952270-78-9

Twenty-four-year-old Hope DeSilva has been released from a three-year stint in a Georgia prison. After returning to her family property in a tiny Georgia town, she decides she's had enough of the poverty, violence, and progound family dysfunction. It's time to get out on her own. She buys a $400 car and heads to find work out west.

After the car breaks down in Colorado, she's given a ride into a mountain town called Wynter where she runs into brash, aggressive police officer Samantha Gains, who has not one ounce of patience or sympathy for a felon in her black-and-white world of right or wrong, good or bad.

But, running from her own family trauma and inexplicably bewitched by the young newcomer Hope, Samantha begins to realize that maybe her strict worldview isn't as simple as it seems. When a freak accident brings the two women together, it will take both of them letting go of their pasts to truly move on.

Take another trip to Wynter and revisit old friends as they work their magic to help Hope and Samantha find their footing—and ultimately bring them home.

*She Who Would be King* - ISBN - 978-1-952270-89-5

Cateline is the seventeen-year-old daughter of a nobleman in fourteenth-century France. It's a time when children aren't seen as those to be loved and cherished, but instead are used as pawns and bargaining chips on the chessboard of control and privilege.

She is married off to a prince in the country of Sursha, a Gaelic-speaking island nation near Ireland. Fergus, her betrothed, is next in line to take over once beloved King Carthac dies. Or is he?

Fallon, the youngest royal child and only girl, has been raised as one of the king's sons her entire life, for reasons she has never fully understood. A natural fighter, she was raised to be a warrior and head the Crown's Elite Guard assigned to protect her boorish brother Fergus.

Forced to fill in for her brother in an unexpected way, an instant attraction between Fallon and Cateline forms. In a game of thrones filled with deception and betrayal, even the most secret love can mean death.

*Showing Mercy (Wynter Series Book 5)* - ISBN - 978-1-952270-94-9

Fifteen-year-old Mercy Faulkner is hit with the hardest blow of her young life when her beloved father is killed in an accident. Now, she must leave all she knows to move with her mother, a hard woman that she feels like she barely knows, to the small mountain town of Wynter, Colorado. Her mother has been offered a job there and a place to live and start over for the two.

Bethany Wynter, seventeen, gorgeous and the granddaughter of the founder of Wynter and early residents, Justice and Thea Kilkoyne, she has everything going for her. She and her twin brother, Billy are at the top of their game - popular, well-loved in the community and dominate in academics and athletics.

But, when the beautiful and shy Mercy shows up in town, a sibling rivalry will begin that will split the twins for the first time in their life.

When World War II hits the shores of the United States, everything changes for everyone. Who will go off to war, who will come back, and will any of them ever be the same?

*Control* - ISBN -

Keller Mitchum has already lived a lifetime in eighteen years. Fully responsible for her five-year-old sister Parker, Keller has seen and experienced things in life that should exist in the most intense fictional plot. Wise beyond her years, she will do absolutely anything to keep Parker safe.

Garrison Davies is a twenty-three-year-old pilot in Massachusetts, working with her father in a small, family-owned cargo business. Independent, feisty, and brilliant at what she does, she makes little time for anything outside of her beloved planes and dogs. Her simple and structured world is turned on its head when a difficult situation lands two unexpected guests into her life and her house.

Garrison tries to make a safe space for Keller and Parker, only partially aware of the horrors they come from. As time passes, it becomes clear that it's not only the past that keeps the two sisters at arm's length. Can Garrison break through Keller's defenses and help her regain control?

## Other Sapphire books from Sapphire Authors

*Dusty Road Home* – ISBN – 978-1-952270-72-7

Melanie Crenshaw has fallen off the proverbial map. Notoriously private on a good day, the world-famous mystery author has gone dark to avoid any public blowback or scandal from her latest failed relationship. Seeking quiet and solace, she retreats to her rural hometown, hoping isolation will be just the atmosphere she needs to finish her novel. But going back home is never as easy as it sounds, especially when a nosy reporter starts sniffing around.

Pulitzer-winning investigative journalist Pilar Stein has seen people at their worst—and has the scars to prove it. After taking time off to heal from a particularly brutal assignment, she's back in the saddle and ready to reclaim her place among the elite of hard-hitting reporters. Unfortunately, her re-entry story—a profile on elusive author Melanie Crenshaw who has suddenly disappeared—seems to lack the teeth necessary to catapult her back to the top of her game.

Appearances are deceiving, of course, and Pilar soon discovers that what she deems a simple fluff piece might well lead to the scoop of a generation…just not the one she expected.

As Melanie fights to maintain her privacy while Pilar takes a backhoe to her past, the two women find themselves torn between their own professional convictions and their growing attraction to each other. And no matter which road they take, it's going to be a bumpy ride.

*You Can't Ourtrun Your Roots* – ISBN – 978-1-952270-82-6

What if instead of meeting someone new, you reconnected with someone from your past?

As Southern as fried chicken and peach cobbler, free spirit Gloria Robinson spent her lifetime building a successful permaculture farm on the tired dirt of former cotton fields in South Carolina. Now widowed, Gloria is certain she'll never find someone new, not in this town. She wouldn't even know how to try. Politically, she fears her years of effort for social justice are slipping backward. She's becoming weary, but she's digging in her heels.

Living in Washington D.C., perpetually single, party girl Anna May Walker floats through life disconnected from her roots in the South. Self-focused, she often ponders how she wronged Gloria in high school. When Anna May's father dies, she heads home to lure her mother to move near her in a retirement community.

Avoiding each other in a small town is impossible, particularly when Anna May's boss unwittingly assigns her to write a story about Gloria's farm. After decades apart, will the old sparks be enough to restart a fire between them?

*First comes Marriage: Morgantown - Book One* - ISBN - 978-1-952270- 80-2

Take one CEO, one pink-haired alien, a secret marriage, vengeful aliens, unexplained deaths, and a bitter sister out for revenge, and two women's lives will never be the same.

As CEO of MartinTech, Brynn Martin is at the top of her professional game. Her personal life is another matter, but she's not in a hurry to break her single status. All that changes on a Tuesday morning when a bombshell is dropped.

At sixteen, Micah Legon fled her abusive family and home world of Vubloxia. Now, at twenty-nine, she's content and settled in her life, running a cleanup business with her siblings. Then one morning, she gets a phone call that changes everything.

A chance encounter six years ago in Las Vegas at a "Meet an Alien" convention comes back to haunt both women. While Micah remembers the day with fondness, Brynn remembers nothing. After meeting again, both women come to an agreement. However, nothing is ever that simple.

Micah makes it her mission to break through Brynn's tough exterior. Brynn makes it her mission to keep Micah at arm's length. Nothing will stop either woman from getting what she wants. The trouble is convincing the other that her plan is the right one.

*Out of the Ashes* - ISBN - 978-1-952270-84-0

When unusual seismic activity is detected on Mount St. Helens, volcanologist Nova "Cano" Kane, along with a team from the United States Geological Survey, is sent to investigate. The year is 1980, and there hasn't been a large-scale eruption on the mountain in over one hundred years.

Dr. Allison "Allie" Albright is a prominent professor at the University of Washington where the seismic activity is being tracked. As more scientists pour into Seattle, she braces for the possible return of Cano.

Neither Allie nor Cano has fully recovered from their breakup four years earlier. Both live with the pain and regret of how their relationship ended. Maybe it's best to leave it in the past and focus on the job at hand.

They must battle the limits of predictive science, the shortsightedness of bureaucracy, and the bias of the media, while fighting their complicated feelings for each other. As Mount St. Helens continues to churn, so too does their attraction.
Which will erupt first—the volcano or their feelings for each other?

*The Serenity Nearby* – ISBN – 978-1-952270-65-9

Veronica Hockmeier's relationship with her girlfriend/ PhD supervisor is on the rocks. A graduate student has died by suicide in her English Department. And her eating disorder has returned with a vengeance. All Veronica wants to do is get out of town for a weekend, and when her paper is accepted at an academic conference on Emily Dickinson, in Dickinson's hometown of Amherst, Massachusetts, Veronica takes this as a good sign.

On the way there, she is greeted with calamity after calamity: an accident on the road, a person from her past, and what appears to be the ghost of a graduate student in her hotel room. When a friendly hotel worker named Bo Wu shows her some kindness, Veronica can't help but fall for the tall woman with a winning smile—even if she does have a creepy collection of items dead patrons have left behind.

When Veronica's passport goes missing and another body turns up at the hotel, she becomes trapped in a nightmare she can't escape from—not without Bo's help.

Printed in Great Britain
by Amazon

48855417R00192